Jonathan Andrews grew up in Leeds, West Yorks   ......ms mie
working and providing for his beloved wife, Maria, and three daughters, Sarah,
Diane, and Shannon. He has been fortunate enough to experience many
interesting roles such as head chef, security manager and even postman!
Jonathan has always had a very keen interest in Roman history and has always
enjoyed reading books about ancient Rome and the Roman empire. As he reaches
retirement, Jonathan now dedicates his time to writing, walking his Polish
lowland sheepdog, Peanut, and socialising with friends and family. *Atticus,
Fighter of Rome Series: A Hero is Born* is the first book of Jonathan's exciting
new series, *Atticus: Fighter of Rome.*

To my beautiful wife, Maria, of over 42 years.

To my wonderful daughter, Sarah, Diane, and Shannon.

To my good friend, Terry Fernly, "Big Tel", who is sadly no longer with us but was a big inspiration and fun to be around.

To lovely sister, Carol, who passed away far too soon. A mother to four boys. Love her always.

Jonathan Andrews

ATTICUS, FIGHTER OF ROME SERIES: A HERO IS BORN

AUSTIN MACAULEY PUBLISHERS™

LONDON * CAMBRIDGE * NEW YORK * SHARJAH

A CIP catalogue record for this title is available from the British Library.

ISBN 9781398482074 (Paperback)
ISBN 9781398482081 (ePub e-book)

www.austinmacauley.co.uk

First Published 2024
Austin Macauley Publishers Ltd®
1 Canada Square
Canary Wharf
London
E14 5AA

Austin Macauley Publishers

About the Book

Emperor Augustus ruled the empire with an iron fist. Many kings and rulers throughout the empire were plotting to take their lands back from Rome. The legions fought to quell uprisings all over the empire. Rome needed a warrior and a true leader of men. The Gods have answered, and Atticus was born.

Introduction

Atticus was born in one of the brothels in the city of Capranica to a prostitute by the name of Antonia. She was very pretty, slim with blonde hair and brown eyes. The owner of the brothel, Aulus, a short fat bald man with a black beard allowed Antonia to keep the boy but only until he was old enough to fend for himself. Aulus did not allow this because he was kind-hearted, he was far from that as could be and only allowed Antonia this courtesy as she was indeed a pretty little thing and by far his best earner. As soon as Aulus saw the boy was fit to get rid of, he would.

Aulus would often shout at Antonia that, "It was time for that brat of yours to leave or I will make him leave myself," and she would cry and beg Aulus not to take away her child.

Late one-night Aulus crept into the shed, where Atticus laid sleeping, covering his mouth so that no one could hear the boy's screams, he snatched the boy and took him away.

In a dark corner down a secluded alleyway, where the homeless slept and rats roamed free, there in the shadows stood a tall, well-built man, a merchant of sorts, who was travelling to Rome. Aulus had arranged for the merchant to take the boy and dump him in the slums of the Aventine, far away from his mother so that he could never return and be a burden to Aulus once more. Aulus had paid the merchant good money for his service, as he saw it, and handed the shaken boy over to the merchant. The merchant looked at Aulus with his dark hollow eyes, never speaking a single word and nodded. He swiftly turned around, boy in arms, gagged, tied, and threw him onto the back of his wagon and off they went into the darkness.

It was still dark when the merchant arrived at the slums and he quickly took the boy into the dark, shit strewn alleyways. He untied Atticus, without a hint of care, and kicked him up the arse. "Go on, boy, before I take my knife to you," he snarled coldly at Atticus, who was only the shy age of four.

The next few months were difficult for Atticus; he had to beg for scraps of food and rummage through waste. He cried himself to sleep every night, missing his mother's loving smile and recalling the warmth of the shed he'd slept in, and how he longed again for that warmth and shelter, but most of all he yearned for his mother's love.

The cold nights were long and cruel and many in the slums didn't always make it from dusk until dawn. "Another meal for the rats," Atticus would say to himself. But Atticus loved to sit and bask in the sun, watching the soldiers marching past from the side of the road in the city, marvelling at their uniforms and plumed helmets of the commanders.

It was at this point Atticus knew what he was going to do. He had a desire like no other, one day when he was old enough, he would join the legions and fight for the glory of Rome. But not only would he fight for Rome, but he would be the best fighter that Rome's legions had ever seen.

Chapter 1

Early in the morning of a mid-summer's day, Castus, the baker returned from the market, carrying a large sack of flour over his shoulder. He opened the door to his small quaint bakery and stepped inside. As he put the sack down on the floor and shouted to his wife Misha, who was a small, rounded lady with rosy, pink cheeks and a very round face and only four foot tall, "It's only me, Misha."

"I'm in the kitchen," she quickly replied with a hint of cheer in her voice.

Castus, who was a tall plump man with grey hair, travelled down the small hall, stepped into the kitchen, and stopped dead in his tracks. Looking towards the table, staring at the boy sitting there chewing on a piece of bread, Castus curiously asked, "What do we have here then, Misha?" eyeing the boy up and down. Atticus was covered in more black dirt than the colour of his own skin, wearing ragged clothes and had the stench of a sewer. The little boy covered in grime sat looking up at Castus; Misha handed the boy some more bread.

"This is Atticus, my love, he's the little boy I have been telling you so much about," she informed Castus, who looked at her with a blank expression upon his face,

"You know the little lad always begging and sleeping amongst the rubbish." Castus still didn't reply, he just stared at his wife with the same blank expression. "Well, I have decided," Misha went on to say.

"Decided what?" Castus finally spoke while letting out a sigh.

"Decided he can sleep on the floor in the storeroom."

All the time Misha and Castus were talking Atticus didn't look up, he just carried on happily chewing on the bread. "Why? You don't know anything about this boy!" Castus exclaimed.

"I know this much," Misha went on to say, "he's called Atticus, he's six years old, got taken away from his mother when he was four and dumped in those dirty alleyways. Nothing to keep him warm at night, no food no money, survived these last two years and didn't join one of those Gangs who come down here taking our money every two weeks. And if we don't pay, they beat us up and smash the windows. That tells me a lot about this lad's character!"

Castus realised he wasn't going to win this argument and so turned to look at Atticus whilst talking to Misha, "Well, you'd better get the soap, some warm water and scrub him. He stinks. I won't have my storeroom smelling of shit." and walked out of the kitchen.

Misha looked down at Atticus with a smile, "Told you, lad, his bark is worse than his bite," and giggled, ruffling Atticus's hair.

"Come on, time to get you washed, my boy," and off they went to the tub in the larder.

"So, Atticus," Misha asked, "where did you live?"

"Not sure?" he replied, so on Misha scrubbed him from top to bottom. When she finished, she threw him a towel. "Dry yourself, Atticus, while I nip next door and get you some clothes to wear." While Misha was gone Atticus rubbed himself dry, thinking to himself how kind and caring Misha was and how one day he would repay her.

Misha returned. "Here you are, lad," with a smile and gave him a brown tunic and a belt to fasten around his waist. Atticus happily put it on and fastened the belt. "Now, lad, you look almost human," Misha laughed. "I'll put some straw in the corner of the storeroom for you to sleep on. Also, during the day, you best be out of Castus's way but be in by seven, no later, mind. We go to bed early because we're up very early to bake the bread and pastries."

The next few days passed by; Atticus still carried on begging. He didn't want to over burden Castus and Misha, so any odd coins he was given he handed them over to Misha. He always kept out of the way during the day and when he wasn't begging he would go watch the soldiers marching to the gates; some were changing the guards, others were going out on patrol up into the hills. Atticus loved the sound of the hobnailed boots crunching on the road as they marched past.

Atticus had stopped looking through the bags of rubbish in the alleyways but always managed to get filthy. The alleys were always strewn with garbage, human and animal shit and smelled of piss but he'd lived in them for the last two years and thought nothing of it.

Atticus had befriended a young girl over the past year while living and sleeping in the alleyways of the Aventine, who was two years older than himself called Julia. She begged for food and any spare coins while living in the alleyways amongst the rats and garbage, but she was very small and frail for her age and always had a cough. Her little blue eyes peered out from her sunken eye sockets and Atticus did his best for her and every morning when he left the bakery with some fresh bread, he would always seek her out and share it with her. She would always look up at Atticus and thank him and do her best to smile but Atticus could see the pain etched on her tiny face and wished he could do more.

The following day the early morning sunlight peered through the cracks in the roof tiles of the storeroom. Atticus was already awake due to the noise coming from the bakery; the local gang thugs had arrived, demanding their protection money.

One voice was shouting at Castus and Misha, "Pay up before I give you both a good hiding and smash the place up," Atticus heard Misha sobbing. "Here, take it, please, leave us."

"Don't worry," shouted the ringleader, "as long as you pay." Then as they left, he turned and growled, "Don't forget we'll be back in two weeks." After paying the gang, it left Misha and Castus with just enough to get by and make ends meet to run the bakery.

Atticus swore an oath to himself that as soon as he was big enough, he would make them regret ever taking money or hurting Misha and Castus; the only people so far in his life to have helped him make his life bearable.

When the gang had left, Atticus went into the kitchen, looked at Misha and said, "If only I was older and stronger, I wouldn't let them hurt you."

She looked at Atticus and said, "I know, lad, but never mind me go on and play or whatever, just don't get into any bother, take that bag of food with you on the table."

So off Atticus went, out and down the alley onto the main street, heading off to find Julia, happy in the knowledge he'd got food for her. She wasn't in her normal spot where she begged so he went into the alley where she slept. He was humming a tune to himself and couldn't wait to share his breakfast with her. As he turned into a tiny alley where she slept fear and shock gripped his face. On the floor behind a pile of rubbish he could see her tiny lifeless body being eaten by rats. He turned and ran out of the alleyways with a deep pain in his chest and struggled to breath. Once in the main street, Atticus slowed down and gasped for air, tears now rolled down his face.

He sat at the side of the road with his head in his hands. He'd faced a hard start to life, but nothing had prepared him for this. After a while, Atticus stood up and wiped his face; he was now more than ever determined to join the legions and make something of himself and become Rome's greatest fighter. Then Atticus walked up towards the main gate, and as he approached the gate, one of the soldiers on guard duty asked him, "Where are you off to, young man?"

"Just off to explore up the road a bit and see what's up there," Atticus replied, trying to smile.

"Well, just be careful and don't get into any trouble, and if I were you, I would go for a swim in the river and wash some of that dirt off you."

"I don't know how to swim," Atticus replied.

"Just be off with you before I kick you up the backside, lad."

So off he went out of the gate and up the road towards the hills, passing some merchants coming down the road heading towards the city. He walked on, the air smelt fresher the further he got away from the city, he began to feel a little bit better.

The sun shone down warming his face, Atticus soon began to feel quite at ease as he wandered further up the road. After walking for a couple of hours up the road passing fields and trees, he noticed a small group of buildings situated on the top of a hill. They were surrounded by a large white wall with a black wooden gate, and to the left he could see rows of vines tumbling down the fields. As he got closer, he could see some people working in the fields tending to the vines; it was getting quite hot now and was feeling thirsty.

As Atticus approached the gate, he sat on a small wall and began to watch the farm workers with the sun on his face and a nice cooling breeze.

After a while, the gate crunched open, making Atticus turn to look, out stepped a very tall man who looked to be in his early fifties but strong looking with big arms and a thick neck. Atticus also noticed a large scar running down his left cheek, and another smaller scar above his right eye, his hair was cut short and was beginning to go grey at the temples. The man suddenly appeared,

"Who are you, boy? And what are you doing sitting on my wall?"

"Nothing, Sir, just watching them tending the vines minding my own business," replied Atticus.

"Stand up when you talk to me, boy, watch your manners or you will get a clip around the ear for your cheek."

Atticus stood up looking up to the big man. "Sorry, Sir, don't mean to be rude."

"Better not be," the man replied, looking Atticus up and down, "What's your name boy and are you looking for some work?"

"My name is Atticus and depends on what work you got." Looking up at the big man.

Romulus smiled looking at Atticus trying to figure him out; he couldn't help but think there's more to this lad than meets the eye.

"My name is Romulus, got so many job offers you can be choosey, boy?"

"No," Atticus replied, looking at Romulus.

"Those scars on your face, did you get those fighting in the legions for Rome?"

"What's that to you, boy?"

Atticus paused before replying and said, "I will work very hard for you every day without fail and do anything you ask of me, if you teach me how to fight," replied Atticus.

Romulus chuckled and asked, "Why do you want to learn how to fight?" Atticus looked up at Romulus staring straight into his eyes without so much as a flinch.

"Sir, I want to fight in the legions for Rome," Atticus then passed for a second before continuing, "I want to be the best fighter Rome has ever seen."

At this point Romulus burst into a fit of laughter, but Atticus never took his eyes off Romulus, not for even a second.

When Romulus finished laughing, looking down at Atticus, into his dark brown eyes, he could see Atticus meant what he'd said.

"How old are you?" Romulus questioned.

"I'm six," Atticus replied.

"You're big for six. I thought you were at least ten. You sure about your age, Atticus?"

"Yes, I'm six, born sometime in June, not sure of the date," he went on to say; Romulus also thought Atticus was quite strong looking for his age.

Romulus asked, "Where do you live and what do your parents think about you fighting for Rome?"

"Got no parents and I sleep on the floor in the baker's storeroom," Atticus explained.

"Oh, I see, so you want food and lodgings as well as training, eh?" Romulus chuckled.

"Won't say no to a bit of food but I'm happy sleeping at the bakers. They've been good to me and in a tight spot at the moment, so I want to keep an eye out for them and one day when I'm bigger I will deal with it."

Romulus thought to himself, '*Unusual for a boy so young to have such a sense of loyalty*'.

Romulus put his hand on Atticus's shoulder and said, "Seems like a fair deal to me, lad. Come on in and I will show you around but mark my words, boy, you will have to work hard and train hard. I don't stand for any nonsense."

Chapter 2

When Atticus and Romulus entered the courtyard, a slave closed the gate behind them and stood guard. As they continued on through the courtyard, Atticus gazed at the wonderful surroundings; a water fountain in the centre, two ornate stone benches to the right of the fountain, some apple trees in a grove to the left further down and a large house was set to the far side behind the stone benches with two steps leading up to the entrance. As they walked on through the garden, they were met by a slender slave girl of about ten years old.

"Atticus, this is Naomi," Romulus explained.

"Good day, master," Naomi replied, followed by a bow of the head to Romulus.

"No need to call me master, Naomi, plain old Romulus will do."

Atticus gazed at Naomi; she'd spoken in a very soft voice and had a beautiful smile, which made his cheeks redden. Atticus, whilst trying his best to hide his blush said, "Hello."

Romulus looked down at Atticus, "Naomi will teach you how to work the fields, tend to the vines, feed the pigs and milk the goats."

Naomi looked at Atticus and thought to herself, '*he needs a bath, he smells*' and she wriggled her nose.

"I think we need to take him to the horse trough and wash him first."

Romulus laughed and said, "Yes, the boy does smell a bit." Atticus looked at them both confused.

"I can't smell anything. What you on about? I had a wash at the bakers last week," he protested.

"Go on then, Naomi, get the soap and take him to the trough. Wash him clean while I go and find him some sandals to wear and a clean tunic." Atticus thought to protest but decided better of it.

So, off he went with Naomi; she stripped him of his clothes and began to scrub him with soap and a brush. It took her almost half an hour to get rid of the smell.

"That's better!" she exclaimed with that soft voice of hers, which made Atticus's cheeks go pink again. Moments later Romulus arrived with a clean tunic and sandals.

"Here you are, boy, try these on for size." As soon as Atticus was dressed, Romulus looked him up and down and stated,

"You'll do." Naomi sniggered and walked off.

"Right, boy, follow me and you can meet my friend Zuma. He will show you how to clean the stables, feed and groom the horses and when I think you're ready I might even teach you to ride one."

"Really!" smiled Atticus, "I can't wait," he yelled.

As they approached the stables, the door opened and out walked Zuma; Atticus looked at Zuma thinking, *'Gosh, I've never seen anybody so big.'* Romulus looked at Atticus gawking and laughed.

"Zuma has that effect on people when they first meet him."

Zuma was a giant of a man standing seven foot tall, black as the darkest night and arms as thick as most men's legs. Zuma bowed his head slightly and said,

"Good day, Romulus," then looking at Atticus, he continued, "and what do we have here?"

Smiling from ear to ear, Romulus, replied, "This, my friend, is Atticus, our new farm boy. Atticus, this is my most trusted friend Zuma," introducing him properly, "who on many occasions has seen fit to save my life."

"And you have saved mine also, Romulus," Zuma butted in with a big smile.

"This young boy in return for a hard day's graft wants to learn how to fight in the legions of Rome," said Romulus.

Zuma paused looking down at Atticus before speaking, "Does he now! How old are you, my little friend?"

Atticus looking up at Zuma replied, "Six and I'm stronger than you think, my very large friend."

Zuma burst out laughing and said, "A boy with a great sense of humour, eh! Don't you think Romulus for one so young."

"He has that," replied Romulus. Zuma then thinking to himself, *'tall for six and looked strong'*. Zuma, who always thought himself to be a good judge of character, decided he liked Atticus and mused, *'There's a strong heart beating in that child and a good one at that.'*

Romulus spoke, "Zuma, I'm off to the city and I will be back in a couple of hours, put a saddle on Lightning, Fury's a bit boisterous for my liking. I'm sure he's upset with me for some reason."

As soon as Romulus had mounted, he set off out of the gate at a good canter, Figo, one of the slaves shut the gate behind him. Figo was a very tall man in his late forties with a slight limp.

"Come on, lad, Zuma said time for you to meet Blaze and Fury." So off they went into the stable.

In the first stall was a beautiful brown mare and in the second stall was a jet-black stallion. "That, my little friend, is Fury. Don't get too close to his hind legs, he kicks out to let you know who's boss. Blaze, the brown chestnut, is far more placid. You won't get any bother from her." For the next couple of hours Zuma showed Atticus how to groom, feed and muck out. "Right, lad, time for a drink. It's been hot work."

On the way-out, Atticus went to the gate of Fury's stall and put his hand up to stroke Fury's face. "Careful, lad!" exclaimed Zuma, "He don't take to strangers. You might get bit for your trouble." But Fury just lowered his head, touching Atticus as he stroked his face. Zuma thought to himself, *'Well I, never Fury's never done that before, not even for Romulus or me!'*, so Zuma didn't say a word and just watched them both getting acquainted.

Outside, the sound of hoofs clattering on the stone flags took Zuma out of his trance, "Come, Atticus, sounds like Romulus is back." So off they went out of the stable; Romulus had dismounted and was leading Lightning towards the stable. When he saw them, he said to Zuma, "What do you think about our little friend? Will he cut it, and do you think he's worth training in return for his hard work?" Atticus looked up at the giant in earnest, waiting for the reply.

Zuma looked down at Atticus with that smile from ear to ear and replied, "Yes, Romulus, he will do just fine."

Romulus shouted for Aramea, and a small fat lady came running out of the house.

"Yes, master."

Romulus looked up at the heavens and said, "Give me strength. Stop calling me master. Put some salted pork bread and cheese in a bag for young Atticus here to take home with him."

"Yes, master," she replied and ran back into the house. Romulus shook his head, sighed then laughed out loud. "One day I will get her to call me Romulus if it's the last thing I ever do." Aramea returned with a small bag containing the food, passing it to Atticus saying,

"Here you are, young man."

"Thank you," replied Atticus.

Romulus turned to Atticus and said, "Well, lad, off you go but be here no later than seven."

"Yes, master," he replied smiling and ducking underneath the palm of Romulus's hand because he was just about to get a clip around the ear for his cheek. Shouting goodbye, he ran out of the gate, not wanting to be home late and get locked out.

Over the next few months, Atticus worked hard every day in the fields with Naomi and in the stables with Zuma, he milked the goats and fed the pigs. In return, Romulus was good to his word and started teaching him how to use the short sword but also how to read and write.

Atticus loved to practise with the sword; slashing, blocking, and stabbing at the wooden poles with arms which replicated the torso of a man. At first Atticus protested about having to learn how to read and write, and about learning to read maps, but Romulus explained to get on in the legions you needed to be able to read and write. Atticus would need map reading skills to find the best ground to fight the enemy, and to be able to get from one place to another in the shortest distance, saving valuable time especially if food and water was short.

Romulus woke up feeling the warmth of the early morning sun on his face through the cracks in the wooden shutters, he climbed out of bed and wandered to the kitchen while rubbing his eyes. Zuma was already sitting at the table, Aramea was stirring a pot above the fire.

"Good morning, master," she said as he entered the kitchen; she took a large wooden bowl and filled it with porridge.

"Sit down, here's your breakfast, nice and hot just the way you like it," she said with a smile.

"Ah, smells delicious," he replied, sitting down opposite to Zuma, "looks like it's going to be another hot day," whilst blowing his porridge to cool it.

"Yes, not a cloud in the sky," added Zuma.

"So, what have you got for young Atticus to do this morning?" Romulus asked.

"He's been here over an hour already. Atticus is in the stables feeding Blaze and Lightning and putting Fury into the paddock to stretch his legs," announced Zuma.

"You know how Fury hates being cooped up."

"Aye, he's got wings for legs that one, and a temper to match," replied Romulus.

"He has that, but Fury's got a love for that boy's company and when they're together it's as if they know what each other is thinking," Zuma continued, "I've often noticed when Atticus is in Fury's stall feeding and grooming him, they have their heads touching each other while the boy strokes Fury's face."

"By the Gods, if I went into Fury's stall he would rear up and kick out at me, he's bitten me on more than one occasion."

This made Zuma go into a fit of laughter, when he'd managed to stop laughing, he finally managed to say,

"Better finish this porridge and give him some sword practise."

Chapter 3

Several more months had passed, and the grapes had all been picked off the vines, Romulus had hired some local girls to press the grapes in large tubs with their feet. Atticus was now seven and seemed to get taller by the month; he'd got long jet-black hair flowing halfway down his back and was as tall as any 12-year-old. Atticus was sitting down on the bench next to the well, watching Naomi and the girls squash the grapes. Zuma came out of the main house and approached Atticus and with that big smile of his from ear to ear shouted, "Hey, Atticus, my little friend, hasn't taken you long to take an interest in girls." Atticus began to protest his innocence, feeling his cheeks go red and warm; Naomi and the girls began to giggle. Zuma shouted, "Come, boy, go and get your wooden training sword. Let's see how much you've improved."

So off went Atticus up to the training ground, glad to get out of sight of the girls. He got his training sword from the strong box, which was kept in the small shed outside the stable, then made his way to the centre. Zuma stood there, waiting, wooden sword in hand, standing at seven foot tall and as wide as any stable door. Even at the age of seven, Atticus was almost five-feet tall and starting to broaden a little with all the hard work and training with Romulus. Atticus took his stance; feet slightly apart, pointing at a forty-five-degree angle and crouched slightly, Zuma told Atticus to raise his sword slightly,

"Ready, boy?"

"Yes, I'm ready," replied Atticus.

Zuma confidently began with a few light lunges towards Atticus for him to block. Even though they were light, Atticus felt the blows vibrate from head to toe. After ten minutes, Zuma began to slightly up the pace with chopping strokes, left and then right, but Atticus still managed to block them, only backing off a little. Then with a quick twist of his wrist Zuma cut to his left and knocked the sword from Atticus's hand.

"Come on, Atticus, keep a firm grip and don't take your eyes off your opponent, not even for a second. Pick it up, lad, get your stance sword up." And on they went lunging, slashing, and blocking while moving around the training square. Zuma was always showing him different moves and feints to get his opponent off balance, all the time Atticus concentrated hard sweat pouring down his face, he could taste the salt on his lips and his lungs felt they were going to burst. This went on for a further twenty minutes when Zuma ended the session.

"Well done lad, time for a drink of water and a well-earned break."

But as soon as Atticus had finished the water, he went straight to the training blocks and began to cut and slash at the wooden poles. Zuma looked at him with a smile. Then off he went to check the girls were squashing the grapes properly.

While Atticus cut and slashed at the wooden posts, he pictured the posts as if they were the gang terrorising the baker and his wife.

A while later, just as the sun began to set, there was a loud knock on the big wooden gate. Zuma went to the spy hole and looked out as he did a voice spoke, Praetorian Paulinus to see Romulus. Zuma immediately opened the gate to let the praetorian soldiers in Paulinus and four other praetorians entered the courtyard; "Atticus, run and bring the master to the courtyard, tell him we have an honoured guest wishing to see him."

Aramea came running out; "Good evening, Sirs, can I get you all something to drink?"

"Yes, some watered wine would be nice, thank you," Paulinus replied while dusting some sand off his tunic and waiting for Romulus to arrive.

Seconds later, Romulus arrived with Aramea carrying a tray with six goblets of wine and a dish of figs.

Putting it down on the stone table in the courtyard, she bowed her head and said,

"There you are, Sirs, and there's one for you master," and backed her way into the house to continue preparing the supper, passing by Atticus who had come back into the courtyard and was standing by the water fountain.

"It's nice to see you, Paulinus, may I congratulate you on your promotion, I see your an Optio now," looking at his uniform.

"Thank you," replied Paulinus.

"What can I do for you so late in the evening?" asked Romulus.

They both sat down beside the stone table, the other praetorians had collected their wine and stood chatting amongst themselves by the gate. After quenching his thirst and wiping his mouth, Paulinus began by saying,

"There's been some trouble further up into the hills, bands of brigands, and maybe some deserters are raiding the farmsteads and pinching livestock."

While Paulinus and Romulus sat discussing what had been happening, while eating the figs and drinking the wine, Atticus had wandered over to the praetorian escort. He began to marvel at their uniforms, and plumed helmets, noting that each one of them carried a shield, spear and a short sword in a scabbard hanging from their belts. The sun was setting, but still bounced off their brightly polished breast plates. Moments later Paulinus and Romulus stood up and clasped forearms.

"Thank you for the warning. We better be on our toes and more vigilant at night," said Romulus.

"Yes, that would be wise and thank you for the wine and figs, must be getting back to the Garrison and make my report," said Paulinus.

"Any sign of trouble, I will send a message at once to the Garrison," replied Romulus. Zuma then opened the gate; Paulinus bid his farewell and the praetorian escort left. Romulus looked over towards Atticus and exclaimed,

"Get some supper from the kitchen, lad, and make your way home or you'll get locked out, it's getting late."

Off Atticus went to the kitchen and reappeared moments later with a small bag of bread and jerky. As he left, Romulus shouted to him,

"Don't be late! I need you hear bright and early and wide-awake tomorrow."

"Yes, master," Atticus replied with a grin and gave him his best Roman salute that he'd been practicing.

"Don't get cheeky, lad or I'll kick you up the arse for good measure." Romulus joked with a smile, all the while Zuma stood in the background laughing.

So off Atticus went, food in hand, running back to town through the shit filled alleys and smell of piss. But all the way back, he couldn't think of anything else but how well the soldiers looked in their fine uniforms.

It was dark now and the lanterns had been lit in the main streets, but there was not much in the way of light in the alleyways, so you had to tread carefully and not slip in some shit.

As he went down the alley, he noticed two boys in the shadows peering out from behind some bags of rubbish. Atticus slowed his pace and the hairs on the back of his neck pricked up, he began to look around for another way to go, but there was nowhere else to go but straight ahead.

Atticus placed his right hand under his tunic and took hold of his club, the club was quite heavy, and approximately ten inches long; Zuma had made it for him just in case he needed to protect himself on the way home at night. As he got nearer, the two boys stepped out and blocked his path, one boy was as tall as Atticus but fat and clearly at least three or four years older than him. The second boy was taller than Atticus by a good five inches but very skinny.

The taller of the two boys began to speak. "What have we here?" smirking at Atticus, the fat boy grinned saying, "Looks like the kid from the bakery." He then began to rub his fist into the palm of his hand.

Atticus had quickly weighed the situation up and planned what move he would make as soon as the time was right.

Then the taller of the two boys spoke, "You have to pay a toll to walk down this alley late at night." And began tapping his fingers into the palm of his hand glaring at Atticus.

"And if I don't?" questioned Atticus.

"We'll give you a bloody good kicking and take what we want anyway!" chuckled the fat boy.

Before he could say another word, Atticus head butted him so hard he crashed to the floor, his nose broken and pouring with blood. He smashed his head as he fell onto the stone flags knocking himself unconscious.

But before he'd hit the floor, Atticus had pulled his club out from under his tunic, and before the tall boy had any time to react, Atticus smashed him with all his might slamming the club across the side of his head. The tall skinny boy collapsed into the sacks of rubbish, he was dead before he hit them, splinters of his skull had penetrated his brain from the force of the blow.

Quickly Atticus looked all around to see if anyone was watching, but there was a deafening silence and no one to be seen. He checked both boys to see if they were still alive, the skinny boy was not breathing and there was a large crack in his skull where the blow had struck, and a thick ooze of blood was dripping out. The other boy was still alive and moaning but Atticus knew the boy had recognised him and would bring other members of the gang to the bakers to kill him and burn the bakery down. So, without a second thought he smashed the club against the fat boy's skull, killing him in an instant.

Atticus then ran down the alley, dodging sacks of rubbish and piles of shit. He turned left into a side alley and ran down it, passing the side of the Three Flags tavern. As he ran down, he almost tripped over a drunk, lying in his own puke. At the end of the alley, he slowed before going into the main street, not to arouse suspicion from any Roman guards patrolling the streets. He then took the long way around, to the bakers, and went in.

Misha was sitting in the kitchen waiting. "Where have you been, lad, it's getting late?" she asked.

"Sorry, some soldiers came to the farm about some bandits raiding farms," Misha interrupted,

"Never mind that now, off to bed with you, I need some sleep."

Off Atticus went to the storeroom, as Misha bolted the door and went to bed. While lying on his bed of straw, staring up at the roof, he began to ponder over his actions in the alleyway. Could he have acted in any other way? Pausing to think, at the age of only seven he'd been forced to defend himself, killing two other boys, but was satisfied the other boys were part of the gang terrorising Castus and Misha, and were nothing but scum. And not before long, Atticus was fast asleep dreaming of joining Rome's legions.

Chapter 4

Early the following morning, Atticus awoke; he could smell the freshly baked bread being taken out of the oven. It was only 05.30am, the sun had only just become partially visible above the horizon. He quickly put his club back under his tunic and out of sight, then made his way out of the storeroom and into the bakery, whilst squinting his eyes to adjust to the light.

"By your up early, Atticus, even for you," announced Misha.

"They told me to be up at the farm early today, must have a lot on," explained Atticus.

"Here you are then," Misha spoke pushing a slice of warm fresh bread with a piece of fruit into Atticus's hand. His eyes widened.

"Oh, thank you, Misha, I'm quite hungry." Atticus seemed to be always hungry these days, with all the extra hard work and training, giving him a big appetite. Since he'd been working at the farm Romulus, occasionally gave him a few coins, even though he was working only for food and training, but Atticus always gave them to Misha to go towards his keep.

"Well, be off with you out of my way, I've lots to do, and you need to be up at that farm," Misha shouted with a smile.

So, off he went out of the side door of the bakery, which led straight into an alley, turning left and after a couple of hundred yards or so, he went into the main street. Walking along after a short while, he came close to the three flags tavern, and as he passed the entrance to the alley he'd run down the night before, three soldiers of the night watch patrol came out. He quickly turned his eyes to the front, and quickened his pace slightly, to get past and on up the street to the main gate. But as he did so, one of the night watch guards; an ugly looking brute, with cane in his hand shouted,

"Hey, you boy, come here now," Atticus thought quickly, better not try to run off.

So, he slowly walked over to the three soldiers. The ugly one who shouted, was slapping his cane into the palm of his hand.

"What's up, Sir?" Atticus asked, putting on an innocent expression.

"Where are you off too early in the morning?" demanded the soldier.

"Off to work, Sir."

"Is that so?" came the reply. "And where is it you work, boy?"

"For Romulus up at his farm, Sir." Then the ugly soldier put his face in front of Atticus, so they were nearly touching at the nose.

"Were you skulking around these alleyways last night up to no good?" His breath stank of stale wine, making Atticus blink.

"No, Sir, was in bed asleep."

"Are you sure?" pushed the soldier, prodding Atticus in the stomach with his cane, "And why would a fine ex-legionnaire centurion like Romulus want to hire a runt like you?" spitting into the face of Atticus, making him wince.

At that point the sound of hobnailed boots crunching on the stone road, could be heard coming towards them. The soldiers turned around to see a section of praetorian soldiers marching up the street, being led by Optio Paulinus who Atticus recognised from last night at the farm.

As soon as the section of praetorians arrived Paulinus shouted, "Halt," and the praetorians stamped their feet as one and stood to attention.

"Praetorians stand at ease," yelled Paulinus, then he walked up to the three soldiers and addressed the ugly looking brute,

"Prictus, what's going on here?" Paulinus demanded.

Prictus saluted and the other two stood to attention,

"Just questioning this boy, there were a couple of lads killed in the alleyways over there last night, not far from the Three Flags tavern Sir," explained Prictus.

Paulinus pressed Prictus for more information,

"Well, I wanted to know what this little runt was doing out so early and had he been in the alleys last night," then he belched out loud, "begging your pardon, Sir." Atticus did his best not to laugh.

"Have you been drinking on duty, Prictus?" Paulinus asked angrily.

"Me, Sir? No, Sir."

Paulinus didn't like Prictus, he regarded him as a lazy drunken bully, always trying to dodge his duties. "And what did you find out?" Paulinus asked while looking at Atticus.

"Told us some cock and bull story about working for Romulus and being asleep all night," replied Prictus.

"And that's Sir! To you," retorted Paulinus.

"Sir, sorry, Sir," said Prictus.

"This young lad you call a runt does work for Romulus and he speaks very highly of young Atticus here."

At this point Prictus' jaw fell open when Paulinus addressed the boy by his name. "I err' umm' err," Prictus stuttered, wondering what to say.

"Close your mouth before those rotten teeth of yours fall out," said Paulinus; several of the praetorians started to laugh.

"Silence in the ranks if you please," continued Paulinus, "Are you sure you haven't been drinking Prictus? Because if I find out you have, you'll be on latrine duty for a month, and as for Atticus here being involved, he was up at Romulus's farm last night when I called to see him."

Paulinus then turned to Atticus with a smile. "Better get yourself up there as quickly as you can young man, knowing Romulus as I do, he will be expecting you early."

"Yes, Sir, he is," replied Atticus, and off he ran as fast as he could.

Five minutes later he was out of the gates and running up the road towards Romulus's farm, not even tacking a second to look back. Soon he was well away from the city smiling to himself thinking that was lucky Paulinus turning up when he did and went on making his way up the road.

Time passed quickly and soon he reached the hills and could see Romulus's farm in the distance. A large group of Roman cavalry came cantering down the road heading towards the city. Atticus had to jump out of the way and off the road, watching the cavalry ride pass he counted at least forty, led by an officer in a fine uniform and riding a beautiful white stallion, and in less than a couple of minutes, they'd disappeared down the road towards the city, not paying any attention to Atticus.

Back in the city, Paulinus had told Prictus and the two other soldiers to go straight to the officer of the watch and make a full report immediately, before going back to their barracks. Paulinus knew all too well that Prictus would soon be drinking a jug of wine and falling asleep. At that moment, the cavalry had returned, pulling up in front of Paulinus. He and his praetorians immediately stood to attention.

"At ease, gentlemen," the tribune on the white stallion said. Paulinus saluted and said, "Good morning, Tribune Marcus Sir."

"Good morning, Paulinus," Marcus replied as he looked down from his white stallion. "Anything to report, Paulinus?"

"Not really. A couple of boys from one of the gangs have been found dead in the alleys behind the three flags, Sir, according to those soldiers of the night watch."

"I see. Make sure they make a full report."

"Done that already, Sir," replied Paulinus.

"Good, carry on then."

"Yes, Sir," Paulinus replied and saluted.

Marcus and his cavalry trotted off back to barracks, and the praetorians marched off up to the gate.

Back up the road, Atticus had arrived at the farm and banged on the door; one of the house slaves opened it and let Atticus in. The courtyard was a hive of activity, there were a couple of wagons already hitched up to two oxen apiece; Romulus and several farm hands were loading them up with amphoras of wine from the cellar.

"Glad you could make it, Atticus," shouted Romulus with a smile.

"Sorry, I'm a bit late. I got held up by some soldiers on the way out of the city," explained Atticus.

"Never mind about that, lad. Go straight down to the cellar and help bring up the amphoras of wine, Zuma's down there. He'll show you which ones."

Atticus immediately ran towards the cellar shouting, "Yes, Sir."

When he got to the bottom of the stairs, he could see Zuma and two slaves in the light of the torches. Zuma was pointing to the amphoras of wine which needed to be taken up and out of the cellar.

"Morning, Zuma!" exclaimed Atticus as he approached.

"Morning, Atticus. Thought you'd slept in, lad." Zuma joked, with that big smile of his, looking at the boy.

"No way, you know me better than that. I'll tell you about it later when were not as busy."

It took them another couple of hours to carry the amphoras of wine and load them onto the wagons; the amphoras had been covered with large tarpaulins to keep them out of sight.

"Why are we taking so many amphoras of wine to the city?" questioned Atticus.

Romulus explained, "All the taverns are stocking up for the arrival of two legions coming back to Rome from fighting in Germania for a three-month rest."

"Oh, I see," replied Atticus.

"They've been replaced by Felix's legions from Thracia, so it's going to be a bit rowdy in the taverns and brothels," Romulus continued.

Zuma then shouted over, "There'll be plenty of soldiers spending their pay drinking and whoring, so there will be plenty of coin to be made."

"And we need to make our fair share," Romulus said smiling. "So this lot will make for a good profit and keep us all fed for a while."

Each wagon had two slaves aboard driving the oxen; Romulus and Zuma had armed themselves to ward off any attempts by robbers to steal the wine and were riding Blaze and Lightning. Aramea was sitting on the back of one of the wagons next to Seema, and when all the wine had been delivered, the wagons would be loaded up with all the fresh supplies. These would be purchased from the market by Aramea and Seema with the help of the other slaves. Romulus had also given Atticus a list of jobs to do on the farm, while they were in the city. Shortly after, they left for the city; one of the slaves bolted the doors and a sense of calm descended on the farm.

The first task for Atticus was to fill the water carriers up from the well and then take them down to Naomi and the field hands to water the crops and vines. This wasn't by any means an easy task; the water in the well was twenty feet down and had to be hand pulled up one bucket at a time, and by the time Atticus had finished his whole body ached from his shoulders to his knees.

He then had to load the water carriers onto the cart and harness one of the donkeys to pull the cart to the bottom of the fields, where Naomi was working. When he got there, he shouted to Naomi.

"I've brought the water; would you like me to help?"

"Yes, please," Naomi replied.

As Atticus looked over at Naomi, he couldn't help but gaze at her beauty; Naomi was slim with blonde hair and blue eyes, her hair hung all the way down her back, and he also noticed her ample breasts rubbing against her dress.

"What are you staring at?" she teased, smiling at Atticus who immediately felt his cheeks redden; he quickly replied,

"Nothing," Atticus turned away and began to water the crops.

As soon as they had finished, they made their way back up the slope towards the paddock, where Fury was enjoying the morning sun, galloping around kicking his legs out behind him. As they approached the paddock, Naomi shouted,

"Look at Fury. He's having so much fun, I've noticed though how much Fury loves having you around, Atticus," and with a coy smile, said, "just like me." Then Naomi ran off down past the stable. Atticus felt embarrassed and lost for words, but he ran after her. Naomi looked back at Atticus and said,

"What's up? Cat got your tongue," she teased.

"Err, no, I'm just trying to remember what job I've got to do next," he mumbled. "Before I practice with the bow and javelin," in an attempt to change the subject.

"I've got to milk the goats and feed the pigs," Naomi went on to say,

"And I've got to clean the stables and get the feed ready for Blaze and Lightning," Atticus replied,

"They'll be hungry when they get back," and off they went.

Just before sunset, Romulus and Zuma returned with the wagons. As they came into the courtyard, Romulus shouted for the house slaves to come and help unload the wagons. Then he shouted for Atticus.

"Take Blaze and Lightning and bed them down for the night, make sure they've got plenty of feed and water."

"Yes, master," Atticus replied with a cheeky grin.

When Seema, the youngest house slave appeared, Zuma asked, "Bring a jug of lemon water and two cups, please, Seema."

"Yes, Zuma, won't be a minute," whilst running back into the house to fetch Zuma's request.

Romulus and Zuma sat down on one of the stone benches and waited for the lemon water to arrive.

"Well, that's been a profitable day, Zuma, my friend, worth all the hard work." Romulus sighed, feeling fatigue setting in.

"I better put the bags of coins into the strong box out of the way as soon as I've had a drink," Zuma said.

"No rush," replied Romulus.

Seema arrived with the cups and water,

"Here you are, Sir," and placed the jug and cups down onto the stone table. Seema then bowed her head to Romulus and Zuma and ran to help the others unloading the supplies brought back from the city.

Romulus chuckled saying, "Wish she wouldn't bloody bow her head makes me feel like a bit of a pompous arse."

Zuma burst out laughing; "Well, if you're a pompous arse that means I'm a senator and I'm about as much a senator, as the boil on a pig's buttocks."

This made them both fall about laughing even more.

After they'd rested and felt refreshed from the lemon water, Zuma took the bags of coins to the strong box, and Romulus went to check everything had been stored properly.

Atticus returned after feeding and bedding the horses down for the night; Aramea shouted, "Suppers ready everybody."

When they were all settled at the table, Romulus asked Atticus. "How's everything gone here today, boy?"

"Everything has been done as you instructed, Sir."

"And what did you practice today?"

"With bow and arrow and javelin," explained Atticus.

"Did you manage to hit the targets, my little friend?" asked Zuma, smiling while eating a chunk of mutton.

"Never missed, my big friend," Atticus proclaimed winking at Zuma. Romulus smiled across the table and said,

"Well, isn't he full of it as usual?"

Zuma laughed, "Yes, might have to put him across my knee and spank his backside." With that big smile from ear to ear, and at that point everyone sitting at the table burst out into fits of laughter.

After the meal was finished, Atticus bid his farewell and made his way back to the city for a well-earned night sleep in the baker's storeroom.

Chapter 5

The next few years passed by quickly; winter came and went, summer passed in the blink of an eye.

Atticus worked hard and trained hard every day never complaining how hard it was. Atticus and Naomi had become very close. Romulus and Zuma had become aware of how well Atticus was mastering the sword, his archery and his javelin throwing was second to none for someone so young.

Atticus was fourteen now, standing a good five foot eight, his jet-black hair was down to his shoulders, and with all the physical work, was becoming very broad and muscular. Zuma kept teasing Atticus, telling him one day while Atticus was asleep, he'd cut his hair short jokingly. Atticus had a typical Roman nose and cheekbones and had become a very striking individual.

Naomi was now eighteen and very good looking; Romulus kept joking it was about time she got married, and she would always reply "never, don't need no man to spoil my day" with a smile.

So, life was good, but "time moved on too quickly" Romulus would often say; it was coming up to his sixtieth birthday which was making him feel very old, but he was fit and very agile still, this had been helped by all the training with Atticus over the last few years.

It was only six in the morning, but Atticus was already hard at work cleaning the stables in the early morning sun; he'd already put Blaze and Lightning into the paddock to graze in the early sunshine. And as soon as he'd finished cleaning the stable, he put a saddle on Fury because Fury needed to run and let some steam off.

Atticus climbed up and sat in the saddle and gently nudged Fury forward towards the fields that led down to the river and forest. Atticus had slung his bow over his shoulder and hung a quiver of arrows over one of the saddles horns, just in case of trouble or he might kill some game for supper.

So off they rode at a canter down the field. At the bottom was a wooden fence and as they approached Fury needed no prompting and charged forward leaping over the fence with ease.

Atticus patted Fury's neck. "Well done, Fury." And on they went, Atticus had a gleaming well-polished sword hanging in a scabbard from his belt that Romulus had purchased for him as a gift for his fourteenth birthday. Atticus was so proud of his first ever sword, he would polish it twice a day and sharpen it every few days. Leaving the stables and paddock behind they rode on down the slopes, and through the brush. Fury picked up the pace to a gallop and charged on down the field towards the river crossing, passing the big oak tree at the bottom.

The ground levelled out and Fury slowed to a trot as they approached the river; they had travelled about four miles since leaving the farm. The river was shallow at this time of the year, so Fury had no trouble reaching the other side. Then they followed the track leading into the forest where Atticus hoped to kill something for supper, realising he didn't have too long to spare. Atticus had promised Naomi, he would help her feed the pigs and milk the goats and that was one of the reasons he arrived so early at the farm to give him a couple of hours for hunting. Atticus slowly nudged Fury forward, quietly working their way between the trees and bushes hoping for any sign of prey.

Fury was even careful not to stand on any small branches to alert any prey close by. After about thirty minutes stalking their way through, they came across a small clearing. Pausing at the edge, just through the trees on the far side was a small wild boar foraging for food.

Very slowly, Atticus knocked an arrow and pulled the bowstring back; the boar was about sixty yards away, and as quick as a flash, Atticus took aim and fired.

The arrow thumped straight into the boar's chest striking its heart, killing it instantly. Down it went; Atticus had become a very fine shot spending hours a day, week in week out, shooting at archery targets. Sometimes he would ride Fury at pace firing arrow after arrow as fast as he could at the targets.

But this was his first kill with the bow. Atticus rode over to where the young boar had fallen. He slid down from Fury and pulled the arrow out. He then took some rope off the back of the saddle, tied the boar's legs together and heaved it on to Fury's back, tying it securely so it wouldn't fall off. He then quickly mounted and set off back to the farm feeling quite pleased with himself.

Half an hour later he rode into the courtyard and jumped down from Fury; Zuma was in the corner chopping wood ready for winter and laying it in neat rows up against the outer walls. Zuma turned towards Atticus and said,

"Well, what have you got there, my little friend?"

"Supper," replied Atticus, "and if you chop enough wood for a fire to roast it on, I might let you have some, my big friend." And he began to laugh.

Seconds later, Atticus had to duck quickly as a piece of freshly chopped wood came flying in his direction.

"Okay, Zuma, you can have as much as you like." He chuckled.

Zuma walked over to Fury with a big smiling face looking at the young boar and said,

"I see you struck it in the heart, impressive for your first kill, it will make fine eating for everyone. I'll get a fire going and set up a spit to roast it on. You'd better take it to the kitchen for Aramea to gut and clean it," said Zuma.

"Can't, I'm already late to help Naomi with the pigs and goats," replied Atticus and turned to run off to the pig pen.

"Any excuse so you can spend some time with that girl. I suppose you want me to see to Fury as well," shouted Zuma and started to grumble to himself, "I don't know, kids today, eh."

When Atticus arrived at the pig pen, Naomi was already feeding them, shooing them away as she threw the scraps of waste, vegetables, and leftovers into the trough.

"You're late," she chastised him.

"I know, I'm sorry, but I've killed a wild boar and we're having a roast tonight," Atticus replied proudly, hoping that would calm her temper, not that she had much of a temper anyway.

"Good, now start milking the goats or I'll never get my work done and hurry up about it."

'No pleasing some women' he thought to himself and got straight on with the milking. As soon as they had finished, Atticus made his excuses and left for training with Romulus.

"Why are you late?" bellowed Romulus.

"What's up with everybody today? Everyone's in a rush to be somewhere else," replied Atticus.

Romulus looked at him.

"Oh, we are a bit tetchy today," replied Romulus with a grin, "start on the blocks, get yourself warmed up, lad, loosen them shoulders and stretch your arms. Then when you're ready, we'll have a proper session. Zuma thinks you're getting pretty good so its best I see for myself, lad."

The last few months of training had been left in the hands of Zuma as Romulus had been busy delivering the amphoras of wine to the taverns and brothels, with the help of several farm slaves and was often too tired when he got back; the town was full of legionnaires filling their bellies getting drunk and shagging plenty of whores in the local brothels.

Romulus had also been to the slave market and purchased a couple of handy looking slaves to guard the farm at night.

Things were getting a bit lively in the mountains a few miles further out with an increase in attacks on merchants travelling into the city to sell their goods; even though there had been an increase in patrols to catch and kill the bands of brigands and deserters.

So, after twenty minutes of warming up, Romulus beckoned Atticus over,

"Right, time for a proper sparring session, boy."

Immediately, Atticus started to circle Romulus, and as quick as a flash, tossed his sword from his right hand to his left hand and back again.

Atticus had practised fighting with his left hand as well as his right and was quite comfortable fighting with a sword in either hand which caught Romulus by surprise.

Atticus feint to the left and then immediately to the right, he lunged at Romulus and then slashed left and right, and then jumped upwards to his left and brought his sword crashing down towards the head of Romulus who had to use all his wits and sword skills to block all the attacks by Atticus.

Then Romulus lunged forward and attacked Atticus, first to the head which was blocked with ease and then to his body, again Atticus blocked it with ease.

Romulus went forward again, slashing left then right still Atticus parried them all without any problem, neither Romulus nor Atticus took their eyes off each other.

Both of them concentrating hard, hadn't noticed Zuma and Naomi had come to watch the duel unfolding.

Romulus had started to breathe heavily in the heat of mid-afternoon, sweat was pouring down the faces of both Atticus and Romulus, both fighters attacking forward and then back peddling, blocking their opponent. But in an instant Atticus spun to his left dived and rolled to the back of Romulus and swept his right leg through the back of Romulus's legs before he had any chance to react, knocking him off balance. Down Romulus fell, heavily onto his back, and before he could move, Atticus had placed his wooden sword at Romulus's throat.

Romulus let out a slight groan from being winded falling hard to the floor, Atticus looked down at Romulus with a smile and said,

"What's up, Sir? Needed to lie down. Were you getting tired?"

Romulus looked up at Atticus and replied, "Well done, lad, now pull me the fuck up."

Zuma then began to clap loudly, but Naomi didn't know how to react and just stood still with her mouth firmly shut, after all that, her master was lying on the floor. But her eyes were full of love and admiration for Atticus. Zuma, with that big smile of his, exclaimed,

"Told you, Romulus, the boy's learning fast."

"I know, I've just found out for myself," dusting himself down, looking at Atticus and beaming with pride.

"Looks like all that hard work and training is paying off."

Romulus then put his arm around Atticus, hugged him and said, "I couldn't be prouder of you; even if you were my son." Romulus had never married and as far as he knew had never fathered any children. Romulus then turned to Zuma and said,

"How's that boar coming along? I'm feeling very hungry after that little work out, smells dam good from over here."

"Just a couple of hours more, Seema is turning it and basting the boar over the fire as we speak," replied Zuma.

"Well, in that case let's all sit out in the courtyard this evening and get Aramea and the other house slaves to set a large table. I want bread, figs, fruit the whole nine yards and open a barrel of our finest wine," said Romulus.

"Yes, and I will make sure the whole household gets washed and changed ready to join the feast," replied Zuma.

That evening, everyone ate their fill of hot roasted meat and fresh bread, fruit and drank plenty of fine wine. The house slaves all loved living and working for Romulus, who they thought to be a very fair and generous master.

And for the very first time, Atticus heard Zuma singing songs from his native homeland, entertaining everyone after the feast.

Chapter 6

The next few weeks passed by; autumn had arrived the nights began to close in and there was a chill in the air. Atticus carried on training hard after his chores were done.

"Snow's coming to the mountain tops and hills. I can feel it in my bones," Romulus mumbled to himself.

Fires were lit in the main house and sleeping quarters of the slaves and farm workers, the larder was full and plenty of feed filled the barn for the animals.

"One thing is for sure" Romulus mused "we're definitely ready for winter."

Zuma with the help of Atticus had chopped plenty of wood for the fires to keep them warm at night through the winter months.

Romulus looked over at Atticus who was cleaning and sharpening his sword and said,

"Better start making your way home. It's going to be a cold one tonight unless you want to sleep here instead."

"Thank you, but I need to check on Misha and Castus. I like to make sure they're all right." Atticus smiled.

Romulus strolled over to Atticus and patted him on his shoulder. "I know they have been good to you over these past few years, and I know you're more than capable but take care." They clasped their forearms and Atticus replied, "I'd better get off then."

"Give me the sword and I will put it away for tomorrow," said Romulus.

"Thanks, and I'll see you early in the morning." Atticus had put a cape on over his tunic to help keep himself warm, and then made his way out of the gate and down the road towards the city.

He'd got a sharp knife hanging in a sheath from his belt out of sight just in case he ran into any kind of trouble.

It was definitely getting colder he could see the trail of vapour coming out of his mouth when he exhaled. He looked up at the night sky, filled his lungs and exhaled to see how far he could blow a trail of vapour. *'Not bad,'* he thought and then started jogging down the road to keep warm.

Upon arriving back at the bakery, he could hear Misha sobbing and quickly went inside. Misha was cleaning and dabbing blood off the face of Castus.

"What's happened?" Atticus asked as Misha turned to face him, he could see bruising appearing under her left eye and a slight swelling on her cheek. Castus had a split lip and blood pouring out of his nose. Misha sobbed and said,

"They wanted more money this time, but we just didn't have it, so they're coming back tomorrow for more."

"How long ago did this happen?" asked Atticus.

"About ten minutes before you arrived," said Castus.

"How many were they?"

"Six of them came and were led by a new gang member I've not seen before," replied Castus.

"When I've gone, bolt the doors and windows when I return, I will knock twice, pause and then knock three times so you know it's me, don't open it for anyone else."

"Oh, don't go," Misha pleaded with Atticus, "I don't want you getting hurt, it doesn't matter, stay."

Atticus looked into her little round face and said,

"I won't be the one getting hurt, they need to be taught a lesson." Atticus then stroked the side of her chin and went out into the night, closing the door behind him.

Atticus knew exactly which way they would go back to their lair and the quickest way to catch up was over the rooftops. So, he climbed up onto the tiled roofs overlooking the alleyways and with stealth, speed, and agility, making as little noise as possible ran and jumped from one roof to the next. It wasn't long before he could hear voices ahead in the alley below.

It was pitch black with very little moonlight, only flickers of light shone through the cracks in the closed shutters of people's windows.

As he got closer, he could see the backs of a couple of them straggling behind the others walking in single file in the narrow alleyways strewn with rubbish and shit. Rats scurried amongst the alleys looking for food, several were eating and clawing the carcass of a dead dog.

Down he dropped to the floor not even making a sound or disturbing the rats feeding, and up the dark alley he went behind them. '*Vengeance is mine,*' thought Atticus to himself. On he stalked the gang, soon the one at the back stopped to take a piss in a corner, Atticus smiled and in seconds put his hand over the mouth of the gang member to stop him making a sound.

He was smaller than Atticus and about sixteen years old, two years older than Atticus. Atticus then quickly put his other hand around his neck and with a sudden twist a snap came the sound, as the boy's neck broke.

Atticus let go and dropped him into his own pool of piss, and continued on up the alley, avoiding the piles of shit on the floor, thinking, '*One down five to go.*'

Soon he'd caught up with the second one; he was quite heavily built, almost six foot tall, the same as Atticus, and also about sixteen. As he passed a side alley, Atticus was on him in a flash, grabbing him around his neck from behind. Atticus had already pulled the knife out of its sheath with his other hand, and he slit the throat of the gang member without so much as a second thought. He then gently dropped him into a pile of shit, blood gushing out of his throat, the last bit of air exhaling from his lungs as he died.

Atticus went on silent, focused, only one thing motivating him: vengeance. '*Two down, four to go,*' he thought to himself.

Moments later he heard a voice calling his comrades and footsteps coming back down the alley. Atticus quickly hid in the shadow of a doorway out of sight; the boy shouted,

"Stop fucking about, you two, it's freezing!"

The boy was scrawny and only about five foot tall. He slowly passed Atticus, peering down the alley and shouted,

"Where the fuck are you?"

Atticus pulled him into the shadow of the doorway hand over his mouth so he couldn't make a sound. He then punched his knife up through the bottom of his back twisting it as it went into the bottom of his lung. The breath of life drained from his body, Atticus pulled the knife out and dropped him in the doorway and on he went. '*Three down three to go.*'

Further up, Atticus could hear the three remaining gang members talking amongst themselves. Atticus hid in the shadows just out of sight and listened, the leader angrily shouted,

"You two, get down that fucking alley and tell that lot to bloody well hurry up! I haven't got all night, I'm freezing my tits off, give me that jug of wine, I'll wait for you around that bloody corner."

Atticus let them pass thinking, '*I will deal with you two later but first time to meet your new leader.*' Atticus quickly and silently dashed down a side alley and up another one to come out in front of the leader, who was standing in a doorway; he was swigging from the jug of wine and belching loudly.

Atticus spoke with a chill in his voice enough to make the hairs on a rat's back stand to attention,

"Now then you piece of shit! It's time for you to answer to the Gods!"

The gang leader stepped out of the doorway looking at Atticus,

"Who the fuck do you think you are?" he growled.

"Your worst fucking nightmare," replied Atticus with the look of death written all over his face stepping forward.

"Piss off if you know what's good for you," came the reply, spitting wine out of his mouth and belching loudly again.

The leader was six foot two, a couple of inches taller than Atticus but very fat and clearly out of condition. He was about twenty years of age; he'd already lost his front teeth and was quite ugly looking. Atticus hadn't seen him around these parts before, and age didn't matter to Atticus, he had trained every day for the last eight years; he was a perfect fighting machine even at the young age of fourteen. Before the leader could continue to speak, Atticus lunged forward, thundering his fist straight into his throat. The force of the punch crushed his windpipe into the back of his neck, the sound of cracking bones broke the silence that had descended in the alley. Down he fell, Atticus just looked down at him watching the last gasps of air coming out of his mouth; the ebb of life slowly drifting out, death had arrived to take him from this world.

Atticus bent down and cut off the large purse of coins hanging from his belt then quickly returned to the alley and went in search of the other two. It didn't take long; they were already coming back up. Atticus had tied the purse of money to his belt and out of sight. As soon as they saw Atticus' fear spread across their faces like a wildfire, they'd obviously found the dead bodies of their companions. They immediately froze, standing still in silence unable to utter any words. Then before they could come to their senses Atticus slashed one of them across his throat with his knife.

The boy who was about fourteen fell to his knees holding his throat trying to stem the flow of blood.

Atticus grabbed the second boy who was a little older, tall, and skinny, pulled him towards him, looking straight into the terrified boy's eyes and coldly said,

"That's the last time you'll hurt anyone I love."

Atticus slid his knife up through the youth's chin so hard, the blade penetrated his brain, killing him instantly. Atticus slid his knife back out and dropped the lifeless body onto the floor, the other one had bled to death lying face down.

Atticus strode down the alley feeling no remorse, turned left, and disappeared into the night.

An hour after leaving the bakers, Atticus had returned. He knocked twice paused and knocked three times again. The bolt inside crunched and the door opened slowly. Castus looked out then stepped back to let Atticus in, locking the door behind him. He turned to face Atticus, looking at him in the candlelight and said with fear in his voice,

"My god, lad, where are you hurt? You're covered with blood."

"Don't worry, Castus it's not mine, calm down, I'm all right."

Misha came running into the kitchen and said,

"Oh, my dear boy, what have you done? Quick get those clothes off for me to wash! Somebody might come. Hurry up, Atticus."

While he was undressing, Misha told Castus to get a bowl of water and soap for Atticus to wash all the blood off himself. Quickly Castus rushed off and returned with the bowl of water and soap, but before Atticus began to wash, he turned to Misha and placed the purse full of money on the table in front of her.

"Hide this! It's for you and Castus, don't spend it all at once. You might raise some suspicion." Then, he quickly began to wash the blood off himself.

Misha replied,

"Bless you, lad, and as soon as you've finished, better get off to bed and blow those candles out we've seen enough trouble for one night."

Chapter 7

The following morning Atticus was up bright and early. Misha and Castus were baking bread and pastries. "Morning, Atticus," said Castus.

"Morning," he replied, rubbing his eyes to adjust to the light.

Misha handed him his clothes saying, "Here you are, they're clean and dry."

As he dressed, they could hear a commotion going on in the alleyway, Atticus opened the door and went outside. Soldiers were running up the alleyway shouting,

"Out of the way. Come on, make way," shoving bystanders and onlookers out of the way.

One of the cloth merchants came walking down squeezing his way past the people crowding the narrow alley. As he approached, Atticus asked him,

"What's going on up there?" trying not to appear too concerned.

"They've found a few dead bodies further up the alleyways, bit gruesome by all accounts."

"Come on, move," shouted another couple of soldiers pushing their way through.

The merchant almost fell over as they barged past and would have done if Atticus hadn't taken hold of his arm.

"Thank you, my friend," said the merchant and then carried on speaking,

"Looks like there's been a bit of a gang fight as to who's turf it is if you ask me!"

"Probably is," replied Atticus shrugging his shoulders, the merchant then went on to say moving a little closer and in a whisper.

"Some are saying it's a demon! Come to make retribution of some sort, being as nobody heard a sound or saw anything."

Then the merchant shivered as if someone had just walked over his grave.

"And anyway, by all accounts, the soldiers don't seem to be really bothered seeing as it's only vermin from the gangs," said the merchant.

And on that note, the merchant bid his farewell and went off down the alley without looking back and disappeared amongst the throng of people.

Atticus turned and went back inside the bakers, Misha whispered,

"Everything alright? Nobody saw you last night, did they?" she had a worried look on her face.

"Doesn't look like it and from what one of the merchant's up there said, nobody really cares!"

"Good," Misha replied, "better make yourself scarce and get off up to the farm or you'll be late!" Atticus nodded and put his clean cape on.

Misha passed him some fresh bread and cheese.

"Eat this on your way and we'll see you tonight."

"Thank you," replied Atticus, as he made his way out and on to the main street and made his way up towards the main gates.

Crowds of people were still gathered at the entrance to the alleyway further up, talking amongst themselves trying to find out what had transpired. As he passed under the archway, one of the guards nodded at Atticus; he smiled in response and off he went up the road at a good pace.

There was still a cold chill in the air even though the sun was out. Just over an hour and a half later, Atticus arrived at the farm. Atticus banged on the door and Figo one of the house slaves opened it saying,

"Good morning, young Sir," and bolted it shut behind Atticus, after letting him in.

Atticus entered the main house and walked down the corridor leading to the kitchen. Romulus was sitting at the table eating his porridge and looked up and said,

"Morning, young Atticus."

"Morning, master," he replied with a cheeky grin.

"Don't start with your bloody cheek, you've just got here," he replied with a smile,

"Help yourself to some porridge and sit yourself down here next to me, I want a little chat before you start your chores."

Atticus got a wooden bowl and filled it up and sat down. Romulus looked at Atticus and asked,

"That trouble on the Aventine last night had it anything to do with you?"

Atticus would never lie to Romulus; he paused before replying, and then began to tell Romulus of what had happened the night before when he'd returned home to the bakery, followed by the events that had unfolded afterwards in the alleys.

Romulus sat and listened without interrupting and when Atticus had finished Romulus sat quietly stroking his chin before responding. Then, whilst looking at Atticus, Romulus spoke,

"In life sometimes we have to take life, whether it be fighting in battle or protecting our loved ones, or those not capable of protecting themselves," he then paused for a moment,

"I've always tried to live my life doing this and never killed anybody who didn't deserve to die or wasn't trying to kill me, so as far as I'm concerned, you've acted with honour in the protection of those you love so there's no more to say." Romulus put his arm around Atticus giving him a slight hug saying,

"Finish that porridge and get to work, we've plenty to do."

Atticus smiled at Romulus and said, "Thank you." He finished his breakfast and went to the stables.

When Atticus arrived in the stable straight away, Fury began to get excited seeing him.

"Now then Fury you seem to be happy to see me!" as he approached Fury's stall. Fury began stamping his front leg and nodding his head vigorously snorting through his nose. Atticus patted Fury on his neck then ruffled his mane,

"Come on then, time for some water and exercise while I clean all this mess up."

He then led Fury out to the field stopping briefly to allow Fury to get a drink from the trough. As soon Fury got through the gate to the field, off he charged, kicking his hind legs, and jumping about shaking his mane. Atticus smiled and went back into the stable and led Blaze and Lightning out for a drink and put them into the field too. He then closed the gate as Fury charged past.

Atticus then began mucking out the stable, cleaning and putting everything back in its place, happy in the knowledge Romulus believed in him. He put in fresh bedding and filled the feed buckets with oats, making sure everything was in order, he then took some blankets out and put them on Blaze and lightning to keep them warm. Fury was too busy charging around, keeping himself warm.

Atticus then went down to the vineyard to help Naomi, there were a couple of farm workers already helping her.

"Hi, Naomi," Atticus shouted as he arrived, "how are you today?" trying to make polite conversation with her. He'd always found it hard talking to her without going red and feeling a warm glow on his cheeks.

"Fine, Atticus, how are you?" replied Naomi,

"Oh, I'm good. What do you want me to do?" No matter how fearless Atticus was when it came to fighting, he was always a little shy around Naomi.

"Over here, help me with these vines," she replied.

After a couple of hours or so she shouted over to Atticus,

"Time to go for lunch."

As they walked back up the fields towards the main house Naomi turned to Atticus saying,

"I suppose after lunch you will be playing with those silly weapons?" She teased and ran off up to the house. Atticus ran after her shouting,

"They're not, silly," he protested, Naomi just carried on running and began to laugh.

Atticus went into the stable and collected the bread and cheese Misha had given him to eat on the way to work but had decided to save it knowing Aramea would have made some hot porridge. He then sat down on a bale of hay eating his lunch, when he'd finished, he went to the paddock and brought Blaze and Lightning back in, putting them into their stalls. It had just started to snow so he shouted,

"Fury, come on, time to get out of the snow."

Fury pretended not to hear and carried on running around at the bottom of the hill. Atticus smiled to himself and shouted,

"I know you heard me, come on or no hunting trip tomorrow!"

Straight away Fury charged up the hill and jumped the fence and came to a stand-still, shaking flakes of snow out of his mane.

"Show off," said Atticus laughing,

"Come on, back into your stall, no more messing around," whilst walking into the stable, Fury following close behind.

By the time Fury was eating his oats and back in his stall, the snow started to really come down. Atticus shut the stable door and ran into the main house. Romulus shouted,

"We're in my private quarters if that's you, Atticus?"

"It is," he replied and went through the kitchen and into Romulus's private lounge. This was a very large room with two large couches, with cushions on either side of a fireplace. At one end of the room was a long table with piles of scrolls and maps neatly piled on it; that was where Atticus had learned to read and write Greek and Latin. A above the table was a large window with shutters at either side. In the corner there was a bust of the emperor Augustus. Hanging on the wall was a wool and silk tapestry depicting a roman battle legionnaire's fighting men with painted faces and above the fireplace was a large tapestry depicting a roman sea battle. Atticus had loved standing looking at them taking in every detail when he was very young and still did. On a small table at the opposite end of the room to the window was a small shrine to the roman Gods, Jupiter, and Mars who both Romulus and Zuma believed in.

"It's a lot bloody warmer in here," said Atticus, walking into the room. Romulus and Zuma were sitting on the couches eating some figs and drinking wine.

"Now then, lad," said Romulus.

Zuma smiled saying,

"Good day, my little friend," not that Atticus was little anymore but Zuma standing seven feet tall, towered over most men.

"Hello, my big friend, hope your neck is not too stiff having to bend down under these ceilings, wouldn't want you getting a permanent stoop" replied Atticus laughing.

Then he turned to Romulus and said,

"Good day, master," with a cheeky grin.

"I'll give you, master," throwing one of the cushions hitting Atticus in the chest. Over the past few years, since Atticus had arrived when all three were in each other's company it became natural to take the piss out of each other on most occasions.

"It's a bit cold out there today for weapons practise," said Romulus.

"It is a bit, but I don't mind," replied Atticus.

"No matter, me and Zuma have come up with a little test for you." They all walked over to the table where a large map had been spread over it.

"What is it?" enquired Atticus. The map showed various mountain ranges, a large forest, a river, trails leading to the forest, mountains and a trail leading to a fort. Romulus began,

"Right, Atticus, you're in charge of a relief column of some eighty men and a small wagon trail consisting of four wagons carrying weapons and supplies for the fort! But there is a large enemy force of three-hundred men, one hundred of which is cavalry, the rest are infantry coming to attack you from the west here!" Romulus pointing at the map.

"You and your men are approaching from here! The task at hand, I want you to position your men, find the best terrain and work out how much time you have before you are attacked. Make your best strategy to save your men and supplies."

Romulus paused for a few seconds, then said,

"It's midday, the sun is at its highest in the west of your position, the enemies ten miles away and closing in, information you have received from your scouts."

Zuma then said,

"You've got approximately an hour before you're attacked, the test starts now!"

Atticus began concentrating, going over in his head all the details of the map; Romulus and Zuma sat back down on the couches, keeping quiet eating the figs, and drinking some of Romulus's fine wine. After about fifty minutes Atticus turned around, looked over at Romulus and Zuma and said,

"Done!"

Romulus and Zuma walked over to the table and looked at the map; Atticus had marked out his columns position and defences. Romulus asked,

"Why not position yourself in the forest?"

"The forest is further to the west, nearer to where the enemy is approaching from. It would be slow and hard to get the wagons off the trail and into the trees, the forest floor is flat, no high ground and not enough time to set up a reasonable defensive position. The greater number of enemy infantries attacking us through the forest at our front." Atticus paused for a moment, "And their cavalry could easily attack our rear from the open ground here." Atticus pointing at the map, "We lose."

"What about here?" Zuma pointed at the map. "On this slope."

Again, Atticus responded,

"Yes, it's on higher ground, a bit further away from the enemies approaching, more time to make our defences but we're open to attack from all sides." Atticus paused again, "Their cavalry could quite easily get to the higher slope there –" pointing at the map – "throw their javelins and fire down arrows onto us while were attacked on the other three sides, eventually we lose." Then Romulus suggested,

"Why not make a dash for the fort?"

"Not enough time, the wagons would slow us down. We'd be caught in the open by a much greater force and slaughtered."

"Then explain why that position you've chosen, lad?"

"It's the furthest away from the enemy plenty of time to prepare a strong defensive position. It's at the base of that mountain no way to attack us from behind or to the left, they couldn't attack us from the right because of the river." Atticus paused for Romulus and Zuma to look over his defensive position.

"Their only option left is a frontal attack; we'd cut them down with our archers. I've placed markers at one-hundred yards, then again at seventy yards for the archers, then again at forty yards we'd throw our javelins. Then just in front of our trench, hundreds of caltrops are waiting for their remaining forces!"

"Nasty bugger." Smiled Zuma.

"I know that will cause disarray slicing their feet taking down those in front and those behind would be pushed over them. Then I would launch our remaining javelins onto them and have my archers attack their cavalry by that time, their losses would be so great they'd have to retreat or surrender. If not, we form testudo march in and kill them all at this point we win! Minimum losses to us."

Atticus looked up from the map and across to Romulus and Zuma waiting for a response. Romulus spoke first,

"Excellent! I like it. What do you think, Zuma?"

"Perfect, it's a shame most of our commanders were as thick as pig shit and didn't give a fuck about our losses," answered Zuma.

"True, but we still had one or two good ones," Romulus replied gazing out of the window. "That snow is coming thick and fast and it's starting to settle quite deep. What do you want to do, Atticus? sleep here tonight or make your way home?"

Atticus replied, "It will only take an hour if I jog keeping me warm. It will help me keep my fitness level up, don't want you two thinking I'm getting soft and lazy."

Zuma smiled and said, "That will be the day."

Then Romulus said, "Tie them rabbit furs around the bottom of your legs helps against the cold, better get yourself off, lad. We'll see you in the morning."

The two guards were well wrapped up and already patrolling the palisade outside as Atticus left and began to jog down the road towards the city. Figo, one of the house slaves, locked the large door behind him.

As he approached the gate, two guards stepped out towards him, one of them spoke as swirls of snow blew around their faces in the dark.

"Who goes there?"

"Atticus returning from Romulus's farm," he replied.

"It's okay," the second guard spoke. "I recognise this lad," speaking to the other guard, "off you go." letting Atticus through the gates and into the great city.

Not long later he was knocking on the door of the bakery, Castus opened the door and said, "Quick, come in, don't let the heat out."

A log fire crackled as it burnt in the fireplace with a large pot hanging over it. As soon as Atticus was in, Castus bolted the door and placed two sacks of flour at the base of the door to stop the snow blowing in under it.

"Bloody awful out there, lad, there's some broth on the fire. It's nice and hot, there's a bowl and spoon on the table and some fresh bread help yourself."

"Thank you," replied Atticus, stamping his feet trying to get some feeling back in his toes.

"Has anything else happened down here today while I've been up at the farm?"

"No, nothing. It's been very quiet once all that commotion died down earlier."

"Good."

Then Atticus filled his bowl with the broth and sat down at the table, pulling a chunk of bread, and dipping it into the broth.

"Misha's gone to bed. She's quite exhausted after all the goings on over the last 24 hours and she's up early tomorrow, mind you so am I." Castus chuckled. "So, I'll say goodnight and see you in the morning, young man," and off he went to bed.

"Goodnight," replied Atticus, and as soon as he'd finished his supper, Atticus went to his bed in the storeroom.

Chapter 8

Spring had arrived Atticus had put the horses out to graze, but all Fury wanted to do was charge around kicking up as much dust as possible. Atticus had cleaned the stables, taken a cart carrying the water urns down the fields to Naomi and the field hands tending the vines and crops of vegetables. He'd helped Seema feed the pigs and milk the goats and was now practising with his swords. Romulus, Zuma and four of the house slaves had set off for the city with a cart loaded up with amphoras of wine for the taverns and brothels of Rome. *'It's been all go since the first thing this morning,'* Atticus thought to himself as he slashed his blades at the wooden post.

It was only a couple of weeks away from June and his sixteenth birthday, almost ten years had passed since he first arrived at the farm. He was planning on joining the legions as soon as he was eighteen, knowing full well he had to be twenty but as he was already six foot two and very broad, he could quite easily pass for twenty. He'd been training every day for the last ten years with sword, bow, javelin, and riding Fury, he could also read and write in both Latin and Greek.

Atticus often rode Fury while standing up in the stirrups not holding the reins firing arrows at targets at speed never missing the centre of the targets. He could quite easily throw a javelin further than Romulus and almost as far as Zuma. He could also fight with a sword in either left or right hand and also with two swords at the same time. Such was his dedication to training with all weapons day in day out. On many occasions Naomi would watch him riding Fury with awe at his riding skills, jumping fences while not holding the reins of Fury and shooting arrows at targets never missing. Naomi made sure Atticus couldn't see her watching him or so she thought, she didn't want him getting big headed. Not only that Naomi didn't want Atticus to realise she'd totally fallen head over heels in love with him, but she also did her best to hide it from everyone.

Early in the afternoon Zuma and Romulus returned from the city, Atticus was at the archery targets practising with his bow. Romulus had gotten the house slaves to unload the goods they had bought from the market. They were also instructed to return the oxen to their enclosure and put the cart away. Romulus and Zuma walked up and lent on the fence behind Atticus and began coughing and farting loudly trying to put Atticus off hitting the centre of the targets set fifty yards away. Atticus laughed out loud and shouted,

"You'll have to try harder than that to make me miss and hit the target dead centre again with ease," turning to face them with a grin. Romulus turned to Zuma.

"Don't you think those targets are a bit close at fifty yards?"

"Looks like it to me," said Zuma laughing.

"Is that so?" replied Atticus with a grin. "Fancy a little wager you two?"

"Depends," asked Romulus.

"I will set two targets side by side at one-hundred yards." Atticus then paused for effect, "And with one pull of the bow fire, two arrows and hit both targets dead centre."

Romulus scratched his head looking at Atticus then said,

"One pull of the bow both targets dead centre 100 yards."

Then Romulus looked across at Zuma. "Don't know about you, Zuma, but can't see him pulling that off," whilst stroking his chin.

"What's the wager?" asked Zuma.

"Ten sesterce each," replied Atticus.

"And where are you getting 20 sesterces if you lose?" asked Romulus.

"Not planning on losing." Atticus smiled in response.

"Really! You're good but I still can't see how you are going to pull it off."

"Worth a bet then," Atticus replied, trying his best to entice them both.

"I'm in," said Zuma.

"Bugger it, so am I," said Romulus.

Atticus walked down to the targets and reset them at one hundred yards side by side, then went to the shed and brought out a longer bow.

Romulus raised his eyebrows saying, "That's an odd-looking bow I haven't seen one that long before."

Zuma looked on with a bit of a wry smile on his face, Romulus said to Zuma, "What do you make of that?"

"Longer bow longer distance but he's still got to hit both targets with a single draw of the bow," answered Zuma.

Atticus took up position and picked some dry grass up, throwing it in the air checking the wind direction even though there was only a slight breeze.

Then he took two arrows out of the quiver, knocked them both side by side and very slightly apart, took a deep breath, filling his lungs.

He held his breath drawing the bow back, needing all of his strength, then aimed towards the target to the right and fired at the same time slightly turning the bow left; both arrows flew to their respective targets. *Thud*! *thud*! Atticus turned bow in hand and bowed, behind him two targets with an arrow dead centre.

"Fuck me," said Romulus. Zuma just stood and clapped his hands together loudly with that big smile of his from ear to ear.

"Worth every sesterce," he said, and from the side of the shed they could hear a small pair of hands clapping furiously.

All three turned to see Naomi who immediately stepped back, tripped over a bucket, fell back with her legs in the air, scrambled to her feet and ran off down the field.

This made Romulus and Zuma both laugh loudly. Atticus just went red in the face.

"Looks like you've got an admirer, lad," said Romulus. "Anyway, it's time for lunch I'm famished. Aramea will be putting fresh fish meat and vegetables on the table as we speak so off to the kitchen they went."

Romulus wasn't the only one hungry, both Zuma and Atticus as usual were feeling hungry. The fresh fish and meat were cooked to perfection and melted in their mouths; they washed it down with several glasses of cold lemon water.

It was coming up to early evening, so Atticus bid his farewell saying,

"I will be here early before you ask in the morning."

"Here, lad, before you go, here's ten sesterces," said Romulus whilst pulling out his leather purse.

"And here's mine," Zuma said, pushing the coins across the table to Atticus.

Atticus set off back to the city, it was a beautiful warm evening. Romulus and Zuma were sitting outside on the stone benches at the side of the water fountain. They were enjoying a jug of wine from the cellar, and some nice dates. Romulus spoke, "I can't tell you how proud I am of Atticus, remember all those years ago when I found him sitting on that wall outside all smelly covered in grime!"

"I do," replied Zuma, "and that cheeky grin and sense of humour, he's grown so fast." Zuma paused to take a drink of wine.

Romulus continued, "Reads and writes, in both Latin and Greek and has worked so hard on the farm, looking after them horses."

"Can't even think of a time when he's ever complained," Zuma replied. "He's going to make a fine legionnaire, even I can't match his riding skills. Let alone the bow as we found out this afternoon," which made them laugh loudly. "And at some expense to us both," said Romulus.

"I struggle to best him with the sword and javelin and if things carry on as they are, it won't be long before he kicks my arse at those," said Zuma, both of them chuckling again.

"Fill these cups up with more wine. I feel like getting drunk," said Romulus.

"I won't complain haven't been drunk in ages." Zuma smiled.

"Do you realise Atticus is 16 shortly?" said Romulus.

"I do," replied Zuma.

"Well, I'm going to adopt him as my son!" Romulus then paused, looking into the face of Zuma for any sign of reaction, Zuma gave none. "And I will also give him Fury. What do you say, Zuma?"

Several moments passed while Zuma swallowed a mouthful of wine, he then began his reply,

"I've known you more than 25 years now, my friend, and in all that time you've treated me like your brother. You have a great heart and a very good judge of character." Zuma paused and took another drink.

"He is without any doubt a very special young man and has a strong will to do the right thing. Great things will come of him, and I believe one day Rome itself will be in his debt." Zuma paused again.

"So, my answer is yes, my friend, you are doing the right thing and now we should get drunk and enjoy the rest of the evening," and so they did.

Chapter 9

It was another hot day. Atticus was in the stable putting a saddle on Fury, ready to go hunting; he'd slung his quiver of arrows over his shoulder and fastened his sword onto his belt. He'd already groomed Blaze and Lightning and put them into the paddock. Seema was milking the goats, Aramea was in the kitchen preparing lunch, Naomi was down in the fields with two of the field hands tending to the vines at the bottom of the slope. Romulus and Zuma had returned from the city and were in the main house. All of a sudden Atticus heard Naomi screaming loudly breaking the silence. The shouts of "Help" coming from the field hands working with her Atticus jumped up onto Fury's back grabbing his bow in his hand holding the reins and rode out to see what was happening. He could see two men carrying off a couple of the piglets running down the field, a third man had Naomi slung over his shoulder making his way as fast as he could towards a fourth man sitting on horseback. He was holding the reins of several more horses under a large tree at the bottom of the field. Atticus rang the alarm bell hanging from a large post outside the stable door, as he set off at speed, his bow in the hand holding the reins. He managed to grab a javelin with his free hand that was leaning up against the side of the shed. Atticus's heart was pounding in his chest as loud as a drum.

"On! Fury on," he shouted as they charged down the field, Fury not really needing any prompting. His sword clattering at his side in its scabbard, the only thought rushing through his head was to '*save Naomi*' and kill anyone who stood in his way. Further down the field he went, passing one of the field hands bloods pouring from a wound to his left arm. On he went, he then noticed a fifth man running as fast as he could spear in hand, Atticus was gaining fast, he was now only a couple of hundred yards behind the group running on foot. They had almost reached their companion holding their horses and means of escape.

Fury was charging forward foaming at the mouth; Atticus was only one hundred yards behind now realising he needed to deal with their means of escape.

Atticus stood up in his stirrups, tightened his knees into Fury's flanks and with all his might launched the javelin straight at the one sitting on horseback under the tree. His aim was true after training day in day out over the last ten years. The javelin flew with such ferocity, punching straight into the man's chest smashing ribs, muscle, and flesh, knocking him backwards pinning him to the tree. The javelin became embedded in its trunk blood sprayed, his scream of death frightening the horses which made them scatter in all directions.

The two carrying the piglets turned and dropped them drawing their swords realising there was no escaping their pursuer.

The one carrying Naomi over his shoulder carried on running trying to escape into some bushes, the raider with the spear was about to throw it at Atticus but was too slow. Atticus had knocked an arrow to his bow and fired, striking the raider in the throat killing him in an instant.

No sooner had he hit the floor, Atticus had knocked another arrow aiming and firing at the one carrying Naomi off into the bushes. And seconds later the arrow struck him in the back of his head with a thud, causing the back of his head to shatter, such was the force. Down he went, dropping Naomi on top of himself the two remaining raiders immediately threw down their weapons raising their hands in the air begging for mercy. Atticus could hear the shouts from up behind him as Romulus and Zuma approached on Blaze and Lightning. Atticus slowly nudged Fury forward towards them with his sword drawn as they screamed again for mercy.

"On your knees," growled Atticus as he toward above them sitting on Fury, who began to stamp the hoof of his right leg into the ground in anger. They both fell to their knees in fear still pleading for their lives. Atticus slowly dismounted dropping down onto his feet all the time not taking his eyes off them for a second. They just knelt there whimpering with their heads hung low, not daring to make eye to eye contact with Atticus. He could hear Naomi sobbing as she got to her feet, Atticus's sword gleamed in the sunlight, slowly he approached them and demanded.

"What gives you the right to steal from my master, Romulus?" Atticus then paused before continuing and began circling the two men. "And causing fear and pain to my friend Naomi."

"Sorry, Sir, sorry," they whimpered.

Atticus then placed the tip of his sword under the chin of the nearest raider forcing his head up and making him look at Atticus. The raider was in his mid-twenties, unshaven, quite broad with a broken nose, the raider just stared up at Atticus daring not to utter a word. Atticus noticed the tattoo of the legions on his arm and began pointing at it with his sword and said coldly with low growl.

"Not only are you thieves but deserters and a stain on the glory of Rome!" Then with the speed of lightning drew back his sword and with one swift stroke took off his head causing blood to spray over the other deserter who screamed out in fear. Romulus and Zuma arrived pulling up Blaze and Lightning,

"Leave one alive, Atticus!" shouted Romulus.

"Don't worry, this one will face justice back in Rome," Atticus replied with a smile. Then Atticus cleaned the blood off his sword on the dead man's headless body and returned it to his scabbard. Naomi ran over to Atticus throwing her arms around him, still sobbing, and said,

"You've saved me!" looking up at him with tear filled eyes, hugging him hard. This took Atticus out of his dark mood and feeling her body against his felt his cheeks redden and struggled to reply,

"Oh, err! You're safe now, no need to worry!" Atticus gently lifted her up stroking her hair and sat her on Fury. Zuma turned to Romulus and said,

"Well, I never, no fear taking on five deserters all by himself, then stands their knees practically knocking going red in the face because a girl puts her arms around him." Both Romulus and Zuma laughed.

"Do stop teasing him," Naomi said with a smile.

Romulus turned to the house slaves who had all arrived, some panting from the exertion of running down the fields.

"Round up those horses and tie this one up and take him up to the courtyard, don't take your eyes off him. I don't want him escaping. Collect the dead bodies, tie them onto their horses so they don't fall off." Then, Romulus paused looking at the dead deserter still dangling stuck to the tree with the javelin,

"Zuma pull that javelin out and shove that body on a horse! And can somebody put that bloody head in a sack. We'd better make sure we take everything back down to the Garrison in Rome early tomorrow."

When they all arrived back in the courtyard, Aramea and Seema ran over to Naomi engulfing her in their arms crying, Aramea saying,

"Oh! My poor lovely Naomi, are you alright?"

"I am now, thanks to Atticus," she replied.

Chapter 10

The following morning, they set off for the city. It had been the first time Atticus had slept at the farm. Romulus had made him bathe to wash all the blood off himself and got Aramea to wash and dry his clothes. They'd tied the dead deserters across their horses, tying the horses in-line together, the surviving deserter was bound and tied to his saddle, being led by Atticus riding Fury. All the captured weapons and the sack containing the severed head were being carried by a spare horse led by Zuma. The sun shone bright in a cloudless sky, the mood among them was quite jovial and as they rode, fits of laughter echoed off the rocks on the sloping hills from time to time as they rode on towards the city. Flies had begun to buzz around the sack containing the severed head, and bodies of the dead deserters and a couple of buzzards circled above hoping for a meal.

As they approached the gate, several of the guards looked towards them, the optio in charge of the guard detail shouted "Halt" and walked over as they came to a stand-still. He then recognised Romulus, but by this time there were quite a few onlookers who were queuing to gain access to the city.

"Good day, Romulus, what have we here?" noticing all the flies buzzing around the dead bodies laid across the horses.

Several more soldiers walked over and stood behind their optio. "Good day, Gaius, how's your father these days?" Romulus spoke.

"Well, I hope he is that, but still as grumpy as ever," Gaius replied, which made them both laugh.

"These buggers are deserters who tried to raid my home yesterday and that one we kept alive for interrogation so I'm dropping them off up at the Garrison," explained Romulus.

"Oh, better not keep you any longer," and shouted, "guards, let these through straight away!"

Atticus nudged Fury forward and on they rode through the crowds of onlookers, some had begun pointing at the dead bodies talking amongst themselves.

As they rode towards the Garrison gates, crowds of people had begun to line the streets, trying to get a glimpse of the row of horses carrying the dead bodies.

When they arrived at the gate several guards blocked their way "halt" came the cry.

"State your business," shouted the commander of the gate.

Romulus replied, "brought some dead deserters and one for interrogation, who'd tried to raid my home yesterday."

The commander was quite short but stocky, clean shaven with very short, cropped hair. The rest of the guard were standing in line to attention behind him.

The commander began to walk between the horses. "Four dead and one alive, I see." Then he turned to face Romulus. "Looks like they picked the wrong homestead," said the commander looking up at the size of Romulus and Zuma sitting astride their horses.

Romulus replied, "Not us," then turned towards Atticus nodding in his direction, "my lad, over there, dealt with them all by himself."

A couple of the guards standing in line began to look across at Atticus while the commander spoke walking towards Atticus sitting on Fury.

"Did he now?"

As he got closer Fury began to stamp his hooves on the road and chomp on his bit.

Atticus patted Fury's neck saying, "Steady, boy."

Romulus laughed and said, "I wouldn't get too close to Fury; he can be a little temperamental at times if he doesn't know you."

"I see all five of them by yourself, how old are you, young man?" asked the commander while keeping his distance from Fury.

Atticus replied, "16, very shortly."

The commander turning to face Romulus. "Sixteen, very big for his age!"

Zuma then spoke out loud, "Yes, he may only be sixteen but he's been trained by me and Romulus from the age of six so you could say it was a bit one sided."

Several of the guards began to mutter among themselves, which made the commander shout, "Silence in the ranks unless you want my cane shoving up your arse."

Silence quickly restored; a large crowd had now gathered in the street behind quietly watching.

"Spurius fetch Centurion Metelus here at once and be quick about it," shouted the commander.

It wasn't long before boots were heard marching towards the gate from inside the Garrison as a group of soldiers led by Centurion Metelus, Spurius was marching just behind him.

Metelus walked straight up to Romulus clasping his forearm saying, "Good to see you're still alive and kicking you old dog." Then looking at Zuma. "Hello, my old friend. I see you're still as big and scary as ever!" which made all three of them laugh.

"Well, I be," said Metelus looking at the horses laden with the dead deserters, Romulus quickly updated Metelus of the previous days' action in detail.

Then Metelus walked amongst the horses of the dead deserters lifting up one of their heads looking at his face wafting away the flies buzzing around it.

"This one's Cyrus, a worthless piece of shit, no loss to the legions, being missing for about three weeks."

Then he walked on lifting another head up. "Well, well! Linus, another lazy cunt been missing for a month no less."

As he walked on to the third, he shouted, "Fuck me! Where's his head?"

Romulus grinned and replied, "In that sack hanging on that horse."

"Spurius, bring that sack here and empty it out onto the floor at my feet."

As the head rolled out Metelus said, "Don't know this bugger." Then he lifted the next dead deserter's head, again saying, "Don't know this one either!"

Metelus then looked at the deserter sat on the horse that Atticus held the reins of, and said, "But I do know that one! Goes by the name of Felix!" as he walked over. "Been wondering where you'd got to, you worthless piece of rat shit."

Metelus then promptly dragged him off his horse causing him to fall heavily onto the floor giving him a good kick as he landed, and said, "Looks like Sirius will be having some fun torturing you tonight," as Felix rolled around on the floor in pain.

Metelus turned to address Atticus, "Well, my lad, according to what my dear friend Romulus has told me, Rome owes you a debt of gratitude."

"It was nothing, Sir! Just keeping my loved ones safe," replied Atticus.

"Modesty as well as a good fighter! Rome needs more like you young man."

"Thank you," said Atticus.

"Romulus would you do me the honour of bringing everything into the Garrison while we lock that piece of shit up for Sirius to play with later. It won't take long to find out what information we can extract from him."

"Right, lads, dispose of these bodies," shouted the commander.

Then Metelus said,

"While there on with that I'll nip up to the pay master's office and collect your reward young man. Rome pays 20 sesterce per deserter dead or alive"

"That's one hundred sesterces!"

"Money well-earned I'd say," Metelus replied, and off he went.

Not long later, he returned with a bag of coins and handed it over to Atticus,

"Thank you, Sir," said Atticus.

Zuma said, "Nice tidy sum, lad. What are you planning to do with it?"

"Give it to Misha and Castus. They need it more than me," replied Atticus.

The deserter's horses had been returned to the Garrison; Felix the surviving deserter had been taken to the cells for interrogation.

The sound of hobnailed boots crunching on the stone road echoing off the buildings became louder as a large group of praetorian soldiers marched towards them. They were led by an officer wearing highly polished armour, and a decorated plumed helmet. Atticus thought to himself 'must be a very high-ranking officer'.

As they arrived, all the soldiers with Metelus stood to attention, Metelus saluted shouting, "Sir!"

The praetorian escort had come to a halt, which consisted of over thirty soldiers all standing to attention.

"Good day, Centurion Metelus. What have you to report?" looking around at Romulus and Zuma, Atticus stood in the background holding the reins of the horses.

"Sir! Good day, Tribune Marcus," then he quickly relayed the events of the morning and also what happened the previous day at Romulus's home in full detail making sure he'd not missed anything out.

"Good, make sure there's a full written report on the legatus' desk!"

"Yes, Sir," replied Metelus.

"Without delay word is spreading through the camp as we speak, don't want him hearing any gossip and hearsay, do we now?"

"No, Sir!" then Metelus saluted and marched off up past the barracks and out of sight.

Marcus turned and addressed Romulus, "Good day, Romulus, how's the retirement? Looks like you're still being kept on your toes," he said with a smile.

"It's good but it's not as lively as it's been lately though." Romulus chuckled.

"And I suppose this is the young man who's acted so bravely and saved the day?" Marcus went on to say while looking across at Atticus.

Romulus replied, "He certainly is, and I couldn't be prouder of him."

Atticus stood still without saying a word, a little in awe at being addressed by such a high-ranking officer of the Roman army.

Marcus stepped towards Atticus, "Well, young man, what made you chop one of those deserters heads off may I ask?"

"Sir, he was a deserter and, in my opinion, had disrespected the legions of Rome and what they stand for," replied Atticus.

"I see, and why didn't you chop the head off the remaining deserter?"

Atticus smiled and replied, "Thought you might need him for interrogation, there could be more out there needing to be rounded up!"

"Very good, very good indeed. I like your way of thinking, young man." Then he turned to Romulus saying, "Thank you, once again. I won't keep you any longer! I'd better get off to the cells and see how that interrogation is coming along." Then immediately, Marcus spun around and walked off to the cells with his large escort marching behind.

"Right, lads, it's time we set off back to the farm! Are you staying at the bakers tonight or is that a silly question?" asked Romulus.

"I'll stay at the bakers and be up early in the morning!"

"Take care," shouted Zuma.

"Yes, we'll see you in the morning," said Romulus while patting Atticus on his back.

"Give me Fury's reins. I will take him back with us."

Off they rode, most of the crowd of onlookers had dispersed, so Atticus walked over to the bakery wanting to tell them of the incident up at the farm.

Ten minutes later he was back at the bakery and as he went in shouted, "It's only me!" Misha came into the kitchen with Castus following close behind.

"Lovely to see you safe, got a bit worried last night when you didn't come home!"

"No need to worry, just got a bit late with one thing or another so I decided to sleep there."

Atticus then told Misha what had happened. "Hello, lad, I bet you're hungry?" said Castus.

"I'm famished and that fresh bread smells lovely," replied Atticus.

"Well, sit yourself down. I've got some nice mutton and cheese to go with it," and off he went into the larder then returned with a plate full saying, "here you are, lad." Misha went off and came back with a cup of wine for him.

"Here you are, Misha, almost forgot." Passing her the bag of money.

"Well, I never! Where did you get this?"

"Let's just say it's for services rendered to Rome," he said with a smile then put a large piece of mutton in his mouth.

"Better hide this somewhere safe," said Misha and she disappeared out of the kitchen, then returned a little later with a big smile on her face.

"We'd better get off to bed, early start as usual but we've also got quite a large order of pastries for one of them senators having a bit of a party. So, finish your food and we'll see you in the morning," said Misha she then gave Atticus a kiss on his cheek, and off they went.

Atticus finished the food, drank the wine, and went off to sleep in the storeroom.

Chapter 11

The following morning Atticus had got up early and was cleaning out the stable, Naomi had joined him and was sitting on a stool watching him groom Fury.

"That horse, Fury," Naomi began to speak breaking the silence, "he loves you like no other, his eyes never stray from you all the while you brush him."

Atticus stopped brushing Fury and looked over at Naomi,

"That's because he knows I love him with all my heart and knows I would risk my life to save his!"

"And I suppose Fury would do the same for you! Is that not so, Atticus?" asked Naomi.

"Why don't you ask him?" said Atticus, Naomi stared at Atticus raising her eyebrows. "Fury wouldn't understand me!"

"Yes, he would come here, stand next to me and put your hand on Fury's face, look into his eyes and ask him."

"Don't be silly, stop teasing me," said Naomi.

"Don't be afraid, trust me!" Then Atticus held his hand out to her.

Naomi hesitated for a moment looking at Atticus, then slowly walked over to him talking hold of his hand.

Atticus then placed her hand onto Fury's face. "Now look into his eyes and ask him."

Naomi looked up at Fury towering above her and gazed into his big brown eyes. "Would you risk your life for Atticus?" Straight away Fury began to nod his head vigorously up and down snorting and stomping his hoof on the floor.

"Told you so," Atticus said with a smile, then Naomi looked up into the eyes of Atticus and asked, "Is that why you risked your life for me yesterday."

"What do you mean?" Going a little red in the face. "You know exactly what I mean did you?"

Then Atticus looked into her face trying to answer.

But his mouth opened, and he struggled to get the words out, "Answer me, Atticus, I want to know."

Then all of a sudden, he blurted out, "Of course I love you, probably from the day I first met you!"

Naomi smiled, kissed him on the lips and said, "Good!" then she promptly turned around and walked straight out of the stable.

Atticus was left standing like a statue, then looked at Fury saying,

"Well, bugger me." He deeply exhaled from his lungs, which seemed to last an eternity.

"What do you think to that, Fury?"

Fury snorted loudly swishing his tail from side to side with excitement, "Aye, that's what I thought!" Atticus carried on brushing Fury down. "Well, that's you finished," he spoke out loud and led him out to the paddock to let some steam off.

As Atticus walked back to the courtyard, there was a loud sound of horses' hooves clattering on the road outside, getting louder as they drew nearer to the farm then more or less stopped outside the large doorway. A loud knock shortly followed., Figo, one of the house slaves peered through the spy hole. Then turning towards Romulus and Zuma who'd appeared from the main house and shouted,

"There's soldiers outside master!"

"Then let them in," shouted Romulus.

Quickly Figo unbolted the door and with the help of Zuma dragged it wide open, it was a very heavy wooden gated door.

In rode Centurion Metelus with several more Roman cavalry trotting in behind and promptly dismounted shouting,

"Greetings, Romulus."

As they clasped forearms Metelus turned towards Zuma and Atticus saying,

"Good day, gentlemen, and what a wonderful day it is!" followed by a smile.

"And what do we owe the honour of this visit my friend?" asked Romulus.

"Well, I've got a proposition for you is there anywhere a bit more private we can go?" asked Metelus.

"Certainly, come we'll go through to my private quarters we won't be disturbed there."

Metelus ordered the cavalry to dismount and rest the horses. Romulus told the servants to bring water for the horses and a drink for the soldiers, then he led Metelus into his private quarters followed by Zuma and Atticus.

As they sat down Romulus enquired if it was alright for Zuma and Atticus to join them.

"Yes, of course! This really concerns Zuma."

Romulus then shouted for Aramea, who quickly arrived in the doorway,

"Bring some wine and pastries, will you please?"

"Yes, master, straight away!" then off she disappeared to the kitchen.

Zuma and Atticus sat on stools by the table, and Romulus sat opposite Metelus on the couches in front of the fireplace.

While they waited for Aramea to return with drinks and pastries, Romulus and Metelus talked and laughed about some of their exploits in the legions they'd shared.

Not long after Aramea returned carrying a tray full of cups of wine and pastries, set it down and quickly left the room, closing the door behind her.

"Right down to business," Metelus said after finishing one of the pastries and slurping down a mouthful of wine.

"First of all, this is a request from Tribune Marcus," passing a letter from him to Romulus, who then read the letter carefully before responding. While the rest of them sat patiently having something to eat and drink.

"I see," looking over at Metelus and asking, "Do you know what's in this letter?"

"Yes," replied Metelus.

"So far there's only tribune Marcus, the legate and ourselves privy to his plan of action."

Romulus turned to Zuma. "Tribune Marcus has requested you to scout for him up in the mountains with a troop of cavalry led by Centurion Metelus."

Zuma sat stroking his chin, Metelus then spoke, "You have vast knowledge of those mountains and terrain and that will be a great help to the success of this mission."

"What information did you gain from interrogating the deserter, Felix?" asked Atticus.

"Glad you asked," replied Metelus. "He sang like a baby before he died, told us exactly where their camp is and how many deserters, bandits and runaway slaves are within."

"What do you say then, Zuma?" asked Metelus after having another drink of wine.

The room went silent as they waited for him to answer.

"They attacked my home and tried to steal, wounded one of the farm hands and tried to run off with Naomi and if it hadn't been for the swift actions and bravery of young Atticus may well have succeeded."

At that point Metelus raised his glass. "To Atticus," he said with a smile then Romulus and Zuma followed suit.

Zuma went on to say, "This is my family, those in the mountains are part of the band of deserters who attacked us, so my answer is yes! I will help you!"

Then Atticus spoke, "Where my big friend goes then so do I!"

"Bloody hell looks like a family outing, so I'd best come along for the ride," Romulus said with a grin and swallowed the rest of his cup of wine.

"Sounds good to me. I've fought alongside both you and Zuma, young Atticus here has proved his worth the other day. So, if you ask me the odds of me surviving this little picnic just got a whole lot better," replied Metelus with a broad smile.

"Now to come up with a plan?" said Metelus looking over at Romulus.

"How many are we up against and what's our forces?" asked Romulus.

"Unfortunately, Tribune Marcus can only spare 50 men at such short notice 40 cavalry all hand-picked by me though and ten good archers."

"How shorter notice do you mean?" asked Zuma.

"We leave early tomorrow," Metelus replied, raising his eyebrows, and looking around the room at everyone.

"And what are we up against?" asked Zuma.

"According to that piece of rat shit, Felix, there's 60 able to fight, about a dozen women and half-a-dozen injured from their raids unfit to fight."

The room became quiet for a few moments, Romulus asked Atticus to spread the map out on the table of the mountains they would be entering, as he did, they all gathered around the table to look at the map.

Metelus pointed at a canyon high up in the mountains and said, "That's where Felix has said there camped."

Zuma looking at the map said, "As you can see there's only one way into attack with numbers but if I were them, I'd have the entrance well protected and with only fifty men our losses could be quite substantial."

"Tricky one if you ask me," said Metelus.

Then Atticus said after taking a long look at the map. "I've got a plan!" Everyone looked towards Atticus.

"Go on then, my little friend, we're all listening," said Zuma.

"Yes, the odds are in their favour one way in, high mountains to the left and rear but here." As he pointed on the map to the right "the map shows these rocks are lower!"

"Zuma, you know this area! Can a small force climb those rocks and get in behind them?"

"Yes, it is possible. Not easy but yes."

"And that forest below will give us cover and a place to hide our horses!"

"Yes," Zuma replied.

"If we split our forces here at this junction well away from the canyon, say me Zuma six archers and four of the cavalry. The rest go towards the entrance to the canyon." Then pausing for his plan to start sinking in.

"Go on, lad," said Metelus.

"Stay out of range of archers they may have guarding the entrance. Build a marching camp on that slope." Pointing again at the map.

"Then what?" asked Romulus.

"Light fires, make as much noise as you can get the attention of the enemy, men singing loud, as if they're all getting drunk, hopefully by this time whoever's up there will think the officer in charge is a complete fool, keep their attention."

"And?" asked Metelus.

"We get in behind them!"

"Then what?" asked Romulus.

"Then we sneak in! Kill as many as we can before becoming detected, even the odds up a bit and when the real fighting starts you charge in. Then between us we can win the fight with as few casualties as possible!" Atticus then stood back from the map waiting for a response to his plan. Silence descended on the room, then after a moment Metelus stood upright after bending over the map walked over to the jug of wine and poured himself a cup.

Then he turned around and enquired, "Anyone else think of a better plan?" looking at both Zuma and Romulus in particular.

"Not me," said Romulus.

Zuma just stood there shrugging his shoulders holding his thick arms out at either side saying, "Me neither!"

"Well, in that case, I'll report back to Tribune Marcus give him a full report, get the supplies we need and meet you outside at five in the morning."

Then he raised his glass and drank the contents all at once, "It's a lovely drop of wine you make, Romulus." Then he put his cup back on the tray and wiped the drops off his chin on his arm and said, "Well, lads, tomorrow it is!" they all made their way out, back into the courtyard.

The soldiers sitting outside quickly stood to attention, "Mount up," shouted Metelus, Figo opened the gate with a struggle and off they rode back to the city.

Atticus said, "I better let Castus, and Misha know I won't be home for a few days, so they won't worry, I'll just say we were very busy up here nothing more!"

"Ride, Fury, you'll be there and back in an hour you need to get to bed early," replied Romulus.

So off he galloped out of the gate, down the road and headed for the city of Rome, and sure enough he was back within the hour, ate supper and went to bed.

Chapter 12

Atticus was up first, he'd fed the horses and saddled all three, filled several canteens with water and hung them from the saddle horns. Fury was filled with excitement, chomping on his bit, swishing his tail about, snorting and shaking his mane.

"Don't worry, Fury we'll soon be off," said Atticus, as he hung a quiver full of arrows from his saddle. He'd put on a clean tunic tied in the middle with a belt where his sword hung in its scabbard. Romulus came out of the main house wearing his armour, a sword hanging from his belt carrying two sacks of food. He then tied them, hanging from his saddle on Blaze who didn't seem to have a care in the world. Blaze just stood still letting his head hang low, chewing some dry grass growing in the courtyard.

Zuma came out wearing a tunic and shawl, "No need for armour," he'd said, "if we're climbing those rocks."

Aramea and Seema were standing watching in the doorway to the house, Naomi came walking into the courtyard and walked over to Atticus. Tacking hold of his hand and said, "Please, take care. I don't know where you're going but by the looks of things, you're going prepared for a fight."

"Don't worry, we won't be all that long," replied Atticus.

"Promise me you'll come back to me safe," asked Naomi, as she looked up into his face with a tear rolling down her cheek.

"I promise both me and Fury will be back soon he answered wiping away the tear." Then off she walked back to her room with a slight ache and a feeling of trepidation inside her stomach.

"Looks like wear ready," said Zuma, at that moment the road outside became alive with the sound of hooves clattering the stone road, and the sound of weapons banging against armour.

"Here we go, lads," shouted Romulus, as they mounted their horses and rode out of the open gate into the road just as Metelus and the soldiers arrived.

73

Romulus had left strict instructions for the household as to their duties while they were gone, making sure the farm was guarded and kept safe at night.

Centurion Metelus rode towards them leading his men, "Good day, gentlemen," he said as he approached, then put his hand in the air shouting "Halt!"

And the troop of cavalry came to a standstill immediately in the road behind Metelus. All three of them joined Metelus at the front. "Forward," shouted Metelus and set off riding at a steady pace.

Romulus spoke as they set off, "Good day, my friend. Take it, everything is in order?"

"It is but nobody knows but us four where we're going at the moment, don't want those deserters getting informed do we now!"

"We don't," replied Romulus.

It had already started to get warm; the sun was now high up in the blue sky burning down on them.

"What a lovely day for a spot of hunting," said Metelus, then nudged his horse to quicken the pace.

After an hour or so Zuma had turned to Metelus saying, "Atticus and I will scout ahead!"

"Keep in sight," answered Metelus.

Zuma and Atticus rode off keeping a distance of about three hundred yards in front.

Metelus and Romulus were quite happy chatting with each other as they rode on, now they were higher up and had made a good distance from Romulus's farm. A nice cooling breeze had picked up which made the ride somewhat more bearable in the heat, apart from the flies buzzing around. The only real discomfort was the cavalry at the back were getting covered in dust kicked up from the horse's hooves and had pulled scarves up to keep the dust out of their mouths.

Romulus was quite happy to be at the front of the dust cloud, thinking '*poor buggers at the back*'. Zuma and Atticus out front had a good view of the surrounding terrain which consisted of low hills and brush scattered about. As they rode on further up the road, a group of wagons and riders had come into sight, as they got nearer Zuma could tell they were traders on their way to Rome to sell their goods at the market, travelling together for safety.

As they passed by, Zuma had asked the driver of the front wagon if they'd come across any trouble. The driver was a fat grumpy bald man in his thirties with a pock marked face, uttered a few words without stopping,

"Haven't seen anything," and just whipped his oxen to keep moving on.

Zuma and Atticus rode past them all as Atticus grinned and said, "He was a bundle of fun," then nudged Fury to quicken the pace a bit.

Zuma shouted to Atticus, "See that summit ahead, that's where we leave the road and head east."

"We better wait there for them to catch up," Atticus shouted back.

When they reached the summit, they pulled off the road slightly. It was a very good vantage point high above the surrounding area of sloping fields, trees, and scattered bushes. Further down he noticed a couple of farmsteads in the far distance, they could see the rest of the troop some five hundred yards behind kicking up dust as they made their way to catch up.

Zuma looked back at them saying, "They must've stopped to speak to those traders as they passed."

"That will have been a waste of time," replied Atticus.

"See those trees to the right all the way down there and further on those hedge rows?" asked Zuma.

"Yes," replied Atticus.

"There's a gap which you can't see from here and on the other side is a trail. I'll make my way down there! Let them know where I'm heading and then catch me up."

"Will do," shouted Atticus.

Then off Zuma rode at a gallop, it wasn't long before Metelus, Romulus and the rest had caught up to Atticus. Zuma had got about halfway down, Atticus quickly told them which direction they were heading then went off to catch up to Zuma. Fury charged down the slope at such a great speed, it wasn't long before they had caught up to Zuma.

"They're coming at a steady pace leaving a nice gap between us," said Atticus.

"Good," replied Zuma. As they went on through the gap where the trail carried on Zuma explained there was a river crossing about ten miles further ahead. They rode on keeping a sharp eye all around.

Zuma then said, "The river crossing will be a good place to rest the horses and let them have a good drink while they catch up!"

"Good," replied Atticus.

It took about an hour to reach the river crossing, on the far side was a large clump of trees to the right and on the left, there were plenty of bushes and rocks starting to appear on the horizon. Atticus and Zuma both dismounted and let Fury and Lightning have a drink at the edge of the river, while they both filled their canteens and had a well-earned drink.

"Needed that," said Atticus, before having another drink emptying his canteen, he then knelt down next to where Fury was drinking and refilled it.

Wasn't long before Romulus, Metelus and the rest of the cavalry arrived. "Halt," shouted Metelus thrusting his arm in the air.

As the troop came to a stand-still, Romulus and Metelus dismounted,

"Well, Zuma, what's our next plan of action?"

"This is a good place to rest the horses. Let them drink and refill the canteens!" Zuma then pointed across the river to the trail ahead. "There's going to be plenty of places to be ambushed so it would be wise to have outriders to our flanks."

Metelus turned towards the troop shouting, "Optio Clictus on me!" Out from the front of the cavalry a young officer nudged his horse forward. He was in his mid-20s clean shaven' with short brown hair, and a small scar on his chin and looked very competent.

"Yes, Sir!"

"I want two lookouts in those trees," and pointed to the other side of the river. "Those on the right and two more up the top of that slope on the left." Metelus then turned to look the way they'd come.

"See up at that ridge on my right."

"Yes, Sir!"

"I want two more lookouts there! Don't want any buggers' surprising us while we rest here for an hour."

As he went to carry out his orders, Metelus shouted after him,

"Anybody falling asleep on watch will get my vine stick that far up his arse, he'll feel it tickling his tonsils!"

"Yes, Sir," replied Clictus.

Romulus laughed and said, "Same old Metelus, lovely way with words."

"True, you taught me well," replied Metelus. This made them both burst out laughing.

Zuma had taken his canteen and filled it up at the river. All the cavalry not on watch duty were watering their horses at the river's edge, sitting on the grass tucking into their rations.

Zuma went up to Metelus and said, "While you're all resting, me and Atticus will scout ahead for a while and return in an hour." Even though Metelus was in charge he was more than happy to let Zuma take the lead.

"What if you're not back in an hour?" asked Metelus.

"That means we've hit trouble," replied Zuma, taking another drink from his canteen.

"Thirsty work this," Romulus said with a smile.

"It's bloody hot," Atticus shouted over while pouring cold water over his head from the river.

Zuma turned to face Metelus saying, "If we've hit trouble, follow the trail straight ahead but take the higher ground on the left and take extra precautions!"

"Very well, see you in an hour," replied Metelus, who then unstrapped his helmet and hung it from his saddle; sweat trickled down his forehead and cheeks running over a scar which had been caused by the chin straps of his helmet. Many Roman soldiers, especially those who'd served in the legions for many years, got these scars, caused by the frequent wearing of their helmets.

Metelus then took hold of his canteen and drank it dry.

"While you're gone, I'll make sure all the canteens are refilled," said Romulus, then both Zuma and Atticus mounted Lightning and Fury and slowly crossed the river. The water was slow moving and only about four foot in depth, so it wasn't a problem crossing and they were soon at the other side.

The two lookouts in the trees had climbed one of them giving them a good view of the trail and signalled everything looked alright ahead.

So off they both went at a gallop up the trail, after travelling for about three miles further along the trail they came to an outcrop of tall rocks where the trail levelled out. They were soon out of sight of the lookouts at the river, the sun burned above them making it feel very uncomfortable.

A couple of rabbits shot across the trail from some bushes on the left, other than the sound of the horses' hooves clattering against the floor it had become very quiet. Zuma and Atticus kept continually looking around, ears pricked listening for the first sign of any trouble, or anything out of the ordinary.

As they reached the far side of the trails summit and began to descend down the other side, they both became aware of thick smoke coming from the direction of a farmstead just coming into view down in the bottom of a valley.

Zuma looked over to Atticus and said, "What do you make of that?"

"Not sure? I can't see too much from here! We'd better get down there and take a closer look."

They nudged their horses leaving the trail and made their way further down into the valley. The farm was about another half a mile down at the bottom of the valley.

Atticus quietly said to Zuma, "See that hedgerow down to our left, that should give us plenty of cover as we make our way closer."

"Yes, I see it," replied Zuma. "I'll follow you over there."

On they went out of sight along the hedgerow making as little noise as possible, several minutes later they came to the end of their cover. They were about 200 yards from the gateway to the farm which was wide open, the ground was flat with no cover and the farm was ringed by a low wooden fence.

The scene unfolding in front of them; in the middle was a wagon with a man tied to it being punched and kicked by another screaming at him, "Where's your fucking valuables?"

A shed was on fire on the far side of the farmyard, and just inside the gate on the right were three more raiders ripping the clothes off a woman laughing as she screamed and pleaded with them,

"No! Please, don't! please, leave me alone, I'm with child," as they attempted to rape her.

Atticus without hesitation had seen enough, took his bow off his shoulder, knocked an arrow. He then charged out of the bush not holding Fury's reins, his knees tucked tight into Fury and standing in the stirrups aimed at the raider punching the man tied up. Seconds later the arrow thudded into the back of his neck, blood sprayed all over the man tied to the wheel as the raider fell backwards.

"Oh, fuck! Come on, Lightning, or we'll be late to the party," said Zuma, he then charged out after Atticus. As they both charged forward, another raider came out of the farmhouse carrying a sack in either hand.

The three raiders stripping and trying to rape the woman hadn't even noticed the death of their comrade. And before the other raider could shout a warning,

Atticus had fired a second arrow hitting him in the throat punching through so hard, the arrowhead came out of the back of his neck killing him in an instant.

On they charged, Atticus had jumped the fence on Fury and landed right at the side of the three raiders attacking the woman. The raider nearest to Atticus turned towards him, fear in his eyes at the sudden appearance of Atticus riding Fury landing at his side. He tried to get to his feet but was far too slow. Atticus had drawn his sword and smashed it down into the deserter's skull, almost splitting the raiders head in two, bone fragments and blood spraying everywhere.

One of the two remaining attackers managed to get to his feet, however it was too late; Fury had come to a standstill and Atticus lunged forward punching his sword through the raider's chest, smashing his ribs. Blood pumped from the hole in his chest as Atticus twisted the sword ripping open his heart, down he went dead before he hit the ground.

Atticus had jumped down from Fury while Zuma was cutting the man free tied to the wheel, blood was pouring from his nose and mouth and had clearly been given a good beating.

Zuma asked him, "Are there any more raiders?"

As the man gasped for air, he shouted, "One more in the house! My children are hiding under the floor in the kitchen, please, save them!" Zuma sprang to his feet and ran off towards the house.

The remaining raider who'd attacked the woman, had fallen backwards with his loincloth tangled around his ankles causing him to trip and fall on his back.

Atticus walked past the woman gathering up her clothes, as he passed her, she shouted to him, "Thank you, Sir! Thank you!"

Atticus then strode over one of the dead deserter's body's, sword in hand pointing it towards the raider squirming on his back pleading for his miserable life.

Atticus stood over him and shouted, "Roll over on to your stomach!"

"Please," the raider squealed.

Atticus growled, "Do as I say, or I'll chop that little cock and balls of yours off!"

Quickly he rolled over in the dirt, his face pressed into the sand covered ground, barely able to breathe, his body trembling with fear from head to toe. "Now spread your arms out if you want to live!"

Straight away he thrust his arms out wide.

"Fury, come here!"

As Fury came to his side, Atticus spoke,

"See this sack of shit, if he moves so much as a muscle, stomp his brains into the ground."

Fury then stomped his right leg into the sand only an inch away from the deserter's face. "My advice to you is don't move because Fury here is very obedient!"

Then Atticus made his way to the house, the woman ran over to her husband, sat on the floor by the wagon and began dabbing the blood on his face with part of her torn clothes.

Atticus entered the farmhouse and went through the kitchen and down a long dark corridor where Zuma stood head touching the ceiling sword in hand. as another raider came out of a side room in front of Zuma. He'd a sword in one hand, and a bag of booty in the other. As soon as he saw the giant Nubian blocking his escape, he began to piss himself. Urine ran down the insides of his legs and a pool of piss quickly formed between them on the floor. He dropped both bag and sword, and began pleading for his life, Zuma without a moment's hesitation thrust his sword forward deep into his stomach and pulled it upwards ripping open his body, spilling his guts all over the floor.

Then Zuma turned and walked back towards Atticus saying,

"There's a couple of children hiding under the floor in the kitchen."

Atticus immediately turned around and they both re-entered the kitchen leaving the dead raider and corridor behind. Under the table they could see a square wooden hatch, Atticus dragged the table to one side, while Zuma opened and lifted the hatch.

As he peered down into the darkness, he could just make out two pairs of eyes staring up at him. The sound of children crying filled the dark room below, Atticus laughed and said,

"Bloody hell, Zuma, you're frightening them to death, my big friend, come on, move out of the way!"

Atticus shouted down in a friendly voice, "Come on up. Your father and mother are waiting for you outside! Quick. Come on, they need to know you're safe."

The sound of footsteps running out of the dark and up the stairs became louder as they got closer to Atticus. Then two young boys about five and seven with blonde hair came out of the cellar, squinting their eyes adjusting to the light. They ran past both Atticus and Zuma and out of the door running to their father and mother with tears of joy. Zuma and Atticus went outside walking over to them, all in a huddle, arms around one another.

The father let go of his wife, but still holding on to one of his boys said, "Thank you for saving my family! How can I repay you, Sirs?"

"No need," replied Zuma.

"Surely there must be some way we can kind, Sirs," said the woman.

"You're alive and we're just glad we were nearby," said Atticus.

Zuma spoke, "You need to bury those bodies and put out that fire before it spreads. We have to go but we'll take that raider with us, so you don't need to worry about him."

"Goodbye and thank you, Sirs," said the man still holding onto one of his boys.

They quickly tied the prisoner to one of the raiders' horses, mounted Fury and Lightning and rode fast back up the valley to the trail.

"We've been gone almost an hour. They'll be wondering where the hell we are," shouted Zuma. And they rode as fast and as hard as Fury and Lightning could take them.

It wasn't long before they were back on the trail, heading back towards the river. As they reached the far side of the trails summit, they could see Metelus, Romulus and the roman cavalry riding hard towards them. Atticus and Zuma immediately pulled up their horses and waved, as they came at speed.

As they arrived Metelus shouted, "Halt!"

"Thank the Gods you're safe," said Romulus pulling up Blaze at the side of Zuma and Atticus.

"We'd started to worry thinking you'd hit trouble!"

Metelus turned his attention to the prisoner tied to his horse. "Looks like they did! What have we here?"

Zuma looking over towards Metelus replied, "We came across a farm further down at the bottom of the valley being ransacked by six deserters."

"Where are they now? Don't tell me the rest got away," asked Metelus.

"They're all dead, probably being buried as we speak," replied Atticus.

Metelus began nudging his horse forward to the side of the prisoner, pulling the gag out of his mouth to keep him quiet, the look of fear etched into his face was clear for all to see.

"Well, if it isn't me old mate Justus," he then punched him hard in the face and if it wasn't for the fact he was tied to his saddle, Justus would have fallen off his horse. Straight away blood poured from his nose and mouth.

Romulus then asked Zuma, "What happened to the other deserters?"

"As we came upon the farm, three of them including this piece of shit behind me were trying to rape the farmer's wife."

As the story unfolded many of the Roman soldiers were listening intently, Zuma carried on speaking. "Her husband was tied to a wheel of a wagon getting a good kicking and before you could say hail Caesar. Atticus charged in, stuck an arrow in the back of his neck and shot a second arrow killing one coming out of the house."

"What about the three raping the woman?" asked Optio Clictus.

"Quiet," shouted Metelus.

Zuma smiled then carried on, "Atticus put two of them to the sword and took this one prisoner, fortunately he'd left one for me to send to the afterlife," finishing the story with a broad smile.

"Fuck me, lad, no flies on you," said Metelus. "But we need to make haste."

On they went passing by the farm down in the valley, Zuma and Atticus had gone ahead scouting. Metelus had sent out riders to cover their flanks as they rode on down the trail, on they went at a blistering pace. The horses' hooves kicking up a cloud of dust high above them as they rode.

Metelus shouted above the noise of the horses' hooves, and clanging of swords, spears, against their armour to Romulus. "When we camp tonight, we'll have a little chat with Justus over there!"

Romulus grinned and replied, "Can't wait."

Up ahead the terrain had become quite rocky, the trail had become only wide enough for two to ride side by side. So, the pace slowed to a trot and the Cavalry thinned out, and to the relief of those riding at the rear in the choking dust, their faces half covered with scarves helping them to breathe the dust cloud more or less disappeared.

After they'd travelled a good ten miles, Zuma pointed over to some high rocks further along the trail to the left. "Up behind those rocks, it flattens out a little, providing a good place to make camp for the night with plenty of cover."

They rode keeping a lookout in all directions for any sign of trouble. As they approached the rocks, Zuma and Atticus carefully nudged their horses up off the trail between them. They came out on the other side and straight away, Atticus agreed it was the perfect place for an overnight camp.

Zuma said, "I'll back track down to the trail and lead the rest up here before they ride past," and off he went.

While Zuma had gone Atticus checked around making sure everything was in order.

It wasn't long before Romulus alongside Metelus, had caught up to where Zuma was waiting. "Halt," shouted Metelus.

Zuma wafted away some flies, buzzing around his face trying to drink off his sweat and said, "We've only got about an hour of light left, up this track off the trail behind me is a perfect spot to camp tonight. Plenty of cover and well out of sight!"

Metelus quickly organised the sentry duties, got Clictus to make sure all the horses were secure for the night. The prisoner Justus was well and truly tied up secure to a tree, two guards were posted to watch over him.

Romulus advised not to light any fires, the soldiers not on guard duty had begun sitting around in groups eating their rations. Some were washing the dust out of their hair, ears and faces, others had fallen asleep more or less straight away.

Zuma and Atticus fed and watered Fury and Lightning, then laid down and fell asleep almost immediately after all the day's exertions.

Metelus nodded to Romulus and said, "Time for a little chat with Justus over there, what say you?"

"Couldn't agree more," replied Romulus.

They walked over to him, kicking him awake, Metelus instructed the guards watching over him to disappear and take a break and not to return for an hour.

The rest of the night passed in near silence, the only sounds to be heard was the odd howl from a wolf, calling out for his mate. In the far distance, the occasional screech of an eagle flying high above them could be heard.

Chapter 13

The following morning before the sun had risen, everyone was busy packing up ready to leave. Atticus and Zuma had already mounted to scout ahead.

Atticus asked Metelus, "What did you find out from that sack of shit, Justus?" knowing full well he'd interrogated him during the night.

"He sang like a chick waiting to be fed by its mother, but nothing really adds to what we already know. I already knew he'd been missing for about a week," pausing while he finished fastening his saddle to his horse. "The only real information we gained were the names of the other deserters you killed."

"I see," Atticus said, with a shrug.

"But at least we know they were not part of that bunch we're after and won't be missed, causing them to be more vigilant."

"True but what have they been up to this past week?" asked Zuma.

"Well, it seems most of the time trying to keep out of the way of any of our patrols until they came across that farm. And the rest is history," Metelus replied with a grin.

"Mount up," came the order from Metelus, and as soon as they were all mounted, he waved them forward and made their way back down onto the trail.

The sun was now high up in the sky to the east, Atticus and Zuma were up ahead a few hundred yards, Metelus had put out riders to their flanks and warned them to keep their "fucking eyes open!"

A few miles further on they crossed a small creek, letting their horses have a quick drink as they went through it. They all then picked up the pace at the other side, riding down the trail which had widened considerably. There were plenty of ruts in the track caused by heavy wagons wetting the trail from the creek, but it wasn't long before the trail evened out making it easier for the horses. Further on they could see the trail entering the middle of a wide dense Forest, about half a mile further on. Zuma turned and looked back to see how far the others were behind.

"Here they come," said Atticus. "Better we wait here for them before we enter that forest."

"Halt," came the shout from Metelus.

Atticus took a drink from his canteen.

"What do you have in mind now, Zuma?" asked Metelus.

"That forest covers the trail for about another seven miles or so, as you can see, stretching all the way to those mountains on either side of it. No way around unless you want to add another couple week to the mission."

"I suppose it's a perfect place for an ambush! But to be honest I can't see too many bands of brigands who'd fancy taking us on," said Romulus.

"Even so we'd better be well prepared for anything," replied Metelus.

"Clictus, on me!"

"Yes, Sir," he shouted while saluting.

"When we enter that forest, I want four flankers either side of us, 50 yards out in good sight of the main force, understand?"

"Yes, Sir."

Metelus took a drink from his canteen.

"If you don't mind, Metelus, I'll join Zuma and Atticus up front just in case of trouble!"

"Good idea," replied Metelus.

"We'll set off and keep a good 500 yards in front, the trails flat so you'll quite easily keep us insight," said Zuma.

Five minutes later the three of them entered the forest, it became very quiet; the light dulled by the treetops, with only flickers of light streaming through any gaps in them.

"What's up, Romulus? Were you missing us?" teased Atticus.

"Don't flatter yourself, lads! Some bugger back there kept farting and it bloody stunk," answered Romulus.

This made them all burst into fits of laughter. As they carried on deeper into the forest Atticus noticed some birds flying out of some bushes and up above the trees, Zuma and Romulus paid no heed and carried on their conversation.

Atticus slowed Fury's pace tucking in behind Zuma and Romulus, then slid off Fury.

"What's up, lad, need a piss?" asked Romulus.

"No, those birds up there were startled by something, or someone keep going on slowly," said Atticus, "here, Zuma," he whispered as he flicked Fury's reins up to him.

"I'm going to dodge into the trees on the left about thirty paces in, make my way up behind whatever's up there. Any trouble I'll make as much noise as I can, if it's nothing I'll step back out onto the trail up ahead, hopefully if it's an ambush they won't see me slip into the forest."

Then Atticus disappeared into the trees.

"We'll let Metelus catch up a little just in case," said Romulus.

"Let's have a drink and let Atticus get up there," said Zuma, taking a drink from his canteen.

Then he laughed out loud as if they were sharing a joke just in case anyone was waiting to ambush them up ahead.

Atticus made his way quickly, but very quietly, up through the trees on the left; he'd gone a distance of about a thousand yards when he began to hear muffled voices talking just in front of him through some bushes. Silently he drew his sword out of his scabbard, and slowly he edged forward towards the voices. As he got closer, he could see five men in Roman uniform, two were lying on the floor, the other three were peering out of the bushes at the trail with their swords drawn. One of them laying on the floor began to moan in pain, and straight away one of the others put his hand across his mouth whispering to him, "Quiet Lucius! try not to make a sound."

Atticus crept up behind the nearest one to him, pressed his sword to the back of his neck and demanded,

"Drop those fucking swords now! Or your friend here dies," growled Atticus.

The two others facing the trail with their swords, quickly turned around to face Atticus, the Roman soldier with his back to Atticus feeling the blade at the back of his neck let his sword fall to the ground.

Then he said to the others, "Do as he says," the other two hesitated.

"Do as I say now," snarled Atticus, both of them finally dropped their swords.

"Now put your hands into the air where I can see them," Atticus said calmly, "Now you crawl over to your mates and do the same," and poked him in the back of his head with his sword gently.

When he reached them, he turned to face Atticus, this was his first glimpse of Atticus and groaned, "Fuck me, bested, by a boy no less!"

The Roman soldier looked like a veteran of many years about 45 years old, unshaven with short-cropped hair going grey at the temples.

"I might be only a boy but trust me, I'm quite capable of sending you deserters to Elysium," replied Atticus.

"We're not fucking deserters," the soldier replied angrily, then Atticus stood up straight, his head above the bushes and shouted.

"Romulus, Zuma, over here!"

No sooner had he shouted the sound of horses' hooves pounding the trail towards him broke the silence.

When they arrived, Zuma was the first to dismount, then with his sword drawn went through the bushes at great haste, followed closely by Romulus.

"Well done, lad, what have we here?" Romulus asked.

"More deserters?" enquired Zuma.

"I've already said we're not deserters!" growled the Roman soldier.

"Well, who the bloody well are you then?" asked Romulus.

"I don't give information to bandits," answered the soldier.

"Bandits!" laughed Atticus.

Then the sound of many horses coming to a halt out on the trail, after Metelus shouted, "Halt!" Metelus quickly dismounted and forced his way through the bushes towards them.

"More deserters, lad?" Metelus asked.

"I've already told these two were not deserters, Sir," noticing Metelus was wearing a centurion's uniform.

"Stand up when you address me and explain yourself," demanded Metelus. As the Roman soldier stood up one of the Roman soldiers laying on the floor began to scream in pain.

"Clictus on me," shouted Metelus, straight away he came through the bushes and quickly saluted.

"Sir."

"Get Titus the medic here at once to see these two wounded soldiers while I get to the bottom of this."

As soon as Titus arrived, Metelus told him to treat the wounded and report to him as soon as he'd assessed them.

"Right, everyone else back out to the trail and give Titus room to work," demanded Metelus.

As soon as they got out of the bushes Metelus spoke, "Not deserters you say? Well, who exactly are you? And why are you hiding in those bushes?" he demanded.

"Sir, my name is Sextus, the two wounded soldiers are Lucius and Publius. These two are Guius and Tiberious. We are from the port city of Ostia Antica, Legion of Legio 11 Augusta, out on patrol, Sir!"

Metelus turned to Clictus. "Bring some water and rations for these men and be quick about it!"

"Yes, Sir!" And off he went.

"Right then Sextus, make your report!"

"Sir, we were patrolling the trail about seven miles out of the forest on the other side in the valley when we were ambushed by a group of bandits at least 30 strong!"

"How many of you were on patrol?" asked Metelus, Clictus arrived with a couple of canteens of water, and some rations passing them amongst the soldiers.

When Sextus finished a mouthful of water, he then carried on with his report, "There were twelve of us, Sir."

"And where are the rest of your patrol?" enquired Romulus.

"Dead as far as I know. We are the only ones who managed to reach these woods. Luckily it was getting dark, so we abandoned our horses and ran into the forest and laid low," answered Sextus, then hanging his head low feeling the pain for the loss of his men.

"Then what?" asked Metelus.

"We could hear them searching through the trees but after an hour or so they gave up unable to see in the dark and rode off," replied Sextus.

"When did this happen?"

"Yesterday evening, Sir!"

Metelus beckoned Romulus, to take a walk further down the trail out of earshot of the others. "Looks like it might be part of the bunch we're after," Metelus said, rubbing his chin.

"Certainly, looks that way probably after the patrols, weapons, and horses!" Titus came marching towards Metelus and Romulus.

"Sir!"

"Yes, Titus, make your report."

"Sorry to report the soldier named Publius has died of his wounds."

Romulus gave out a deep sigh. "The other named Lucius will make a full recovery, I've stitched a nasty wound to his left arm and bandaged it up."

"Good but it's a pity about Publius though, but we must make haste," replied Metelus. He then marched back to the others followed by Romulus and Titus.

"Clictus," shouted Metelus.

"Sir," replied Clictus. "Get the dead soldier Publius buried!"

"Yes, Sir," then Clictus turned shouting.

"Thaddius, Linus! Bring your shovels quick!" and strode into the bushes.

Metelus walked back to Romulus and said, "There's no time to waste, can you three scout ahead and we'll catch you up as soon as we've finished here?"

"Will do! Come on, lads, mount up let's get cracking," shouted Romulus.

Zuma and Atticus quickly mounted and set off with Romulus, soon they came to the edge of the forest, and the trail headed towards a valley on the right.

After a mile Atticus shouted,

"Look over there!" and pointed to a slope on their left. They could see a couple of wolves, ragging at the remains of what looked like a dead body. As they rode towards them, two vultures were flying above in a wide circle, Atticus knocked an arrow to his bow and fired, killing one of the wolves, and the other wolf ran off with its face covered in blood.

Not a great deal of flesh remained but the shreds of clothing were that of a Roman soldier.

"Poor bastard! That's no way to end your life," said Romulus.

"We can't do anything now for him, better keep going," said Zuma, and off they rode back to the trail.

Further on they came across three more dead bodies of Roman soldiers; Romulus noted all their armour and weapons had been taken. Another short distance laid the remains of a half-eaten horse with birds pecking away at its bowels. They just looked down in silence as they rode on past.

"Keep a sharp eye out, lads, don't want any nasty surprises," said Romulus.

Further on they came to some fairly high rocks, with small bushes sticking out from time to time, running along the left-hand side of the trail.

As they approached the far side of the rocks the trail split into two, Zuma pulled up Lightning, turning to look back down the trail, Atticus and Romulus followed suit. It wasn't long before Metelus and the rest pulled up at the side of them. Sextus and the surviving soldiers of the patrol had joined them instead of riding straight back to Ostia Antica. They wanted revenge for their fallen comrades and nothing or nobody would stop them from doing so.

"I take it you saw the dead bodies back there?" Romulus said to Metelus.

"Aye, we did," he replied with a sigh.

"No time to bury what's left of them now, we'll see to that later on the way back, if need be," Metelus replied, while wiping sweat off his brow.

Then Metelus turned his attention to Zuma and enquired, "Is this where we part company?"

"Yes, we should hit that other forest by nightfall and begin our climb up behind them," replied Zuma.

"How many men do you need?" asked Metelus.

"Atticus, I, five of your best archers and four more soldiers good in a fight at close quarters should do," replied Zuma.

Sextus asked, "May I be one of those soldiers?" looking at Metelus. "Sir," he then added.

"That's up to Zuma and young Atticus. Here they are in charge of that assault," replied Metelus.

Sextus looked over to Atticus and Zuma in eager anticipation, Zuma replied, "Fine by me. Welcome to the party!"

"Clictus, get the rest of the men for Zuma at the double," shouted Metelus.

Ten minutes later, he returned with the men. "Right, men, you answer to Zuma and Atticus! Understand?"

"Yes, Sir," came the cry.

"We'll make that camp as arranged and make as much of a diversion as possible, good luck, boys, and we'll see you in the middle," said Metelus with a smile.

Off they went making their way to the forest, as they went Sextus looked over at Atticus, thinking, 'everybody seems to have a lot of faith and respect for that young man', then returned his eyes back to the trail and rode on.

Zuma rode in front with Atticus, setting a good pace to make up for lost time.

The evening began to close in, and the sun disappeared behind the mountains, and the sky began to darken. The night sky fell as they approached the forest, Zuma slowed the pace as they entered the forest at the base of the rocks after a few hundred yards further in he pulled Lightning to a stop.

"Right, boys, we need to be as quiet as we can from here. Don't want to give away our position," whispered Zuma. Atticus nodded in response.

All the soldiers who'd been wearing armour, had left it with Metelus and the main body of men. It wasn't long before they came to a clearing, Zuma dismounted and waved to the others to do the same.

As they huddled up Zuma quietly spoke, "We'll tie the horses up here," and asked one of the soldiers, "What's your name?"

"Decimus, Sir," he replied.

"I need you to stay here and guard the horses, the rest of you follow me and Atticus." Atticus patted Fury and whispered in his ear to behave as he left.

They came out of the edge of the forest at the base of the rocks, Atticus found a gap and a place to start the climb up. The rocks were quite steep and if anyone fell further up, they probably wouldn't survive the fall.

It was a quarter moon, and there wasn't much cloud cover, so they weren't in total darkness. This would help with the accent up the rocks, but also meant they could be seen if they weren't careful. Atticus slowly began climbing and the rest followed looking for footholds and jagged edges to hold onto and pull themselves up. It was hard work, sweat poured down the forehead of Atticus but up he climbed, stopping occasionally, and listening for any sound coming from above. As they reached the summit, they could hear singing and shouting in the distance, echoing off the rocks. Atticus smiled and whispered to Zuma, "Sounds like Romulus and the rest have made camp!" Zuma nodded with a grin. As they went further in, over the summit they could see the glow of fires in the night sky from Romulus's campfires, and more fires within the deserter's camp.

From the camp Romulus and Metelus, could make out the shadows of men high up on the rocks, looking down towards them from the canyon entrance.

"Looks like we've got their attention." Metelus laughed.

"Good, let's hope Zuma and the lads haven't been discovered," replied Romulus. Even though it sounded like a drunken party was happening, everyone was armed and ready to charge into the canyon as soon as the order was given.

Back on the summit, they were now overlooking the deserters camp down in the valley below and so far, hadn't been detected.

Just below them Atticus spotted two lookouts, but both were looking across towards the noise at the canyon entrance. Atticus nodded to Zuma, and pointed to the one on the left and whispered,

"The one on the right is mine."

Then they both slowly climbed down behind the two lookouts without making a sound, Atticus drew his blade, looked over at Zuma and nodded. They both grabbed their foe from behind, covering their mouths and slitting their throats before they could make a sound. Atticus and Zuma pulled the bodies out of sight and hid their bodies in some bushes.

Atticus turned around and looked up at the summit and waved the others down, Sextus was the first to arrive.

Zuma looked at Atticus and whispered, "So far so good, what's next?"

"See that ridge over there on our left?" Atticus replied and pointed.

"Yes," Zuma replied.

"That's overlooking the canyon entrance." Zuma nodded in agreement. "Set the archers there with all that cover they will be able to protect us, as we make our way through the camp to the entrance."

Atticus waited patiently for Zuma to reply, as Zuma surveyed the ridge, he then whispered to Atticus, "Looks like a perfect place to me."

"Archers over here," Zuma spoke quietly, carefully they made their way without making a sound to the side of Atticus.

Zuma then said while pointing to the ridge. "Make your way over there and cover us as we go through the camp below."

"Yes, Sir," came the quiet response from the archers.

Then they set off quietly through the bushes towards the ridge.

"When they're in position, we need to make our way down amongst those tents and kill as many as we can without being discovered," said Atticus.

"Don't want to alert that lot at the entrance," replied Zuma.

"Look down there, they've erected a barricade across the entrance," said Atticus.

"I see it," Zuma replied.

"We need to shift that wagon in the middle to one side so Metelus and Romulus can lead the charge into the camp unhindered," said Atticus.

"Come on then, lads, looks like the archers are in place," whispered Zuma.

"If we do this right and with a bit of luck from the Gods, our casualties will be minimal," said Atticus.

So off they went like wolves in the night stalking their prey making their way down the slope into the camp.

As they made their way down in silence, hidden from view of the camp by many rocks, bushes, and trees, Atticus thrust his arm into the air and quickly crouched down. Straight away Zuma and the rest followed suit.

"Look there between those trees," said Atticus, pointing further down on the left.

"I see him," whispered Zuma.

The figure of a man swaying slightly taking a piss, could be seen about 50 yards away from them.

"Looks like he's pissed," said Atticus with a grin.

"Let's hope most of them down there have had plenty to drink," Sextus said in a low voice, as Atticus took his bow off his shoulder and knocked an arrow.

"Don't you think he's too far and all those branches are—" but before Sextus could finish, Atticus had already aimed and fired, the arrow punched into the man's neck, killing him almost immediately.

Zuma turned around looking at Sextus and whispered,

"No need to worry. I've never seen him miss!" then he smiled and looked back down to where the man had fallen out of sight.

Nobody moved a muscle, waiting for any sound of alarm but none came so on they went weaving their way around the rocks and bushes. Slowly but surely making progress towards the camp. Then Atticus again signalled for them to stop; a little further on were two more of the enemy leaning against a rock sharing a jug of wine, oblivious to the noise still being made outside their camp.

One of them had even started to snore, falling asleep as they watched.

"Fuck me, they deserve to die," said Sextus in a hushed voice.

This time Atticus knocked his bow with two arrows, aiming at the one still awake drinking from the jug of wine. As he fired, he quickly moved the bow left towards the other deserter seconds later *thud, thud,* was the only sound that could be heard, as the arrows struck into the throats of both men killing them in an instant. On they went; as they passed the dead bodies, Sextus and one of the other soldiers dragged the bodies out of sight.

"Better not get overconfident lads still a long way to go," said Zuma.

Soon they reached the edge of some bushes about five yards from a row of tents and stayed just out of sight as voices could be heard on the other side; "Come on, you lot, sober up for fucks sake, can't you hear that racket out there?" a voice shouted.

"Who the fuck put you in charge?" said another.

"Never mind, who's in charge? If we're not fucking careful, we'll all be dead by morning, now get your weapons and man that fucking barricade."

The sounds of men collecting their weapons and complaining could be heard, but it wasn't long before silence was restored.

Quickly, Atticus followed by Zuma and the rest reached the first tent, Atticus drew his knife and cut a hole in the back of the tent and looked in. Inside was a man asleep with his head towards the back of the tent, Atticus lent through the hole with his blade and quickly slit his throat while covering his mouth with his other hand; the only sound was a gurgling noise as he choked on his own blood.

Straight away Atticus reversed back out as Zuma made his way to the next tent. Atticus and the others followed. As they all crouched behind the tent, Zuma cut a hole from top to bottom, as he looked inside, he could see two women tied up back-to-back to each other and gagged. And as he looked in, one of the women, who was in her early thirties with brown hair, also had bruising on one side of her face, and dried blood under her nose, was clearly startled at the sight of Zuma. He quickly put a finger to his mouth and gave a reassuring smile, which seemed to work straight away, and she nodded back to Zuma.

At the front of the tent looking out, sat a man on guard. Zuma crouched down, and quietly passed the two women with his blade drawn, grabbed the guard pulling him further back into the tent with his hand over his mouth. Zuma then punched his blade into his throat, blood sprayed all over the tent. Zuma dropped the dead man and turned towards the women cutting them free, ushering them out of the back of the tent.

Atticus took their gags off. "Thank you," they whispered, and the women who saw Zuma come through the back of the tent grabbed his hand. "I'm Lydia and this is Julia," who clearly was still in shock. Julia was at least fifty with red greying hair, and also had a very black eye and bruising to both cheeks.

Zuma spoke quietly and asked, "How did you both end up here?"

"I've been staying with my friend Julia and her family, when her home was attacked two weeks ago, as I have lost my home. My husband was a violent drunk, owed money he could not repay and was killed for not paying, so my home was taken away from me!"

"We must keep going," Atticus interrupted.

"Yes, you ladies hide in these bushes and don't come out, I'll come back for you quick go now," said Zuma.

As soon as they were hidden, Zuma, Atticus and the others made their way to the next tent. Atticus pointed to the rocks on the far side of the camp where a guard stood looking towards the entrance, the guard wasn't very alert and stood scratching his arse.

"Fuck me, these lazy fuckers deserve to die," said Sextus again.

Atticus aimed and fired an arrow which struck him in his temple, slicing into his brain and down he went without a sound. Zuma cut open the back of the tent,

"Empty," said Zuma.

They went through the bushes towards the barricade; they were now only about sixty yards from it.

"I count eight behind that barricade," said Zuma.

"I hope those archers of ours haven't fallen asleep," Sextus voicing his concern.

"Better not of," replied Atticus.

"But just in case, I'll cover your charge towards the barricade from here," he went on to say while taking his quiver of arrows from off his shoulder, placing it on the floor beside him and knocking an arrow ready to fire.

"All hells going to break loose as soon as we charge," said Zuma with a grin.

"We need that wagon moving, lads, as quick as we can so Romulus and the rest can join the fight unhindered," said Atticus.

"Ready, lads," said Zuma, as they all took their swords out of their scabbards.

"NOW," shouted Zuma.

Off they went charging towards the barricade. Atticus shot an arrow killing one standing behind the wagon; cries of 'alarm' came from the rocks on the other side. A spear hurled towards Zuma and the rest of them as they charged the barricade, but it struck the ground harmlessly.

The archers on the ridge began firing arrows at the enemy amongst the rocks killing anyone daft enough to raise their heads above their cover.

Atticus killed another two running towards the barricade striking them with arrows, as Zuma arrived smashing his sword into the head of a short stocky man defending the barricade, bone and flesh splattering the other defenders.

Sextus and the others were all engaged in hand-to-hand fighting, the sound of steel crashing against steel echoed out loudly. Atticus who had run out of arrows drew his sword ready to join the battle. As he did, an enemy began to bare down on him thirty yards out to his right. But to his left he saw Zuma was fighting two opponents to his front and hadn't seen a third about to stick a spear into his back. So, without any hesitation took his sword into both hands and raised it above his head then launched it with all his strength at the enemy about to attack Zuma from behind. The sword flew through the air spinning as it went, punching straight into the side of his head embedding deep into his skull. The force of the blow knocked him sideways dead before he hit the ground.

Atticus spun around to meet his attacker just in time, as the attacker lunged at him snarling and shouting, "Die, you bastard!"

Atticus quickly sidestepped the lunge and stuck his knife into his chest, striking his heart killing him. Blood sprayed all over Atticus's face and body. Atticus quickly picked up the dead man's sword and charged towards the wagon in the centre of the barricade. The archers on the ridge were doing a fine job, as arrows were continually flying above their heads across the canyon at the enemy in the rocks at the far side. All manner of hell had broken loose, the sound of horses' hooves thundering towards the canyon entrance could now be heard.

"Quick, drag this wagon out of the way," cried Zuma.

All of them took a hold dropping their weapons and pulled the wagon to one side. Any attackers who tried to stop them were quickly sent to their death, by the archers above. The bandits and deserters backed off out of sight and ran between the tents in fear for their lives. No sooner than the wagon was pulled away, Metelus, Romulus, and the Roman cavalry charged through, killing anyone daft enough to stand in their way. The cavalry then began to charge through the rows of tents; their blood lust was up and without mercy they began to kill the deserters retreating to the rear of the valley. Romulus dismounted at the barricade where Zuma, Atticus and the rest were standing with their backs to the wagon, their swords back in their hands ready to kill.

"Glad to see you all alive, thank the Gods," shouted Romulus.

Sextus had walked over to the dead deserter that Atticus had killed and retrieved his sword still stuck in the side of his head.

"Here's your sword, Atticus! That was some fucking throw," shouted Sextus, Romulus looked at Atticus as Zuma put his hand on Atticus's shoulder.

"You saved my life, little brother."

"You'd have done the same for me!" Atticus smiled.

Sextus turned to Romulus and Zuma. "Young Atticus, here is one of the bravest lads I've seen! His fighting skills are second to none, and It's been an honour to fight at his side."

Zuma shouted, "It's not over yet on me, lads, let's get up amongst those rocks and weed the buggers out and finish this."

Up they went climbing through bushes and over small rocks, the odd arrow whizzed above their heads as they went. Small rocks were now being hurled down at them from higher up, but arrows fired from their archers soon came to bare, and it wasn't long before the enemy were killed.

They came across the dead bodies of deserters, who'd been struck by arrows, any still alive were quickly put to death. Two more were found hiding in some bushes but quickly threw down their weapons and surrendered. Sextus told Gaius to tie them up and march them down to the men at the entrance.

"Yes, my friend," came the reply from Gaius.

The battle amongst the tents seemed to be coming to an end, several deserters had put their hands in the air and surrendered, while many more lay dead on the floor.

The prisoners were now being rounded up and made to kneel down in a circle at the entrance. Zuma and Atticus descended back down to where Romulus and Metelus were standing.

"Well done, lads," said Metelus as they approached.

"Clictus on me," he then shouted.

"Yes, Sir," came the reply as he arrived and saluted.

"At ease, lad, lighten up a bit we're not on parade," said Metelus calmly.

Clictus smiled. "Sorry, Sir."

"Get some men together and search this camp from top to bottom, I want to be out of here within the hour, so be quick about it," ordered Metelus.

"Right away, Sir!" And quickly gathered a dozen men together and began the search,

"Sir," came a shout from behind the tents as two Roman soldiers appeared dragging Lydia and Julia.

Zuma stepped forward shouting, "Let go of those ladies immediately unless you want my sword between your ribs!"

Both soldiers quickly let go in sheer fright of the venom in Zuma's voice.

Lydia quickly ran over to Zuma and grabbed his arm, Julia followed her slowly still in shock and stood beside him.

Metelus seeing the look of anger in the face of the giant Zuma, said, "Good day, ladies, may I apologise for any rough handling by my men and how did you come to be here?"

Lydia still holding Zuma's arm very tightly answered, "Julia, my friend, here, her home was attacked while I was staying with her and her husband, she had a younger brother living and working there also." She then paused and held Julia's hand. "They killed them both and took us captive about two weeks ago."

"I'm very sorry to hear that," replied Metelus, then shouted. "Titus!"

"Yes, Sir," he replied as he came running to Metelus.

"Attend to these ladies' injuries, please, then see to the wounded soldiers and give me a full report as to any injuries and how many are dead!"

"Straight away, Sir," replied Titus. He then took his medical bag off his shoulder.

"Ladies, my men will make sure you are as comfortable as possible and will tend to your every need. Zuma here will be your escort for the journey back to Rome!"

"Thank you," replied Lydia, feeling a little more at ease while holding Zuma. Julia just stood tears filling her eye's, which began dropping down her cheeks.

Atticus broke the moment of silence and said, "I'll go back over the top and fetch our horses. We'll meet you at the front of the canyon."

"Good, take Sextus and four other soldiers to help," replied Metelus.

The archers came down from the ridge, carrying one of them who'd been killed. Clictus arrived saluting and made his report.

"The camp and surrounding area have been fully searched. We have eight deserters, four runaway slaves and two gladiators as prisoners, Sir."

Titus then gave his report, "We have four wounded, but will all make a full recovery and with that archer we have only three dead Sir, we've counted forty-nine dead deserters, some of which are runaway slaves, Sir!"

"Excellent news, now get everything ready to leave," answered Metelus. "Yes, Sir," they shouted and went off to carry out their duties.

Metelus then turned his attention to Romulus saying, "Well, to be honest I never expected the mission to be so successful, that plan of young Atticus's has worked a treat."

"Yes, thank fuck, must admit though I think I've aged a good ten years waiting outside in that camp wondering what the hell was happening in here," replied Romulus smiling.

"I will put everything in my report to Tribune Marcus, might be a medal up for grabs." Metelus laughed.

All the dead deserters were piled high and set on fire, two horses were hitched to the wagon and all the captured weapons were placed in the back. The wounded who couldn't ride were laid down in the wagon, Lydia and Julia sat up front next to Zuma who'd told Metelus he would drive the wagon and protect the ladies.

"Mount up," shouted Metelus, and signalled them to move out.

As they left the canyon, Atticus was waiting with Sextus and the soldiers sitting on Fury while holding the reins of Lightning.

Romulus joined him and said, "Well done, lad, your plan saved lives today, not only that, by all accounts your fighting skill and bravery have not gone unnoticed."

"Only making sure we all got back alive and I'm glad we saved those ladies, but I'm bloody hungry," replied Atticus.

Romulus laughed saying, "You are always hungry, in fact you probably eat more than Fury." He then tapped Atticus on his forearm as he rode beside him with affection.

"Still many men are alive today due to you and that makes me proud!"

"You made me what I am so the credits yours," replied Atticus.

The prisoners were all tied up in a long line behind the wagon with guards on either side. As Atticus and Romulus rode on, Atticus smiled and said, "Looks like Zuma's quite taken by his new companion."

"He is, I can see a little twinkle in those eyes of his," answered Romulus, while looking over at Zuma.

Their attention hadn't gone unnoticed as Zuma shouted over,

"What are you two buggers talking about?"

"Err, nothing," replied Romulus.

They both nudged Blaze and Fury faster, laughing as they galloped to the front towards Metelus. Lydia sat there smiling looking up at Zuma, Julia was still very withdrawn into herself, even though Lydia was doing her best to cheer her up.

Several miles further on Sextus joined them up at the front.

"If it's all right with you, Sir, me, and my lads will head straight back to Ostia from here?" asked Sextus.

"That will be fine, have you got enough water and provisions?" asked Metelus.

"Yes, thank you, Sir," replied Sextus.

"Good then, we'll bid you farewell," said Metelus.

"Once again thank you for everything, especially you Atticus," replied Sextus, who nodded his head in response. Sextus then saluted and shouted right lads with me and rode off towards Ostia.

It wasn't long before they arrived at the place, they'd made camp on their way out.

"Best make camp here again. It will soon be night fall," said Romulus.

Metelus agreed and shouted, "Clictus on me!"

"Sir," answered Clictus.

"We'll make camp here again secure the prisoners." Romulus explained, "Set guards and post sentries!"

"Right away, Sir!"

Zuma helped the ladies down and got some blankets for them, then lit a fire; there was no need to hide their whereabouts, Metelus had said.

As the soldiers all sat down around their campfires, the mood was very jovial, some had already started to sing, and others were sitting around talking and laughing amongst themselves. Romulus and Atticus joined Zuma and the ladies.

Zuma passed his canteen to Lydia, who in turn offered it to Julia who smiled saying, "Thank you," she seemed to be more at ease with all the singing and laughter going on.

It wasn't long before they all huddled around the fire laying down and falling asleep; Lydia had curled up at the side of Zuma.

The following morning everyone was up early getting themselves ready for the final stretch of the journey. The sun was up as they rode on towards the city of Rome and Romulus's home.

The journey back was hot; Lydia and Julia had fallen asleep in the back of the wagon even though it was a bumpy ride.

They arrived outside Romulus's farm just before sunset, Lydia and Julia having nowhere to go, no money or clothes, and after discussing their predicament with both Romulus and Zuma, they had accepted Romulus's offer of a home and a place to stay, for as long as they wanted.

This made Zuma very happy he had felt a desire for Lydia's company he hadn't felt for some years.

"Right then, lads, I will make my report to the tribune and come and see you when I'm off duty next. But me and my men owe you all a debt of gratitude for the success of this mission," said Metelus. He then saluted and shouted, "Forward," and set off towards the city, followed by his men and prisoners.

Chapter 14

The gate to Romulus's home swung open, as they rode into the courtyard the whole household was there to greet them. Atticus jumped down from Fury and was immediately engulfed in the arms of Naomi. She began to cry with tears flowing down her cheeks she didn't care who saw. She then began kissing him hard on the lips and cried out, "You're safe! I've been terrified with worry these past few days."

"Well, I'm home now," Atticus gently replied.

Romulus dismounted to the cheers of the whole household, Zuma led Lightning in holding Lydia's hand, with Julia walking by her side. Both of them were a little uncertain as to what to expect, but soon realised this was a happy household and felt very much at home.

"Welcome home," came the shouts from everyone; Aramea and Seema were literally jumping for joy clapping their hands.

Romulus shouted, "Come everyone into the main house, Aramea Seema bring food and wine, let's feast tonight."

Everyone filled the large kitchen, surrounding the large table that was quickly being filled with food and jugs of wine.

Naomi held Atticus back before going in and asked,

"Haven't you got anything you want to ask me?"

Atticus looked a little lost and asked, "Like what?"

"Oh, Atticus," she scolded, "must I spell it out for you?"

Atticus smiled while teasing her and replied, "No, because I already know."

"Know what?" Naomi quipped.

"I know you love me, and I know we'll spend the rest of our lives together," answered Atticus with a smile.

Naomi's mouth fell open and for once didn't have a quick reply.

Atticus cupped her little face into his big hands and gently kissed her on her lips, and said,

"Come on or we'll miss the party." Then, he took hold of her hand and led her into the kitchen where voices full of laughter filled the air.

Romulus raised his voice to be heard,

"Quiet, please!" and the room slowly became silent.

"I've got a little announcement to make," then Romulus paused.

Everyone was now paying full attention.

"Tomorrow is the first of June and many of you will know ten years ago a scruffy little boy of only six arrived outside my door!"

"Not so little for his age," interrupted Zuma, shouting with a big grin on his face, which caused a lot of laughter around the room.

Romulus paused again and looked at Atticus before continuing. Atticus who was now looking a bit embarrassed, still holding Naomi's hand, and looking back at Romulus.

"Over these past ten years, he's worked hard in the fields and stables and as soon as his chores were done trained even harder with both me and Zuma!" pausing again, looking around the room as many of the household nodded in total agreement.

"And the only time he's ever complained is when I told him at such a young age he'd have to learn to read and write!"

Zuma then burst out laughing. Others around the room began to laugh too. Romulus carried on, "His commitment to his training with all manors of weapons has been second to none," then Romulus paused and took a drink of some wine.

"Because of this and his bravery, he's saved the lives of some of you in this room and I could not be prouder of him than I am today!"

"Please, Romulus, that's enough I've only done what anyone else would," Atticus protested.

"Well, just a couple of other things if I may?" then Romulus picked up a scroll off the table.

"This document is for you, Atticus. It states that you are my adopted son and the heir to my estate."

Atticus began protesting again. "I don't deserve this surely?" asked Atticus.

"You do! Both me and Zuma have discussed this and are in full agreement. Oh, and by the way for your birthday, Fury is my gift to you," announced Romulus.

Loud cheers erupted all around the room Atticus put his arms around Romulus and asked,

"Does this mean from now on I call you father?"

"If it pleases you," answered Romulus.

"It does," replied Atticus.

Zuma walked over saying, "It's nothing more than you deserve."

Atticus thanked Zuma and looked back at Naomi, who smiled at him, her heart filled with love and affection for Atticus which was apparent for all to see.

The celebrations went on into the early hours, Atticus had told Romulus he would let Castus, and Misha know he would be moving into Romulus's home but would still visit them and make sure they were safe.

Finally, everyone went to bed except the guards patrolling the palisade and buildings. It was a warm evening and high up in the sky soared an eagle circling the farm.

Chapter 15

Two days after Atticus had moved into Romulus's home permanently, Optio Clictus, along with a Roman escort, came and paid Romulus a visit, to inform him that he, along with Zuma, and Atticus, had been invited to see Tribune Marcus at the Praetorian barracks on Thursday at noon.

Atticus had gone hunting, riding Fury across the river and deep into the woods, home to wolves, bears, deer, and wild boar. So, it was wise to be ready for anything. It wasn't long before Atticus came across a small deer. He'd already bagged a couple of rabbits which were hanging from his saddle. Quietly he knocked an arrow to his bow and slowly pulled back the string made from whale hide, and fired, striking the deer in its neck. It bolted off before falling dead about fifty yards further on through the brush.

As he led Fury through the trees towards the deer, Fury became very alert pricking up his ears and started back stepping slightly, pulling up his head.

Atticus gently patted his neck saying, "Steady boy." He then whispered in Fury's ear, "What's got you spooked, Fury?"

Then all of a sudden, a brown bear came charging at them, smashing its way out from behind some large bushes; the sound of branches snapping, and leaves spraying in all directions filled the air. Atticus quickly aimed and fired an arrow punching into the bears chest, still the bear charged growling and snarling, foam dripping from its mouth. Atticus then fired a second arrow hitting the bear again in its chest, the bear charged on blood pouring from its chest. The bear was now only forty yards away bearing down on Fury and Atticus; Fury reared up slightly but held his ground. Again, Atticus fired an arrow, punching into the bear's throat making it howl with pain. The bear then stood up on its hind legs, eyes glaring in anger as it reared up and snarled bellowing out a thunderous roar. His fur thick with blood pouring from its wounds. It then began charging towards them again, but this time its legs started to buckle under him, and finally the bear crashed head-first into the ground, kicking up dirt and dust into the air. The bear then blew out its last breath, dying no more than ten yards away in front of Fury and Atticus.

As the bear laid still, Atticus jumped down from Fury and shouted.

"Fuck me," Fury snorted and stamped his foot into the dirt in triumph. Atticus realised the bear was young and not fully grown but was still an awesome sight.

Atticus spoke out loud, "Well, Fury, how are we going to get this bugger back home?" He then stroked his chin while looking down at the bear deep in thought.

Atticus then drew his sword and began cutting at branches. Soon, he had made a large stretcher tied together with some vines he'd cut, then fastened it to the rear of fury and with a struggle taking almost an hour, was able to drag the bear onto the stretcher. Atticus took hold of Fury's reins and shouted, "Come on, Fury!"

Between them, they began to drag the bear out of the forest towards home. Slowly and after a couple of hours, breaking now and again to give Fury a rest, the farm became a sight for sore eyes.

"Nearly there, Fury," encouraged Atticus, as they made their way up the fields past the rows of vines full of grapes glistening in the sun.

One of the farm hands came running over, his name was Alepo, a Thresian about twelve years old. As soon as he saw Fury dragging the dead bear ran off towards the main house shouting, "Atticus has killed a bear," repeating his shout over and over again. Soon, Fury and Atticus reached the side of the stable, as Zuma and Romulus approached with most of the household following behind.

"Bloody hell," shouted Romulus, as Optio Clictus stood at his side, eyes wide open glaring at the bear.

Clictus shouted, "By the Gods I've never seen a bear this close up dead or alive before!"

Atticus untied the stretcher from Fury, and took the deer and rabbits off Fury's back, dropping them onto the floor.

Zuma asked, "What happened, my little friend?"

Smiling quickly, Atticus told everyone the events of the day's hunt while he unsaddled Fury.

"Can't wait to tell the story to Metelus," said Clictus.

Atticus told Alepo to fetch some buckets of cold water and pour them over Fury to cool him down. Clictus bid his farewell needing to get back to the Garrison and make his report to Metelus.

"Anyway, Zuma, my big friend, thought you and Lydia would like a nice bear skin rug for your room," said Atticus with a grin.

Zuma laughed and answered, "I'll get a couple of the lads to skin it and peg it out to dry in the sun."

"Looks like we'll be eating some bear steaks tonight, Alepo take those rabbits to the kitchen and gut them."

"Yes, master," he replied.

"Figo."

"Yes, master."

"Carry that deer in for Seema and Aramea to deal with – looks like we'll have plenty of venison for a while," added Zuma.

And after everyone had gone about their tasks, Romulus turned to Atticus and said, "We've all been invited to see Tribune Marcus, at noon on Thursday."

"What for?" enquired Atticus.

"Some sort of thank you regarding that little mission of ours."

"That will be fun, a bit of gratitude in the right place won't go amiss," said Zuma.

"Looks like we're going up in the world." Romulus laughed.

Chapter 16

Thursday morning, Atticus woke early feeling a little bit apprehensive towards the trip into Rome to visit the tribune. He'd eaten breakfast alone, then went to see to the horses, it was another blue, cloudless sky. Fury was full of excitement as usual on seeing Atticus walk into the stable.

Naomi came running over and asked, "How long will you be in the city?"

"Not sure, why?" replied Atticus.

"I just want to spend some time with you all to myself," she replied, taking hold of his hand.

"I'll be all yours as soon as we return!" Then he gave Naomi a long kiss.

"Good," she answered, then left to go down to the vineyard for the day's work.

"Right, come on, Fury, let's get you ready," shouted Atticus and he began grooming Fury.

An hour later he'd groomed and saddled all three horses and led them into the courtyard. Romulus and Zuma came out of the main house laughing aloud. "What's funny?" enquired Atticus.

"Aramea just clouted Zuma with her broom for complaining about his breakfast portion being too small and it broke," said Romulus.

"You can buy me a new broom while you're in the city you big oaf," shouted Aramea, from inside the house.

"Bloody hell, I think we need to fuck off sharpish, lads." Romulus laughed.

"Figo! Get that gate open," shouted Zuma, and out they rode down the road still laughing loudly.

The city gates were crammed with merchants waiting to be allowed in, and others leaving. One of the merchants began to complain about having to wait so long to gain entry but was quickly put in his place by a very large soldier on guard duty tapping him with the butt of his spear.

As they waited in turn, Optio Clictus noticed them, "Tiberius," shouted Clictus.

"Yes, Sir," came the reply from the large soldier who had dealt with the merchant.

"Let those three through," pointing in the direction of Romulus, Zuma, and Atticus' direction. Tiberius walked towards them moving people out of the way.

"Come this way, follow me," he beckoned to Romulus.

As they nudged their horses forward out of line, the merchant who'd complained was about to argue but as he turned around looking to see who was being allowed through, clamped his mouth shut as soon as he saw the size of the three riders coming forward.

"Good day, can't keep the tribune waiting, can we?" Clictus said grinning.

"Good day, Clictus," replied Romulus with a smile.

As they rode passed into the city Tiberius asked, "Who's that?"

"That's Romulus, Zuma and the young one at the back is Atticus!"

"So that's Atticus, the one all the lads are talking about," replied Tiberius.

"That's him," answered Clictus.

"How long have we got before we see the tribune?" asked Atticus.

"About an hour, why?" replied Romulus.

"If it's all right with you both. I'd like to visit Misha and Castus?"

"Yes, that will be fine. I need to take a quick look in the market for some nice silk for Julia to make herself a fine garment to wear and a new broom for Aramea," replied Romulus with a grin.

"We'll meet at the Garrison gates in an hour no later," said Zuma.

And off they all went. Misha and Castus were fine, no-one from the gangs had been anywhere near, not even for money.

Soon, they all met up again at the gates; Romulus had a bag tied to the back of his saddle and a broom wedged under his saddle.

"Is Misha and Castus well?" enquired Romulus.

"Very happy," replied Atticus.

"Is that the silk for Julia?" asked Atticus pointing at the bag.

"It is," replied Romulus, "and what did you get for Lydia? My big friend."

"Nothing much, just some nice smelling perfume stuff," Zuma replied with a smile.

"Better not keep the tribune waiting," said Romulus.

Centurion Metelus met them at the gate,

"Good day boys, follow me!" shouted Metelus; quickly they dismounted and led their horses past the guards at the gate.

"Tie the horses up here!" said Metelus.

On they strode, past the large training ground full of soldiers going through their paces.

"Atticus," came a shout from the training ground.

It was Titus, the medic doing his drill. Several of the Praetorians marching began to turn to look around but were quickly chastised by a burley centurion, threatening to stick his vine stick up their arses.

Atticus waved to Titus and carried on following Metelus, "Looks like you're getting quite a reputation, my little friend," teased Zuma.

As they approached Tribune Marcus's office, Metelus said, "Wait here, lads, won't be long!"

Quickly Metelus went up the steps, returning the salute from the two guards standing to attention and went in. As they waited, Zuma brushed some sand off his tunic, it was a fine deep blue garment sporting a large silver broach. Romulus was wearing a red tunic with a well-polished bronze breastplate. Atticus had put on a cream tunic tied in the middle with a thick leather belt fastened up by a large bronze buckle.

Romulus chuckled and said, "Don't we all look very smart?"

Then Metelus returned and said, "Tribune Marcus is ready to see you follow me."

Inside they passed down a narrow corridor, and at the bottom stood a praetorian guard who immediately opened a door leading into Marcus's office. Tribune Marcus sat behind a large desk and in the corner sat a bald man wearing spectacles, busy writing. Each corner of the desk had carvings of eagles painted gold, and in front of the desk several stools had been placed in a neat row.

"Please sit down, gentlemen," said Marcus pointing at the stools.

"First of all, may I congratulate you all on the successful outcome of the mission!"

"Thank you, Sir," replied Metelus on behalf of them all.

"Hopefully things will quieten down for a while up there, we've enough problems with those goat fucking Parthians, raiding along our eastern boarder if you pardon my expression." Romulus and Metelus both chuckled.

"Not only that but those hairy arse buggers in Germanica are causing us a bit of a headache as well!" This time Atticus couldn't keep his composure and burst out laughing. Marcus just looked at Atticus with a broad smile, at that moment a side door opened and in walked a very finely dressed woman with blond hair all platted and curled in a bun on top of her head.

"Oh, sorry, darling. I didn't know you had visitors?"

"Gentlemen, may I introduce my wife, Aurelia." Straight away they all stood up and bowed their heads.

"Pleasure is all ours," replied Romulus.

"Is there anything I can do for you?" asked Marcus.

"No, dear, it can wait until you're free," she replied, then smiled towards everyone and left the room.

"Back to business, it's quite exceptional to have lost only three men and a couple of men wounded," said Marcus, pausing for a second.

"And you will be pleased to know it's got the attention of my legate Quintus Lucious Valerian, who has invited us all to a meeting with him as soon as you arrive!"

This made Romulus look towards Atticus and raise an eyebrow.

"So, we'd better make haste! Don't want to keep him waiting, do we?" said Marcus and stood up.

"Follow me if you please, gentlemen!"

And off they went, up through the Garrison passing many buildings including a large bathhouse. Any soldiers they passed quickly stood to attention and saluted. Then ahead of them in the centre of the Garrison stood a large building, it had four stone pillars above a series of stone steps, with two large ornate doors painted gold. Two praetorian guards stood at the bottom of the steps while a further two were standing outside the doors at the top of the steps. As they went up the steps, the guards stood to attention and saluted; the guards at the top quickly opened the doors, and once inside they were then escorted down a long wide corridor. Each side of the corridor was lined with statues, and busts of previous emperors. At the end of the corridor were two more gold painted doors with guards standing at ease, one immediately banged on the door and went in, their escort politely asked them to wait. Both doors were opened wide and a voice inside shouted,

"Enter!"

As they went in, Atticus looked around at the splendour of the room; all around the room very lavish tapestries hanging from the walls showing Roman battles. Some depicted battles being won by the Roman navy at sea, statues of the Roman Gods Mars and Jupiter lined the room with a bust of the emperor Augustus. A large desk sat in the centre with several lavish couches were placed in front, and either side of the desk sat a golden eagle. Hanging on the wall behind the desk was a purple tapestry with S-P-Q-R in bold gold letters in the centre.

Tribune Marcus and Centurion Metelus saluted, Romulus Zuma and Atticus bowed their heads politely.

"Welcome, gentlemen. Please be seated!" Quintus spoke, gesturing towards the couches.

"May I introduce our guests, Sir?" asked tribune Marcus.

"Certainly, it's always good to know who's is addressing!"

"Thank you, Sir! May I first introduce to our guests our legate Quintus Lucius Valerian. This is Centurion Metelus," who then stood up and saluted and sat down again. "And on his left is Romulus, former 1st Centurion of the Legio 10 XX Veleria Victris, and his companion Zuma, and this is Romulus's son Atticus." Marcus then sat down.

"Ah! So, this is the young valiant Atticus that has come to my attention!"

Atticus stood and bowed politely saying, "It's an honour to meet you, Sir!" before sitting back down.

"Well, you have all done a great service to Rome!" Quintus then paused to read some notes on his desk.

"And you, young Sir! I'm told, planned the details of the mission?"

"I helped a little," Atticus replied.

"Nonsense, you're too modest. I have the full report of the mission here in front of me written by Centurion Metelus!"

Quintus then paused and shouted, "Bring wine for our guests!"

Shortly after a door opened and two servants entered carrying trays of wine and glasses.

"Place them on my desk!"

The servants quickly did as they were told and poured out the wine filling six glasses, bowed and left.

"Metelus do me the honour and pass the wine to everyone!" which he did straight away, while licking his lips.

Quintus raised his glass and toasted, "To the honour of Rome!"

"To ROME," they all replied and took a drink.

Quintus then put his glass down. "I also have a letter, here in front of me from the legate of the Legio11 Augusta, based in Ostia Antica no less." He then paused for a drink of wine.

"Thanking you for the rescue of the surviving members of one of their patrols and also in Metelus's report it further states you saved a family, being attacked by deserters!"

Again, Quintus paused for another sip of wine and looked directly at Atticus, as a loud knock at the office door boomed.

"Enter," shouted Quintus.

In marched two praetorian soldiers, each carrying a purple cushion in front of them, which they placed on the desk saluted and walked back out.

"Stand gentlemen," demanded Quintus, all five quickly stood upright,

"Tribune Marcus, will you please do me the honour!" said Quintus with a smile.

"With pleasure, Sir," replied Marcus.

First, he picked up a glass medal and pinned it to Centurion Metelus. He then picked up a small silver box and presented it to Romulus. Marcus then presented a silver box to Zuma. Then as he turned to pick the final item up Quintus said.

"Let me, Marcus, if you please."

Marcus passed it over to Quintus, who then walked around his desk and stood in front of Atticus.

Quintus presented Atticus with a small gold eagle pinning it to his tunic and said, "This is given to you with the full gratitude of the people of Rome."

"Please be seated."

After they sat down, Quintus then filled his glass with wine, and also offered some more wine to his guests.

When he was seated, Quintus asked Atticus, "How old are you?"

"16," Atticus replied.

"And what are your plans for the future if you don't mind me asking?" enquired Quintus.

"As soon as I'm old enough I will be joining the legions to fight for Rome," answered Atticus proudly.

Quintus smiled at Atticus's enthusiasm and said, "Good! Rome needs fighters of your calibre!"

Quintus then drank the contents of his glass, tied up the scroll he had been reading and looked over his desk at his guests with admiration and said,

"Well, that concludes our business for today, thank you again but I have urgent matters that I need to attend to, Tribune Marcus will show you out."

He then promptly turned around and left the room, after he'd gone Tribune Marcus led them all outside and back down to their horses.

"Right, gentlemen, duty calls but don't get too comfy you never know when I might need your services again!" he then smiled and went back towards his office.

When he was out of sight Metelus said, "Told you there might be a medal in it," and laughed, looking, and admiring at the glass medal pinned to his chest. "Wait till the lads in the officers' quarters get an eyeful of this!" Metelus rubbed it in the sunshine trying to make it sparkle even more which made Romulus chuckle at the sight of his friend's happiness.

Atticus was still in awe at the gold eagle pinned to his tunic; Romulus took the two silver boxes and put them in the bag on his saddle.

"Wait till the ladies see our little trinkets." Romulus laughed.

Metelus clasped forearms with them and said farewell.

Quickly they mounted up, and off they rode out of the Garrison nodding their heads at the guards and made their way home.

Chapter 17

The morning after their visit with Marcus and Quintus, Atticus was up early; he had put the horses out to graze and cleaned their stalls. He was now on the practise range throwing javelins at the targets fifty yards away, sweat dripping from his forehead. Naomi crept up behind him trying not to be heard but as soon as she got close, Atticus spun around and picked her up laughing. "How did you know I was there?" she screamed.

"Easy, I could smell you," he teased. "Well, do I get a kiss this morning?" she asked, which he promptly did, long and hard.

"Better now?" he asked.

"Mm, a little," she replied.

"Don't forget to come and help me in the fields," said Naomi, as she walked off,

"When do I ever?" he replied smiling while picking another javelin up and throwing it at the target.

Zuma walked up to the practise field, "Good morning, my little friend. Are you sure you know which end of those javelins you aim with," he joked.

"Morning, my big friend, I see! Now that you have a beautiful woman, you can't get out of bed early anymore?" Atticus replied with a grin.

"You ought' to try it sometime now, you're old enough." Zuma teased laughing.

"And the way you and Naomi are getting on when's the wedding?"

Atticus for once didn't have a quick reply, "I err' don't know what you mean?" he eventually replied.

"Come now, my little friend, it's plain to see that you love and adore Naomi and she loves you more than life itself."

Atticus thought for a second before replying, "I'm just waiting for the right time to ask father, there's been a lot happening lately, how about some sword practice after I've helped Naomi down in the fields?" in an attempt to change the subject.

"Yes! I've got things to do in the wine cellar first but should be finished about the same time as you, so we'll get straight to it," he replied.

"Great, I'll meet you here in a couple of hours," replied Atticus.

Evening soon came as they both walked off the training ground after sword practice.

Zuma joked, "I'm getting too old for this!"

"You will never be too old, my big friend!" replied Atticus, trying to catch his breath. They could both smell the aroma of venison cooking.

"That smells bloody good," commented Atticus.

"It does, I'm famished," replied Zuma, as his stomach rumbled loudly.

They entered the house and went straight to the kitchen where Aramea and Seema were preparing supper. Romulus was sitting at the table drinking a glass of cold lemon water. "Here you are, boys!" passing them a glass each of the water. Both Atticus and Zuma were still sweating heavily from practise.

"Looks like you two need a drink. It's still very warm out there," said Romulus.

"It is," replied Zuma.

"Supper ready yet Aramea?" asked Atticus.

"Won't be long, sit yourselves down," she replied.

In walked Lydia and Naomi, "Where's Julia?" asked Romulus.

"She won't be long. She's brushing her hair after bathing," replied Lydia.

Seema put the fresh bread, and pastries on the table, as Julia, wearing a new long tunic she'd made from the silk Romulus had brought back from the market, walked in. It was sky blue in colour with a small gold circle in the centre.

"You look beautiful," commented Romulus, Atticus looked over at Zuma and winked with a smile and spoke,

"Father seems to have become an expert when buying silk on his trips to the market for the ladies."

"Must be, all the time he spends there lately." Zuma grinned.

Romulus puffed out his cheeks saying, "I don't know what you're on about."

"Stop teasing you too." Lydia smiled.

"Right, sit yourselves down, ladies, your supper's ready," said Aramea.

Over the course of the next few weeks, Atticus rode into Rome to visit Misha and Castus, and on several occasions had noticed various members from the Aventine gang hanging around. They seemed to be taking notes of his whereabouts and watching him, not realising Atticus was well-aware of their presence and was always on his guard. Atticus was always well armed, but at the same time Misha had told him the gangs never bothered them anymore and seemed very happy.

Romulus and Zuma had taken a wagon that was loaded full with amphoras of wine, to the city, so Atticus tagged along to go see Misha and Castus.

"I'll see you both later at the three flags when you make the wine delivery!" said Atticus.

"Yes, we'll be there in about an hour, we're delivering to the officers' quarters first at the Garrison, Tribune Marcus is entertaining some of his wife Aurelia's senatorial friends on Friday," replied Romulus.

"An hour it is then at the three flags," said Atticus.

Atticus walked from the bakery leading Fury, as it wasn't too far to the three flags, he could see Romulus's wagon at the alleyway entrance. Figo was sitting on the driver's bench keeping an eye on it; Atticus tied Fury to the back and asked him if Romulus and Zuma had taken all the wine inside that was to be delivered. Figo explained that there was one more amphora to be delivered and pointed to the one at the back, Atticus picked it up and carried it up the alley. He could see a couple of the gang's foot soldiers hanging about in the shadows but as soon as they saw him, they quickly disappeared.

As he went on, he could hear some commotion coming from where Zuma and Romulus were delivering wine; inside was a couple of very drunk legionnaires arguing with Thaddius the owner. Zuma said to the drunken legionnaires, "Time to go!" in a deep low voice, enough to make most men look up at the size of Zuma and piss off rather quickly, but these two were too drunk to have any common sense.

Atticus entered and passed the amphora of wine to Thaddius. "Thanks, lad!" As Atticus turned and looked at the two drunks, one of them, a stocky, short, thickset, bald man in his late thirties, standing in front of the other said, "Who the fuck are you looking at, boy?"

Romulus who was sitting on a stool behind Zuma at the bar just put one of his hands over his eyes and shook his head. Atticus in a flash raised his leg and kicked him in his balls; the soldier's hands fell to his groin, grabbing hold and groaned in pain, Atticus then punched him in the face, knocking him back into the other drunken soldier with enough force to knock them both to the floor. A third soldier who'd been watching, sitting at one of the other tables, stood up holding his hands up and quickly apologised for his friend's drunken behaviour. Thaddius walked from behind the counter with a bucket of cold water and promptly threw it over the two drunken soldiers. Thaddius then helped them up, ushering them out of the door, followed by their companion still apologising for their conduct.

Zuma smiled and said, "I had it all under control."

Thaddius put three cups of wine on the bar and a bag of coin which was payment for the wine delivery, and said, "Here you are, lads, sorry for those drunken buggers."

"I think I was in that state a couple of times in my younger years," Romulus said with a grin.

Romulus then swallowed the cups contents in one gulp and smacked his lips together; Zuma and Atticus followed suit.

"We'll be off now, see you in two weeks," said Romulus, and all three made their way out and back to the wagon where Figo sat waiting.

Business was good, not many other Roman's had cottoned on to the idea of fermenting wine; most of the wine at the moment was being produced in Armenia.

Over the next few weeks, life at the farm was good, though the work was hard. The love between Atticus and Naomi continued to grow stronger, for all to see, and to the amusement of both Zuma and Atticus, a strong bond had grown between Romulus and Julia. She was a completely different person to the one they'd rescued. Lydia and Zuma were too, practically inseparable. On more than one occasion Romulus had joked it was becoming a right little love nest. Centurion Metelus and Optio Clictus would often call in when passing on patrol and give any updates on what was happening with the legions.

Autumn and winter gave way to spring. The taverns were full of legionnaires getting drunk, so Romulus was making a nice little profit. Another field of vines had been planted and were now bearing good quality grapes, according to Romulus as he checked them alongside Naomi.

Chapter 18

Atticus's seventeenth birthday came and went, as the days and months seemed to pass in the blink of an eye. Atticus trained hard after work was done every day without fail, his body was slab of pure muscle; he now stood a mere six foot six, still half a foot shorter than Zuma, but was just as broad. His long black hair was tied in a ponytail and hung halfway down his back; both Zuma and Romulus teased him, telling him that his hair will be cut off as soon as he joined the legions, but he always replied, "A small price to pay for the glory of Rome." He was now carrying two swords with the words death before dishonour etched down their blades and was more than capable of fighting with both swords at the same time.

Many occasions he would spar with Romulus and Zuma, at the same time even though Romulus was now in his early sixties, he was still as strong as an ox, and a very skilled swordsman.

Zuma was a seven-foot giant of a man, strong thick muscled arms and able to defeat most men with the sword.

But both men struggled to keep up with Atticus's speed and agility, as Atticus sparred with them both at the same time.

Back in the city of Rome on the Aventine, the leader of the most powerful gang was a very ruthless, nasty piece of work, known as One Eye. He had lost an eye while fighting for the leadership of the gang. He also had a scar running the full length of the left-hand side of his face.

He was in his mid-30s, just over six foot tall but very overweight, and was frustrated that many of his gang were afraid to collect protection money from the shops, and businesses down at the bottom of the Aventine hill near to the bakers. Many of his gang members have been found dead amongst the shit strewn alleyways over the past several years down there.

One Eye had his suspicions but had no real evidence of who, or what had sent them to the afterlife. He didn't believe like some, that it was an act of the Gods. Several legionaries were on his payroll giving him any information and any warnings they saw fit, but still he had no evidence about their deaths.

When One Eye had enquired about Atticus, he'd been quickly warned off. If one of the gangs ambushed and killed Atticus and the culprit found, Tribune Marcus would march his praetorians up the Aventine and kill every last one of them, and burndown down the Sheep's Head Tavern where they were based.

So, One Eye was planning for an assassin called the Wolf from Sicily, to come and kill Atticus without any trail leading back to him; he'd sent three of his most trusted men to make contact and arrange payment for his services.

Back on the farm, it was another beautiful day. Naomi had been pestering Atticus to take her on his next hunting trip with him and Zuma.

"Morning," shouted Naomi to Atticus running over towards him in the stable; her hair was shining golden in the sun, and her big blue eyes staring at Atticus, which just made his heart beat a little faster at the very sight of her. It was quite obvious who was in charge of this relationship.

"Are you taking me on your hunting trip with Zuma today?" asked Naomi with a smile.

Atticus grabbed a hold of her as she jumped up into his big strong arms, Atticus replied teasing her, "Oh, I see your only really excited to see me when you want something!" as he swung her around in a circle.

Naomi screamed, "Don't be silly now, put me down. You're too rough!" and as he put her feet back on the ground she gave him a long passionate kiss, sliding her tongue inside his mouth.

"I will ask Zuma, but I don't think he'll complain because it's a perfect excuse for him to take Lydia along."

"Good, I've finished my chores, so your father won't mind. I'll go get ready and tell Lydia," she replied, and ran off before Atticus could reply or change his mind.

As she got outside the stable door she was met by Romulus. "His father won't mind what?" he asked with a smile.

"To go hunting," she replied with a courtesy and carried on running towards the house.

"You two look as happy as pigs in shit." Romulus laughed.

"So, when are you going to grow some balls and ask me to sanction your marriage?" asked Romulus, without giving Atticus any warning, taking him by surprise.

"Err, just been waiting for the right time," answered Atticus, a little sheepish.

"Well, the time is right! And the answer is yes, lad, I couldn't be happier for you both!" Romulus smiled.

Atticus threw his arms around him and said, "Thank you, Father! I can't thank you enough!"

"Just let go of me would be a start, you're crushing my ribs," replied Romulus laughing.

Fury began kicking his stall door, "Don't worry, Fury! You can come to the wedding," shouted Atticus, then both Romulus and Atticus burst out laughing. Romulus strolled back to the house as Lydia and Naomi came running out carrying a basket of food.

"Have fun," said Romulus, as they ran past all excited.

Atticus had let Fury out and was placing a saddle on him as Zuma came striding in, then followed quickly by the two ladies giggling.

"They both can ride Blaze," said Zuma, while putting a saddle on Lightning.

"You look rather happy, Atticus," said Lydia.

"I am," he replied with a beaming smile, almost as big as one of Zuma's smiles.

"Why's that then?" she asked.

"I'll tell you all why! When we've set off on the hunt."

"Tell us now," pleaded Lydia.

"Soon, when we are on our way," teased Atticus.

"That's not nice keeping us in suspense!" Naomi butted in.

"Well, you'll just have to wait," he teased them again and jumped up onto Fury and rode out of the stable laughing.

Quickly Naomi and Lydia mounted Blaze and rode after Atticus shouting, "Slow down! Wait for us!"

Zuma just rode on after Atticus, laughing at the ladies' protests.

Atticus slowed down Fury's pace to a trot and let the ladies catch up, Zuma rode Lightning alongside Fury and Atticus, still chuckling.

"Well," enquired Naomi.

"Well, what?" teased Atticus.

"You know exactly what, stop teasing!"

"My father has agreed to us being married," Atticus said out loud.

"A wedding," Lydia screamed. Zuma looked across at Atticus raising an eyebrow with a grin.

"I can't wait," Lydia exclaimed at the top of her voice.

Atticus turned and looked at Naomi who was sitting behind Lydia on Blaze. She didn't say anything, she just smiled at Atticus blowing him a kiss.

Zuma said to Lydia, "If you make any more noise, you'll scare all the animals away and we'll not have fresh meat for supper."

They entered the forest and began the hunt, three hours later they rode back out with only a rabbit to show for their toil.

Zuma complained to the ladies and said, "No wonder! All that noise you made!"

Naomi just laughed and cried out, "I'm too happy to care!"

Zuma looked up to the sky for some inspiration. Atticus noticed Zuma looking up and laughed saying, "You won't get any help from the Gods with these two!"

"Yes, you're probably right Atticus, so next time they want to come. The answer is no!"

Lydia looked at Zuma and gave him a scowl saying, "If that's the case, next time you start snoring, you can sleep in the barn then!"

Everyone burst out laughing even Zuma couldn't help but laugh.

When they arrived back at the farm, Romulus and Julia had just returned from the city. Julia was clutching a small bag containing perfume and spices.

Atticus and Zuma stabled the horses and gave them fresh feed and water, then went into the main house and on into the kitchen, where the ladies were all excitedly talking about the up-and-coming wedding.

When they entered the kitchen, Romulus laughed and said, "Is that all you got from the hunt? One tiny rabbit."

Zuma smiled and sat down, tossing the rabbit on the table in front of Romulus; "I see you've been taken around the shops again."

"Err, well, I didn't have much choice seen as those two went hunting with you," Romulus replied with a sigh.

Julia looked at Zuma and said, "We met up with Tribune Marcus and his charming wife Aurelia and went to the Forum Cuppedinis, so I've ordered something nice for the wedding."

Zuma smiled and said, "I hope Romulus behaved himself walking around that place full of luxury goods with all those senators and their wives wandering about?"

"He did! He had no choice," Julia said with a giggle.

It was a very warm evening, so they all sat outside drinking wine and talking into the early hours before going to bed.

Chapter 19

Two weeks later, Atticus had gone to the city riding Fury to visit Misha and Castus after the day's work was done. It was early evening, still warm in the evening sunshine. As he pulled up Fury outside the bakers, he noticed two legionnaires in an alley to his right. They were talking with two men he knew from the gangs, but he could see a third wearing a long tunic with a hood hiding most of his face further back in the shadows. Atticus was quite sure, even though the man's hood was covering part of his face, he didn't recognise him from around here. Atticus was always on his guard and ready for trouble. Fury had pricked up his ears feeling a little uneasy, which was always a good indication of trouble.

So, as Atticus dismounted, he stroked Fury's neck, whispering, "Easy Fury easy, I know."

The two soldiers walked out of the alley and stood on the far side of the road, a little to his left behind him, just out of sight in a doorway.

The stranger was the assassin Wolf from Sicily, who was dressed in the long-hooded tunic. He was a tall, slim man in his late twenties; one side of his face was disfigured with burn scars he'd received in a house fire as a child, which had killed his parents. His hair would not grow on that side, so he shaved his head bald. His nose was long and pointed, as was his chin, which made his facial looks not pleasing to the eye.

Atticus stood with his back to the alley where the Wolf was now standing, at its entrance giving the impression he hadn't a clue what was going on. Atticus carried on whispering into Fury's long black ear, "Stay calm!" still stroking Fury's neck and not turning to face the inevitable threat.

The Wolf was looking over at Atticus, weighing up his prey after seeing him for the first time. He noted the size and stature of Atticus but made the mistake of thinking that due to Atticus's youthful looks, that he was nothing more than an overgrown boy. Then as he walked out of the alleyway carrying a jug of wine pretending to be nothing more than a drunk and thinking to himself, '*This should be one of his easiest ever pay days I've ever received.*'

A couple walked out of the bakery making their way home, the lady recognising Atticus, said "Good evening," smiled and walked on. Some traders who had finished for the day sat on a cart travelling past down the street heading out of the city. Other people passed by going about their business and were not paying any attention to Atticus or the Wolf.

Dark clouds had appeared from over the hilltops, blotting out the evening sun. A young boy was across the street begging from passers by making their way home. Then a loud crash of thunder broke the relative silence, and a bolt of lightning flashed across the evening sky as the rain began to pour down, bouncing off the floor. The sudden crash of thunder made the young boy almost jump out of his skin, as he looked up at the dark clouds descending above the street.

Atticus out of the corner of his eye had noticed the two soldiers were now shifting from one foot to the other and were looking very nervous. Atticus had concluded that the two soldiers had been paid to witness Atticus's death, and he knew whoever the man wearing the long-hooded tunic was, would soon make his move.

"Hey! You," the Wolf shouted,

Atticus ignored him and didn't turn around, he just carried on stroking Fury's neck. The Wolf then waved his jug about from side to side in an apparent show of drunken behaviour moving closer to Atticus.

Still the rain poured profusely and bounced off the floor creating large puddles in the road. The Wolf's sword swung in its scabbard as he walked further forward to the back of Atticus.

"Hey, you boy! You with the ponytail, who looks like a girl! I'm talking to you," shouted the Wolf, pretending to slur his words and smashing the wine jug on the floor.

Thunder boomed loudly again, and another bolt of lightning lit up the dark sky. Atticus slowed his breathing and was fully focused. He could hear the sound of footsteps splashing in the puddles, getting very close behind him.

Several people running home through the rain stopped to look at the scene unfolding, still Atticus didn't move a muscle. The soldiers kept looking at each other from the shadows across the street, feeling very uneasy, not knowing quite what to expect. But as quick as a flash of lightning; Atticus spun around on the balls of his feet drawing one of his swords, at the same time he quickly side stepped to his right, and before the Wolf could even pull his sword out of his scabbard fully.

Atticus had taken another step forward and punched his sword all the way through the chest of Wolf, up to its hilt, startling the two Roman soldiers.

"Fuck me!" one of them hissed to the other, unable to comprehend what had just happened.

Atticus grabbed Wolf's tunic, pulling him towards himself and held him tight only an inch away from his face. Blood filled Wolf's mouth and began to run down his pointed chin, his eyes bulging wide open as his last breath left his body.

As the Wolf died, Atticus said quietly, "Whatever they paid you, it wasn't enough!"

Atticus then stepped back, pulling his sword out of Wolf's body, letting him drop to the floor as another crash of thunder and a bolt of lightning struck. The Gods were watching from above, pleased with the skill of their disciple below 'Atticus fighter of Rome'.

Blood poured out of Wolf's chest, creating a red stream, as it joined the pools of rainwater as more rain drops bounced off the dead assassin's lifeless body, his eyes staring up at Atticus.

The two soldiers watching still couldn't believe their eyes. Atticus bent down and cleaned the blood off his sword on the tunic of the dead man's body.

"Come on, let's fuck off," whispered one of the soldiers, who was a short, stocky, unshaven man in his thirties, but as they started to slip away, Atticus shouted, "Don't you fucking move!" pointing his sword towards them.

The rain had stopped just as quick as it started, and the dark clouds disappeared. The two soldiers froze with fright at the command from Atticus, after seeing how quick Atticus had killed the assassin; not daring to take another step. Atticus then strode over towards them; they were both a foot shorter than Atticus, and both looked down at the floor not wanting to make eye contact with Atticus. Fury had snapped his rein tying him up outside the bakers, and began rearing up, kicking his front legs out into the air.

Then Fury came to the side of Atticus and pounded his front hooves into the wet ground in front of the two soldiers, spraying them with mud and making them jump back a step. This also made them look up at Atticus and Fury.

"Easy Fury," Atticus calmly spoke.

Fear had gripped the faces of the two soldiers, one of the bystanders who'd been watching had run up to the Garrison gates, shouting an alarm. The sound of marching soldiers splashing through the puddles in the road got louder as they came towards them, led by Centurion Metelus.

"Halt," came the shout from Metelus.

Atticus turned to face him and said, "Greetings, my friend!"

"Greetings," replied Metelus and clasped his forearm, Metelus turned to look at the dead body lying in the rain swept road.

Atticus had taken hold of Fury's broken reins. "Well, what's happened here, Atticus?" enquired Metelus while adjusting his chin strap.

The two soldiers were now standing at attention, not daring to move a muscle, and a dozen praetorian soldiers who'd marched with Metelus were also standing to attention, several of which were looking over at the dead body of Wolf.

Atticus replied, "The man lying dead over there was very drunk and for no reason wanted to pick a fight with me!" Atticus paused for a moment looking at the two soldiers, "So I had no option but to defend myself resulting in his death."

Metelus looked at Atticus raising an eyebrow, Atticus turned to look at the two soldiers again. "Isn't that so? You two saw everything!"

The short, stocky one replied; "Yes, Centurion Sir! Just like he says."

The second soldier added, "That's the way it happened, Sir. I saw it all!"

Metelus grunted whilst glaring at them. He then turned and smiled at Atticus; "Follow me, Atticus! Let's have a look at this dead body, shall we!"

Atticus walked over with Metelus to the body of Wolf and out of earshot of everybody. Metelus spoke quietly looking around making sure no one was listening, "Right, lad, what really happened?"

"I don't know who he is, but my guess he's a paid assassin!" Atticus bent down pulling a heavy purse off Wolf's belt, handing it discreetly to Metelus so nobody else could see. Atticus still had hold of Fury's broken reins, which helped block the view from the other side of the street.

"And those two soldiers have been paid to witness my death, I'm sure of it," Atticus went on to say.

Metelus paused and looked about. "Right, we'll keep that between us and the Tribune Marcus, we'll let everyone think he was a drunk. Those two will make a report to that fact and at some point, I'll deal with them when this all quietens down!"

Metelus and Atticus walked back over to the soldiers. "Right, you two. I want a written report on my desk within the hour or you two will be on latrine duty for a month," shouted Metelus.

"Yes, Sir," came the joint reply and off they ran.

"Spurius!"

"Yes, Sir," replied Spurius.

"Get a couple of men to help you carry that piece of shit lying in the road back to the Garrison!"

"Yes, Sir," came the reply.

"Right, Atticus, I'll be off! I'll come and see you up at Romulus's in a couple of days," said Metelus.

"Better get over to see Misha and Castus and get off home! It's getting late," replied Atticus.

Back at Romulus's, Atticus told Romulus and Zuma what had happened in the city but wanted to keep it amongst themselves as he didn't want Naomi worrying for nothing and retired to bed.

Chapter 20

Romulus had just gotten back from a trip to the city with Julia. Zuma and Atticus were still out hunting, and Naomi and Lydia were down tending to the vines with several of the farm hands.

It was coming up to harvest time and Romulus was itching to produce more wine and refill his wine cellar; there was still plenty of wine, but he liked the cellar to be well stocked.

Romulus had been to visit the magistrate regarding the up-and-coming wedding of Atticus and Naomi, as it wasn't long before Atticus's birthday. He'd also been to the Garrison to have some armour made for Atticus, a surprise for his birthday.

Back in the city, Tribune Marcus was having a bit of a heated discussion with his wife Aurelia, over a trip she wanted to take to Ostia Antica. Merchant ships were due to arrive from the far eastern area of the empire, and she wanted to be there as the ships arrived. The ships were bringing silks, perfumes, spices, Persian rugs, wines and much more. Marcus was happy for her to go but was insisting on a large praetorian escort to accompany her for her own safety.

"Why don't you approve of having an escort?" asked Marcus.

"Oh! They get in the way, pushing everyone about, it spoils all the fun, especially when I'm walking around looking at the stalls," she quipped, feeling rather frustrated.

"That may be! But I can't have you wandering the countryside with only a couple of servants," pleaded Marcus.

"Why not?" she retorted.

"Because, my dear, it's too dangerous," Marcus replied, now feeling a little exhausted with the conservation.

"Sometimes, Marcus, you can be a little overprotective at times." She sighed.

"I'm not! I only want to keep you safe my love!"

As Aurelia paced up and down the room; now feeling she was not going to win this argument, she suddenly spun around facing Marcus.

"Darling," she said smiling.

"What now?" groaned Marcus.

"I've an idea!"

Marcus looked up at her from behind his desk raising his eyebrows, waiting for her to speak.

"You know that lovely man Romulus and his lady Julia?"

"Yes, I do," he answered, realising where the conversation was now going.

"Well, I was thinking maybe if you were to ask him and that other big fellow Zuma and his lady Lydia to accompany me with a couple of servants?" Aurelia paused again, wanting to let Marcus contemplate for a second, then went on to say, "You won't need to worry, I will be quite safe in their hands."

Marcus didn't answer straight away, he just sat behind his desk scratching his head.

"Well?" she pressed for an answer.

"Under one condition!"

"Anything, darling, if it makes you happy," she teased.

"As long as Romulus's son Atticus goes along! I hear from Romulus he's about to get married sometime soon. So, there will be three of you ladies to wander around quite unhindered!"

"Wonderful! Isn't young Atticus that boy who's a bit of a hero by all accounts I hear from your soldiers?"

"He is now stop bothering me! I need to get these reports finished for the legatus!"

"Yes dear" she smiled and clapped her small hands in excitement as she left the room feeling very happy with herself finally getting her own way.

When Aurelia had left his office, Marcus said to himself out loud, "At least I'll have peace and quiet for a day when she's gone!" Then, he carried on finishing the reports for Quintus the legate.

The following day, Aurelia arrived at Romulus's home with a small praetorian escort; Optio Clictus banged on the large door.

Figo looked out of the spy hole and shouted, "Master! There's soldiers and a young lady at the door."

Romulus came out of the main house shouting,

"Well, open the bloody door and let them in quick!"

Romulus then went to help Figo pull open the heavy door. As soon as the door was opened wide enough, in rode Aurelia followed by Clictus and the rest of the escort.

"Greetings, Aurelia, and what do we owe the pleasure of your company?" asked Romulus.

Clictus had quickly jumped down from his horse and went to help her dismount from a wonderful white pony.

"Oh, I was getting bored listening to all those soldiers marching about so I thought I would visit Julia and Lydia," she replied laughing.

"They'll be happy to see you," replied Romulus.

Clictus clasped forearms with Romulus and said, "It's good to see you."

"And you also," Romulus replied smiling.

"Figo, fetch water for the horses," shouted Romulus.

"Come, follow me, Aurelia, they are sitting in the lounge." But, before they had managed to reach the entrance to the house, Julia and Lydia came rushing out smiling.

"It's lovely to see you again so soon," said Julia embracing Aurelia.

"It is. I can't wait to tell you both why I'm here! I'm so excited."

"Hello, Lydia," Aurelia said, kissing her on the cheek.

Off they all went into the house and through to the lounge; they sat down, chatting amongst themselves.

Romulus went to the kitchen and asked Aramea to prepare food and wine and take them through to the lounge. He also sent Seema out to the soldiers with some watered wine and figs.

Zuma arrived from the stables, hearing of the visit of Aurelia.

"Well, what's going on?" he asked Romulus.

"Not sure yet," he replied.

"Better go to the lounge and find out," said Zuma.

Romulus and Zuma walked in the lounge as the girls were giggling amongst themselves. Julia looked up at Romulus and enquired, "Can we all go to Ostia tomorrow with Aurelia?"

"Do I have a choice?" chuckled Romulus.

"No, not really," replied Julia with a smile.

"Good day, Aurelia. It's a pleasure to see you," said Zuma bowing his head.

"Hello, Zuma," she replied.

"So, what's happening in Ostia tomorrow?" asked Zuma.

Aurelia quickly relayed the conversation she had had with her husband Marcus the day before. Lydia looked at Zuma smiling and asked, "Can we go?" but before he could answer in walked Aramea with a tray of food, followed by Seema carrying a tray of wine and glasses. They both set the food and wine down on the table, bowed and walked back out.

"Lovely, I'm quite peckish with all the excitement," said Aurelia, quickly picking up a pastry.

"I'll pour the wine," said Julia, taking hold of the wine jug. She began to fill the glasses Romulus and Zuma both sat down on a couple of stools. Zuma then smiled at Lydia, nodding his head in answer to her question she attempted to say earlier.

As they all sat drinking wine and eating the food, in walked Atticus followed by Naomi. Romulus stood up, "Aurelia, may I introduce my son Atticus and his future wife Naomi."

Atticus bowed his head saying, "It's a pleasure to meet you!" Naomi curtseyed politely.

"Sit here, Naomi," said Romulus pointing to his stool.

"Thank you," she replied, sitting down.

"Aurelia is Marcus' wife," Romulus informed Atticus.

"It's about time I met you, young man! Everyone seems to be talking about you back at the Garrison. And my husband Marcus is insisting you and Naomi accompany me on a trip to Ostia tomorrow! So, I hope you're available?" enquired Aurelia.

"We will, I can't wait," said Naomi, before Atticus could even open his mouth to reply.

"Good, that's settled then," answered Aurelia.

"I think us boys will go stretch our legs a little and let you ladies do the organising," said Romulus.

"All right, my dear," replied Julia, smiling.

Outside Atticus talked with Clictus and the other praetorians, as Zuma and Romulus discussed the trip to Ostia.

An hour later, Aurelia came out of the house, followed by the girls still laughing with each other. Aurelia bid her farewell to everyone and rode out of the courtyard, followed by Optio Clictus and the praetorian escort.

Chapter 21

The following morning, they all arrived early at the Garrison entrance and were quickly met by Tribune Marcus, his wife Aurelia with Centurion Metelus. Romulus and Atticus were riding Fury and Blaze. Figo one of the house slaves drove a wagon with Lydia, Julia, and Naomi sitting in the back on some large cushions, all chatting excitedly amongst themselves.

Zuma was riding Lightning at the rear of the wagon.

"Greetings to you all," said Metelus while Tribune Marcus was giving his wife a kiss on her cheek and telling her to take care of her purse in the crowds at the market.

Julia shouted to Aurelia, "Good morning," as Naomi and Lydia waved frantically from the back of the open top wagon. Aurelia rushed over to them and asked her husband to help her up.

"Let me, my lady," said Metelus, and took her hand helping her onto the seat in the wagon.

"Thank you, Centurion," Aurelia said, sitting with the girls who were now all lost in conversation about the trip.

Metelus looked up at Romulus and said, "Didn't know you liked shopping so much, or is it what you do now at your age, my friend?"

"Just what I need this time in the morning," Romulus sighed.

"Some clever bugger taking the piss!" which made them both start laughing.

Tribune Marcus had walked over to Atticus and clasped his forearm saying, "Greetings, young man, please take extra care with my wife. She can at times be quite oblivious to things happening around her!"

"Don't worry, Sir. I'll protect her with my life," answered Atticus with a reassuring smile.

"I know you will," replied Marcus.

"Best make haste," shouted Romulus; Figo nudged the horses forward pulling the wagon, and off they all went, as the ladies' waved goodbye to the Tribune and Metelus.

As Marcus and Metelus walked back through the Garrison gates, Tribune Marcus said to Metelus with a cough, "Peace and quiet at last but don't tell Aurelia I said that!"

"Oh, no, Sir! Wouldn't dream of it, Sir," Metelus replied smiling.

It wasn't long before Atticus and the group were out of sight of the city, heading along the road to Ostia,

"Another warm day," said Lydia while fanning her face.

"It is, but it's nice to get away from the hustle and bustle of Garrison life, even if it's only for a day." Aurelia laughed.

"How long will it take us to get there?" Lydia asked Zuma, who was still riding behind them.

"At least another three hours or so I would think," he replied, while patting Lightning on his neck.

"We should be there well before midday, my lady," answered Figo as he manoeuvred the wagon down the road, using his whip to move the horses on at a quicker pace.

A patrol of marching legionnaires passed them, led by an officer on horseback who tilted his head in acknowledgement as he passed.

"Don't worry, ladies, we'll have you there in plenty of time to browse the stalls," shouted Romulus.

"You mean plenty of time for you to browse?" joked Atticus.

"Bleeding hell, you've been listening to that bugger Metelus!" laughed Romulus; Fury shook his head about and snorted.

"See, even Fury agrees with me," Atticus laughed. Romulus was about to reply but Atticus butted in first.

"Don't start swearing in front of the ladies. You'll only get in bother with Julia," grinned Atticus.

Romulus closed his mouth firmly shut with a smile.

There hadn't been too many more travellers on the road so far, but that would probably change the nearer they got to Ostia Antica.

They were keeping a good pace and a couple of hours later they could smell the salt of the sea air. There was a nice breeze picking up cooling their faces; Aurelia had brought each of the ladies a fan to keep the flies at bay. The road had started to climb up hill. Another road had intertwined with theirs, and so the road became wider, and was now getting busy in both directions, with people making their way to Ostia and merchants heading in the opposite direction towards Rome. Many people who were walking towards Ostia, kept having to jump out of the way of wagons being pulled along by oxen and horses being ridden fast in both directions.

As they reached the brow of the hill, the walled city of Ostia came into view with the immense Mediterranean ocean behind it. The harbour was full of boats of all sizes, including many Roman warships with their decks filled with men readying them for sail. These warships protected the merchant vessels from being attacked by Celician pirates.

To the left high up on the hills was a very large fort; "What fort is that? enquired Julia."

"That, my dear, is Ostia's Garrison fort, which holds our returning legions from battle!" answered Romulus.

"It's very big," said Lydia.

"It has to be. Sometimes, there will be at least four legions re-equipping, recruiting, and training replacements for their lost comrades," said Zuma.

"And at the same time, it will be housing further legions waiting to depart for battle and, according to Tribune Marcus, General Maximus will be returning shortly from Alesia in Gaul, having successfully put down that uprising last month," said Romulus.

"I hear Maximus is one of our most successful generals at the moment and is highly regarded by the emperor," said Aurelia.

"He is indeed," replied Romulus. "He will want to train new recruits to fill his four legions back up to full strength as soon as possible." Romulus went on to say.

"I see," replied Lydia.

Atticus was taking a great interest in what Romulus and Zuma were saying, but at the same time he was looking at the fort thinking how splendid it looked high upon the hill.

Naomi had shouted, "Look at the sea! Isn't it wonderful?"

Aurelia asked Naomi, "Is it the first time you've seen the ocean?"

"Oh, yes! I've never seen anything like it before in my life!" She gasped.

"It's the first time I've seen the ocean as well," said Atticus riding alongside the wagon looking over at Aurelia.

"I'm so glad we came then," replied Aurelia.

As they reached the walled city of Ostia's main entrance, there was a large contingent of guards on duty checking everyone entering or leaving the city. Suddenly there was a shout from the gate, "Atticus! Romulus! Zuma!"

It was the voice of Sextus, who walked over to them queuing to gain access to the city. Lucius, Guius and Tiberius, were also on guard duty, all from the battle with the deserters, and were also looking over towards them waving as they checked people in and out of the gates.

"My! My," said Romulus, looking at Sextus now wearing the uniform of a centurion.

"I see you've gone up in the world." Atticus laughed.

"Wasn't my idea, I normally like to stay in the background and don't like giving orders so to speak, but it pays good and no latrine duty," Sextus replied with a grin.

Atticus jumped down from Fury and slapped Sextus on his back and said, "It's good to see you, my friend," and they both clasped forearms.

"Tiberius," shouted Sextus.

"Yes, Sir!"

"Hear that, lads – Sir." Sextus grinned, which made Zuma laugh as he joined them. "Take charge here while I escort Romulus's party inside!" Sextus continued to Tiberius.

"Yes, Sir," Tiberius shouting his reply.

Once they were inside and out of the way, Romulus helped the ladies down from the wagon with the help of Zuma. Atticus had taken the reins of their horses.

"Sextus, may I introduce Aurelia who is Tribune Marcus's wife?" Romulus stated.

"Good day, my lady," Sextus answered while bowing his head.

"Good day to you, Centurion," Aurelia replied with a smile.

"And this is my lady Julia, who, if you remember, we rescued that day," Romulus further explained.

"I do indeed!" Sextus bowing again in acknowledgment.

"And this is," Sextus broke in – "The lovely Lydia and, let me guess, is Zuma's lady friend?"

"Yes, I am," Lydia announced proudly.

Then Sextus turned to look at Naomi and asked, "Well, young lady, who are you if I may ask?"

"I'm Naomi, pleased to meet you, Sextus, and I'm to marry Atticus," she replied.

"You look a perfect match, and what do we have the pleasure of your company in our city on such a fine day?" enquired Sextus.

"We've come to buy goods arriving from the east and have some fun along the way," answered Aurelia smiling.

"You've definitely come on the right day then, there's been at least a dozen merchant ships arriving early this morning already," Sextus replied.

The streets leading to the harbour were crammed full of people making their way to the market stalls which sprawled the full length of the harbour's ships moorings and beyond.

"You can leave your wagon and horses just over there at the livery, I will also get a couple of my men to keep an eye on them until you return," said Sextus. "And may I recommend, when you fancy a nice jug of wine and some food, a tavern down near the harbour called the Merry Sailor."

"I hope it's fit for the ladies?" asked Zuma.

"It most certainly is, the owner is a Greek called Adrian, a very fine friend of mine so be sure you mention my name and you will receive the finest wine and food to be found anywhere in Ostia," proclaimed Sextus.

"Thank you," replied Aurelia.

"Let's be off then," said Romulus.

"Figo, you stay here with the wagon and horses, the soldiers Sextus is sending, won't be long," said Atticus.

"I'll see you before you leave," Sextus shouted while making his way back to the city's gate.

"Come, follow me, girls, no time to waste," shouted Aurelia, filled with excitement.

And off they went, making their way through the throngs of people filling the streets towards the market. As Atticus approached the edge of the harbour looking at one of the triremes moored up, he heard the voice of a beggar asking for coins from passers-by. He turned to see an old man of at least seventy years old, sat holding a small dish up in front of him for people to drop an odd coin in. Atticus then noticed the man was also blind; his eye sockets were nothing more than scarred skin tissue. His hands holding the dish were all twisted and disfigured. Atticus took out his leather purse from under his tunic tied securely to his waist with a thick leather strap. He then took several coins out and bent down to place them in the man's dish, as he did the old man took hold of Atticus's hand and gripped it tight. The old man smiled and said, "Thank you, Atticus for your generosity."

Atticus looked down at him bewildered and asked, "How do you know my name? You've never met me, and you have no eyes to see!"

The old man kept a firm grip on Atticus's hand and answered, "The Gods showed me who you are, and Mars watches over you night and day, your destiny is written in stone at his feet. You, young man will be!" The old man gripped Atticus's hand even harder. "The sword of Rome!"

Atticus felt a burning sensation in his hand then the sensation travelled up his arm all the way to his heart. The old man smiled at Atticus and let go of his hand, in the palm of Atticus's hand was a piece of red Jasper glowing brightly.

"That's a gift from the Gods! Carry it with you always," demanded the old beggar.

"I will," replied Atticus.

The old man then simply carried on begging for more coins. Atticus then bid him farewell, turned and walked over to where Naomi was waiting, looking at a small table full of spices. Atticus felt as if he was under some sort of spell and was finding it hard to take it all in.

"What's wrong, Atticus? And what's that in your hand?" asked Naomi.

"It's a gift from that old man over there," replied Atticus.

"What old man?" enquired Naomi,

Atticus turned to point at the beggar, but as he looked to where he'd been sitting only moments earlier, there was nobody there.

"Didn't you see him talking to me?" asked Atticus.

"No, but I wasn't paying much attention. I was looking at this table of spices!"

Atticus looked all around for any sign of the beggar but there was none. Atticus was blissfully unaware that the Gods were watching over his destiny to become Rome's greatest fighter.

"Come on, Atticus, let's catch them up," Naomi shouted and took hold of his hand leading him after the others.

Atticus still had all manner of thoughts floating around in his head. Crowds of people were already engulfing the stalls, bartering for the best price for the goods on sale. Aurelia was loving every minute.

"The atmosphere is lovely," she stated as she began looking at all the goods on offer, and it wasn't long before she'd found some beautiful Persian rugs.

"I must have one of those to brighten up my married quarters at the barracks," Aurelia said. "How much?" she pressed the merchant who was a short, dark-skinned man wearing a scarf wrapped around his head and a long golden gown.

"For you, my, lady 100 sesterce!"

"Don't make me laugh," shouted Romulus standing behind Aurelia.

Atticus and Naomi were looking at another Persian rug on the same stall while Romulus negotiated a price for Aurelia.

"I'll give you 40 sesterces," Romulus barked.

"Oh, come now, Sir! These rugs are of the highest quality," the merchant replied, before pausing for a moment, while smiling and rubbing his hands together.

He then slapped the palm of his hand on his counter and said, "For you though, I will accept 75 sesterces!" he then began rubbing his hands together again.

Romulus scratched his chin while Aurelia seemed to be enjoying the whole thing taking place, her eyes wide open staring at Romulus and the merchant.

"50 and that's my final offer, take it or leave it," said Romulus as he turned and pretended to walk off.

"Wait one moment, Sir," said the merchant with a sigh. "50 it is!"

"We'll have this one as well for 50," shouted Atticus.

The merchant quickly agreed, Aurelia took out her purse and gave the merchant his money. Then clapped her hands, clearly exited with her purchase and having fun. Then she put her purse back in a small basket she was carrying. Romulus then paid for the rug for Atticus and Naomi saying, "A present for your wedding!" with a smile.

Zuma took hold of the rugs which had been rolled and bound by the merchant and carried them underneath one of his thick muscled arms, as if they weighed nothing.

Julia and Lydia were negotiating a price for some perfume at another stall further on. Aurelia quickly caught up with them and began looking at all the perfumes and smelling the different fragrances. A small boy who was begging amongst the crowd had seen Aurelia put her purse in the basket and was waiting for her to be distracted so he could steal it. Atticus had noticed him, and realised an older youth set further back in the crowd was goading the boy on and was getting quite agitated with the lack of the small boy's progress. The boy now squeezed through the throng of people and attempted to steal the purse making a grab for it out of Aurelia's basket, but Atticus was far too fast for the boy. He hadn't seen Atticus come from behind and quickly grabbed the boy's arm, lifting him up off the ground. Atticus held the boy with his legs dangling in mid-air the boy began shouting, "You're hurting me!" as he cried out in pain. "Let go of me," cried the boy again.

Atticus saw the older youth run off and disappear into the crowd as people turned to watch the commotion unfolding.

Aurelia asked Atticus, "What's happened?"

"This boy just tried to steal your purse," he replied.

The boy still hanging in mid-air protested his innocence and cried, "You're mistaken, Sir, I wasn't trying to steal it! Please put me down, you're hurting me!"

Naomi whispered to Atticus, "Please put the boy down, my love." While she took hold of Atticus's free hand and gently squeezed it.

Atticus lowered the boy to the ground but kept hold of his arm, not giving him any chance to escape into the crowds of people. Most of the onlookers weren't taking much notice anymore and got on with their own business. The boy was now sobbing tears were rolling down his cheeks, Atticus had noted the boy had a black eye and many bruises to his arms and legs. The boy's tunic was torn in many places and was filthy. He was very skinny and had dirty brown matted hair.

"Tell me the truth now, boy, no more lies," demanded Atticus.

Zuma, Romulus, and the ladies were now all standing around the little boy, eagerly awaiting his reply, the boy only hung his head low and was clearly shaking with fear.

"How old are you?" asked Atticus.

"Seven," the boy finally replied, still sobbing as tears flowed down his cheeks.

"And what's your name?" asked Atticus.

"Alesandro," he replied while wiping the tears from his cheeks.

Atticus had now let go of Alesandro's arm.

"Why are you stealing?" asked Atticus now in a quiet tone.

"They make me," answered Alesandro.

"Who makes you?" Naomi enquired.

"The older boys in the gang and if I don't, they beat and hurt me," this made Alesandro cry again.

"Was that one of them I saw goading you to steal Aurelia's purse?" asked Atticus.

"Yes, Sir," he replied.

Naomi knelt down in front of Alesandro and said, "No need to cry, Alesandro!" She then took a small cloth from her bag and began to wipe the tears from his cheeks. Alesandro winced as she rubbed his face.

"Sorry, did that hurt?" asked Naomi.

"Yes," replied Alesandro quietly.

Naomi then noticed one side of his face was swollen, Aurelia had also knelt down at Naomi's side. Aurelia then said, "It's wrong to steal, Alesandro, what would your parents say?"

"I haven't got any parents and like I said to this big man, if I don't steal, I get hit and they only let me sleep in their barn if I have stolen something for them," replied Alesandro doing his best to stop sobbing.

"That's no excuse. We should hand him to the authorities," Zuma said.

"No, Sir, please don't. They will chop my hand off!" this time Alesandro began to wail uncontrollably.

"Oh, Zuma, now look what you've done," scolded Lydia.

"You don't know what it's like to have nothing or no one to take care of you," cried Alesandro.

"I do," answered Atticus, remembering the couple of years he spent living in the alleyways amongst the decay of dead animals and shit in the slums of Rome.

Romulus looked at Atticus realising he knew exactly how the boy felt.

Alesandro looked up at Atticus in bewilderment and asked, "How do you know?"

"I lived on the streets for two years from the age of four! Yes, it was hard, but I didn't join the gangs on the streets of Rome or steal!"

Romulus now interrupted and put a hand on Alesandro's shoulder, "Well, lad, you have a choice to make and a quick one!"

"What choice?"

"You can come with us back to Rome, work for me at my farm and vineyard and in return you will be fed, given an education, and a roof over your head with a proper bed to sleep in."

Romulus paused to let his words sink in, Alesandro looked up and asked, "Why would you do that for me? After I tried to steal this lady's purse."

"Because my father is a good and honourable man," interrupted Atticus.

Alesandro looked up at Romulus hoping it wasn't a dream. "Thank you, Sir. I would love to, but I don't deserve your generosity," replied Alesandro.

"Right, then come with us, we all at times deserve a second chance at life, the ladies here have a lot of things to buy still," said Romulus, smiling across at Julia.

"Yes, come on, girls, don't want to miss out, do we?" said Aurelia, who quickly found another stall full of interesting items, and was quickly joined by Lydia and Julia as they went looking around the stalls. Atticus had lifted Alesandro up and sat him on his shoulders to the amusement of Naomi.

Lydia smiled at Zuma and said, "See, that feels better for us all don't you think my love?"

"It does!" and he returned her smile.

After another couple of hours, Aurelia and the girls had now filled several bags with all manner of goods, which Romulus and Zuma had the pleasure of carrying, as well as the two Persian rugs.

"I'm ready for wine and food, is anybody else?" asked Romulus.

"We are famished after all that fun," replied Aurelia.

"Better find the Merry Sailor then," said Atticus.

"It's further on down there," shouted Alesandro and pointed, while sitting on Atticus's shoulders. The thought of having something to eat overwhelmed him, because he hadn't eaten anything for almost two days now.

"Sounds like someone else is hungry," said Zuma, looking at Alesandro with a smile from ear to ear. Alesandro felt a lot more comfortable in their presence and smiled back. It wasn't long before they arrived at the entrance to the Merry Sailor and went in.

It was very busy inside, but they were able to find a table large enough for them all in a corner of the main room. Several more rooms were set back leading

143

off from the main room and were full of off duty legionnaires and marines from the Roman war ships.

"Sit yourselves down here ladies and sit Alesandro in between you," said Romulus. It was quite noisy, but the atmosphere seemed to be full of lots of laughter.

"Me and Atticus will go sort some food for us all, meat, fish, bread, and fruit. Will that be sufficient?"

"Wonderful," replied Aurelia.

"Don't forget the wine," said Julia.

"As if he would," said Zuma laughing.

So, Romulus went with Atticus to the counter, two young girls were serving jugs of wine and taking food orders.

A girl of about fourteen and very bonnie, asked, "Yes, Sirs! What can I get you?"

"Is the tavern owner Adrian about?" enquired Romulus.

Then a voice bellowed from a room in the back, "Who wants to know?" and out walked a very fat man in his early fifties; he had short black hair with a thick black beard and stood behind the counter.

"Good day, Sir! My friend Sextus recommended this wonderful establishment to us," replied Romulus.

"Is that so, and who are you two?" asked the fat man.

"My name is Romulus, and this is my son Atticus."

The fat man's eyes opened wide, and his demeanour completely changed. He held out his hand towards Romulus and clasped forearms. Taking Romulus by surprise.

"It's a pleasure to meet you, fine gentlemen, Sextus speaks very highly of you both and if I remember rightly, he also spoke highly of, let me think, oh yes somebody who goes by the name of Zuma!"

"Yes, my friend, Zuma is sitting over there looking after the ladies," replied Romulus.

"I'm honoured to meet you. Yes, my name is Adrian. I'm always a little weary of strangers asking for me so I must apologise for my earlier manner!"

"No need to apologise I can quite understand," replied Romulus.

"What can I get for you?"

"Some wine, fresh meat, fruit, fish, oh and some bread would be nice," replied Romulus.

144

"Go, sit down, my friends, I will personally see to it myself."

No sooner as they'd sat down the young girl came over to their table carrying two jugs of wine and several glasses.

"Here you are ladies and gentlemen," and placed the tray in the centre of the table.

"Could we have a glass of lemon water for young Alesandro please?" asked Lydia.

"Yes, my lady," then she turned and rushed off back behind the counter.

"Excuse me, ladies and gentlemen, sorry for the interruption," a tall slim legionnaire had approached their table and bowed his head very slightly.

"How can we help you?" asked Zuma.

"I couldn't help but overhear your conversation with Adrian. My name is Cyrus, I'm the brother of Gaius, one of the soldiers you rescued in the forest, and I would like to express my eternal thanks to you all."

"No need we were just happy to be in the right place at the right time," answered Atticus.

"That maybe so, but all the same may I salute you, and wish you good fortune, the name of Atticus is already on the lips of many, a soldier as a brave warrior."

After he saluted, he then returned to his two comrades who'd been watching from the counter and carried on with their conversation.

"Well, Atticus seems your name is not only known in Rome," said Aurelia.

"Don't know why?" answered Atticus, shyly having a drink of his wine.

"Well, I know this, my husband can't wait until you join the Roman army," Aurelia went on to say.

"Here you are, honoured guests," said Adrian, as he placed a large tray of food down on the table. Alesandro's eyes lit up at the sight of so much wonderful food and his little stomach let out a rumble.

Naomi passed him a plate and said, "Come on, tuck in," but Alesandro didn't need any encouragement and grabbed a large chunk of mutton and a piece of bread and ate frantically.

"Slow down, you'll make yourself sick," said Julia with a laugh.

"Thank you, Adrian, everything looks wonderful and smells gorgeous," said Lydia, as they all got stuck into the food and wine. The young girl arrived with the lemon water for Alesandro.

"Anything you require, please let me know," said Adrian as he turned around and went back behind the counter, following the girl to serve several more soldiers who had just arrived. Alesandro gulped down the lemon water and burped loudly which made them all laugh, his face even with his black eye and swollen cheeks was a picture of happy contentment.

When they'd finished their food and wine, they bid their farewell to Adrian thanking him for everything; Aurelia had tried to give him payment, but Adrian respectfully declined.

The afternoon sun glared down on them as they walked back to the wagon.

"It's going to be a hot journey home," Lydia commented as they approached the livery where Figo and a couple of soldiers were waiting in the shade.

Zuma placed the Persian rugs in the wagon, Atticus and Romulus put all the bags of goods in too, as Romulus stated, "Better be making our way if we want to reach Rome before dark."

Fury was excited to see Atticus as usual. Sextus had walked over from the city gates as soon as he saw them approach.

"I hope you have enjoyed your visit?"

"We have. It's been wonderful," replied Aurelia.

"And what have you here?" looking at Alesandro.

"This is our newest member of our family, Alesandro," answered Julia.

"Is he now, I hope he knows how to behave himself then."

"He does," replied Naomi with a smile.

"I wish you all a safe journey home, and it's been a pleasure to see you all again," said Sextus.

The road out of the city was very busy, so the going was quite slow to begin with which seemed to annoy Romulus a little as he moaned, "We'll never make Rome before dark at this rate."

But after an hour, when they'd passed by the other road leading away from Ostia, their road became relatively quiet. Alesandro had fallen asleep in the arms of Naomi. Julia and Aurelia were looking through the bags of goods they'd bought while Lydia talked with Zuma who was riding Lightning at the rear of the wagon.

It was now early evening, and they were approaching the halfway stage back to Rome.

"We should reach Rome before dark hopefully, now we're well clear of Ostia," said Romulus to Atticus.

Figo had kept the wagon going at a good pace. The horses had been well fed and watered back in Ostia, and they had rested for the return trip and were still quite fresh.

Fury pricked up his ears and side stepped. "Wait, stop the wagon," shouted Atticus, "something's got Fury spooked."

The terrain was very hilly on both sides of the road with several trees and rocks jotted around.

"Listen!"

"To what?" asked Julia, all the ladies were now looking all around up at the hills feeling a little uneasy.

"Quiet," whispered Atticus, "there it is again."

The sound of clashing steel could be heard over the top of the hill to the left. Another wagon came to a stand-still behind them containing a man, three small children and a woman; the man shouted over, "What's going on up there?"

"Not sure, stay in your wagon and get your family out of sight," replied Zuma.

Then suddenly a horse bolted over the hill towards them, clearly in panic and without its rider. Atticus quickly rode towards it and managed to grab one of its reins pulling it to a stop.

"Woah, boy easy, here, father, hold the reins while I ride up there and take a look."

"I'll come," said Zuma.

"No, best I go alone you and father protect the ladies and Alesandro. If I need help, I will raise my arm but only one of you come."

"I will," stated Zuma.

"Here Figo take one of my swords just in case." and off Atticus charged up the hill, all ready with his bow in hand and arrows in his quiver hung over his shoulder.

"Be careful," screamed Naomi, as he rode off.

"Don't worry, Atticus knows what he's doing, but we need to be ready for anything," shouted Romulus, who had now drawn his sword.

"Lay down in the wagon everyone and keep out of sight," said Zuma while drawing his sword out of its scabbard, and riding Lightning to the side of Romulus.

Atticus had now reached the brow of the hill and could see a fight taking place below. There were several dead horses, and at least a dozen dead bodies lying around at the bottom. Atticus could also see a man protecting a young boy, who was cowering behind a small rock. The attackers were all wearing black garments with black head scarfs and charcoal painted around their eyes. Three of which were on horseback and a further four attackers were on foot, fighting with three men defending the man and boy who seemed to be dressed like merchants of some sort. Atticus quickly raised his arm signalling to Romulus and Zuma, and then charged down the hill to join the fight. Zuma had seen Atticus's hand raised up in the air and immediately charged up the hill as fast as Lightning could go, with his sword swinging in mid-air.

Atticus, charging forward down the hill, knocked an arrow, aimed, and fired, killing one of the attackers on horseback; the arrow punching into the riders face and blood sprayed as he fell sideways off his horse, hitting the ground dead.

One of the other attackers on horseback quickly turned to face Atticus charging down the hill and charged up towards him, sword waving above his head.

Zuma had now appeared over the brow of the hill and charged towards the fight. The attacker now charging at Atticus shouted a warning to his comrades. Atticus was now bearing down on him, the horse rider dressed in black quickly raised his sword to defend himself. Atticus smashed the sword with such force the blade broke in two, and before he could recover, Atticus had swung his sword backwards at him as he passed, slicing through his neck, and chopping his head clean off.

The horse ran off, still carrying the headless corpse up the hill, passing Zuma as he joined the fray, charging towards the remaining horse rider dressed in black. He was now trying to escape with his life, riding his horse up through some rocks and bushes, but Zuma had cut him off. The look of fear all over his face, as Zuma smashed his sword into the top of his head, bone fragments and blood flew into the air as the sword split his head in two.

Zuma turned to see Atticus killing another one, this time on foot; Fury had kicked the man to the ground and Atticus had jumped down from Fury and embedded his sword into the man's chest. Atticus turned around and could see only one attacker in black now remaining, and the man protecting the boy, who was still cowering behind the rock screaming with fear. Dead bodies were strewn all around, blood staining the sand beneath their feet; silence had replaced the sound of clashing steel as, Atticus walked towards his foe.

The surviving attacker in black, who had tattoos of stars and half-moons below his right eye, spat on the floor in front of Atticus, as he curled his lips. Rather than be captured, he looked into the face Atticus and said in broken Latin "fuck you, Roman pig!" He then slit his own throat, dying as he hit the floor.

Zuma rode Lightning slowly to the side of Atticus and said with a smile, "Wonder why he was so eager to die?"

"That had crossed my mind my big friend," replied Atticus, looking up at Zuma clasping his forearm and smiling back.

On the other side of the hill, the horse carrying the headless corpse had appeared over the brow of the hill and galloped fast down heading towards the two wagons. More travellers had now gathered behind the wagons for cover, the headless rider was now causing alarm among them. Several of the women cowering behind the wagons began to scream with terror at the sight of the headless horseman. The horse carrying the body came to a stop in front of the wagons and the body finally slipped off the horse, slumping to the ground.

"Sounds like it's all gone quiet over there," said Romulus.

"Quick, go find out if Atticus and Zuma are safe?" said Naomi with alarm.

"Figo, watch over the ladies and the boy."

"Yes, master," he replied, still holding one of Atticus's swords.

Romulus galloped off towards the top of the hill.

"Who are you?" enquired Atticus, as the man and boy came out from behind the rock. The man was in his late thirties, with a well-kept beard, and was wearing a fine silk blue gown with a white head scarf around his head. The boy looked to be about twelve years old and was also wearing fine clothes but with fear still in his eyes had to be coaxed out from behind the rock.

"I am Abdi-ILI, and this is my son Abil-ILI, may your Gods look down on you with greatness for saving our lives," he then bowed, touched his lips, then nose and put out his hand towards them.

Zuma and Atticus turned around as the sound of horses' hoofs came from behind; Romulus pulled Blaze to a standstill. "Glad to see you two are safe, the ladies were beginning to worry a little," said Romulus, while looking around at the many dead bodies.

Atticus turned to face Abdi-ILI and his son, and asked him, "Where have you come from?"

"I am a merchant from Mesopotamia, my boat is in Ostia and have been to your city of Rome to admire it's great wonders with my son, and members of my crew for protection."

Atticus had a gut feeling he wasn't telling him the full story. He walked over to one of the dead attackers and began searching his body for any clues as to who the attackers were. Zuma had begun to do the same; like Abdi, they all had the same far-eastern skin colour of olive brown. Atticus looked back over at Abdi-ILI and asked him, "Why did they attack you?"

"Probably to rob us, I can't think of any other reason as to why."

Atticus walked over to a horse belonging to one of the attackers which was now happily grazing and took hold of its reins.

"Here you'll need this to get back to Ostia, but my advice to you is to stay on the road, don't try any more shortcuts."

"Thank you once again for saving our lives, I am eternally in your debt!" Abdi-ILI bowed again, touching his lips, nose and put his hand out, then when he stood upright, he took a large gold ruby ring off one of his fingers, presenting it to Atticus.

"This is for you, so you will always remember this day and my gratitude."

"No need. I would have done it for anyone," replied Atticus.

"Please take it. I would be offended if you didn't, my honour requires it my eternal friend."

Atticus looked at Zuma who nodded for him to accept the gift.

"Thank you then. I will always wear it," replied Atticus.

Zuma helped the boy up onto the horse, then his father sat behind him ready to leave. "What about the bodies?" asked Zuma.

"Wolves and buzzards have to eat the same as us, and we've no time to bury them, we're already late. It's going to be dark when we arrive back in Rome, Marcus won't be too happy," replied Romulus.

Up the hill they all rode, Zuma had collected up all the weapons lying around and fastened them to another spare horse he'd found grazing in some bushes. At the other side of the hill Abdi-ILI and his son headed down the road towards Ostia. Zuma tied the two spare horses to the back of the wagon, as Aurelia questioned Romulus. Naomi had clung to Atticus, relieved he was back safe.

"Come on, no time to waste, ladies, get back on the wagon." Romulus stated, and off they rode. Figo using his whip to motivate the horses pulling the wagon.

Romulus and Atticus rode in front, and Zuma took his position behind the wagon and spare horses.

"What do you make of his story son?" asked Romulus, as they headed back to Rome.

"Something didn't quite add up to me," replied Atticus.

"Go on."

"Well, those men in black who he said were robbers are not from around these parts."

"That's true, so what's your gut telling you?"

"It's telling me those men were not robbers, someone sent them to kill him and his son."

Romulus went quiet for a while as they rode on, mulling over what Atticus had said.

Aurelia had shouted, enquiring, "How long will it be before we get to Rome?" noticing the evening was now closing in and the sky was beginning to darken.

"Not long, we should be there in less than an hour," replied Zuma.

"Good, my back is aching with all this bouncing around in the wagon."

Naomi and Alesandro were fast asleep; "I don't know how they manage to fall asleep so easily." Julia smiled.

"I can't believe how much has happened in one day!" exclaimed Lydia.

"Yes, but it's made our trip a lot more interesting and exciting, don't you think? I wonder what my husband will make of it all when I tell him tonight." Aurelia laughed.

It was dark as they approached Rome's city gates, centurion Metelus was at the gates waiting for them to arrive, with a look of relief on his face as soon as he saw them.

"Get lost, did you? The Tribune's been marching back and forth from the barracks to the gates over and over the past two hours. He's ordered me not to leave the gate until you have arrived," said Metelus.

"Oh, he does fret too much sometimes," shouted Aurelia from the wagon, "What harm could possibly come to us ladies with these men to look after us!"

she went on to say. "Help me down, Centurion, will you? I would like to walk the rest of the way and stretch my legs."

"Yes, my lady," replied Metelus, helping Aurelia down from the wagon.

Romulus and Atticus dismounted and began to unload Aurelias goods she had purchased from Ostia.

"Better get a couple of your lads to carry her belongings back to her quarters," said Romulus, patting Metelus on his back.

"Who's the young boy asleep in the wagon?" asked Metelus.

"Long story, I'm sure Aurelia will fill you in with the details on the way back to the barracks no doubt," replied Romulus.

"I will. It's been such an exciting day!" exclaimed Aurelia.

"Let the Tribune know myself and Julia will come and see him tomorrow," said Romulus.

"I will," replied Metelus.

"But we need to get back home. It's dark and getting late," answered Romulus with a yawn.

"Come on, you two lazy buggers, carry the lady's bags and the Persian rug!" shouted Metelus to two soldiers standing to one side.

"Yes, Sir," came a quick reply.

Romulus and the rest of the group made their way to the gates and left the city behind. The lanterns and torches lit the area well at the gates, but it wasn't long before the road became very dark. Zuma had lit some lanterns and hung them from the wagon which gave a good amount of light to see where they were going. Atticus had taken a torch from one of the guards at the gate and rode in front, lighting up the road a little. Everyone was wide awake and kept a watchful eye out for robbers. Alessandro was the only one still asleep in the wagon. A couple of hours later they reached the farms gate.

Romulus banged and shouted, "Come on, get this gate open!"

Soon they were all inside; everything was put away and the horses were fed and bedded down for the night. Alesandro slept in Naomi's room until a room was properly organised for him. Romulus, Zuma, and Atticus shared a jug of wine and talked over the day's events before retiring to bed.

Chapter 22

Work began early the following day; Aramea had gotten up early and made a large breakfast for everyone. Alesandro was up and began to explore his new surroundings.

"Well, Alesandro, what do you think of your new home?" asked Naomi.

"It's lovely" he replied with a smile.

Julia walked across the courtyard to where Naomi was sitting with Alesandro. "Take off that dirty tunic Alesandro, I've made a new one for you, let's see if it fits!"

Naomi helped him take off the dirty tunic full of holes; as the tunic was lifted, Julia and Naomi looked at each other in horror. His tiny body was covered in bruises, bite marks and scars from old wounds. There was even a nasty burn scar on his chest, which looked as if it had been done by a heated knife. A tear flowed down the cheek of Naomi as she gently felt his body checking for any broken bones and infection but was relieved to find none.

"What's up?" asked Alesandro.

"Who did this to you?" enquired Naomi.

"The older boys because I kept telling them I didn't want to steal."

"Aramea," Julia shouted; moments later she appeared out of the main house and ran over.

"Yes, my lady, what is it?" and as she got nearer put her hand to her mouth in shock at the sight of Alesandro's tiny body.

"Heat some water, not too hot though and bring it here straight away with some Aloe."

"Yes, my lady," and she ran back into the house, her eyes filled with tears.

"Don't worry, Alesandro, we'll soon have you cleaned and dressed, do you feel any pain?" asked Julia.

"A little, but I'm not bothered," Alesandro replied, sitting on a bench swinging his legs.

Aramea returned with a bowl of water, soap, a large cloth, and Aloe, and handed them over to Julia and Naomi. Naomi quickly got to work washing his body and hair very gently. It wasn't long before she'd finished. Julia gently dried him and then applied some Aloe.

"Right, young man, try this tunic on for size now," said Julia. Naomi helped him to get dressed.

"That's better. It's perfect, what do you think, Naomi?"

"Wonderful," she replied.

"Right, I'm off to get ready, Romulus is taking me to visit Aurelia and Marcus." Julie exclaimed.

"While you're gone, I will show Alesandro our animals, and take him down to the vineyard," replied Naomi.

"Where's Zuma and Atticus?" asked Julia.

"They went hunting first thing this morning, and should be back soon," replied Naomi.

"Come on, Alesandro, follow me," Naomi said, and as they walked over to the pig pen, Naomi spoke softly to Alesandro, "Atticus will never let anyone hurt you again you can be sure of that."

"Will he chop their heads off like he did to that bad man yesterday?" asked Alesandro.

"Probably," she answered with a gentle smile looking down at him.

Romulus had saddled Blaze and one of the other horses for Julia to ride and left for the city. On the way, Julia told Romulus about Alesandro's injuries to his body, which had made Romulus angry.

"I've seen some terrible things in war over the past years, but I don't like it when the little one's get hurt," said Romulus.

They arrived at the Garrison a little before midday; one of the guards at the gate addressed Romulus, "What is your business here today?"

"We've come to see Tribune Marcus and his wife Aurelia; my name is Romulus."

"Yes, he's expecting you both, I will get someone to escort you," as he turned the Centurion Metelus arrived and said, "No need, I will escort them."

"Yes, Sir," the soldier replied.

"Good to see you both."

"Good day Metelus," answered Romulus.

"And how is the lovely Julia?"

"Very well, Metelus, thank you."

Romulus dismounted and helped Julia down. "Cyrus," shouted Metelus to one of the soldiers at the gate.

"Sir!"

"Take Romulus' horses to the stable if you will and make sure they get some water."

"Yes, Sir."

Metelus escorted them through the barracks to the Tribune's quarters, "That was some trip you had yesterday, that lad of yours doesn't muck around when there's a bit of trouble to sort out."

Romulus looked at Metelus smiling and answered, "He has a great sense of duty to help others, even at the risk of his own life and as you know the Gods favour the brave."

"They do indeed. I almost feel sorry for Rome's enemies when he joins the legions!" Romulus looked at Metelus and raised an eyebrow.

"I said almost!" Metelus exclaimed, and they both burst out laughing.

"You two are so incorrigible at times when you get together," said Julia, which only made them laugh even louder.

One of the guards on duty outside the Tribune's quarters knocked on Marcus's door as they approached, letting him know they'd arrived. Then he saluted Metelus and said, "Go straight in, Sir," and opened the door for them.

"Sir," saluted Metelus, "your guests have arrived." Metelus then spun around and marched back out, winking at Romulus on his way.

"Good day to you both, and how are you today? Julia, I hope you have rested and recovered from your day in Ostia I hope?"

"I am, it was wonderful thank you."

"Galactus," shouted Marcus; a swarthy looking man wearing spectacles appeared from behind a desk in the corner of the room, he looked a little overweight from lack of exercise and had very tanned skin, with greying hair. He answered, "Yes, my liege," rubbing his hands together and dribbling down his chin as he spoke.

"Inform the lady Aurelia that Romulus and Julia have arrived."

"Yes, my liege," replied Galactus, still rubbing his hands together and dribbling down his chin. He then turned and left the room.

"Bit of a strange one that if you don't mind me saying," said Romulus.

"He is a little, but he's good with numerals and writing, and above all does as he's told without question, I purchased him from a slave market in Gaul last year."

Marcus walked over to a table and asked, "Would you like some wine while we wait for Aurelia?"

"Yes, that would be wonderful," answered Julia.

"Yes, thank you," replied Romulus.

Marcus passed them both a glass full each and poured one for himself, "What's Atticus up to today?"

"He's gone hunting with Zuma," replied Romulus.

"I hear you've acquired a new member to add to your household, a young boy by all accounts?"

"His name is Alesandro," answered Julia.

Then the door swung open and in walked Aurelia, "Hello, my dear. I've just poured our guests some wine would you like a glass?"

"Yes, darling," Aurelia answered.

Marcus filled a glass and gave it to Aurelia. "Come, sit down, everyone," said Marcus.

"I thought while you and Romulus have a drink and talk about whatever you men do! Julia and I could go visit the Campus Martius."

"Yes, of course, I'll get Centurion Metelus to escort you both," replied Marcus.

"Galactus! Go fetch Centurion Metelus."

"Yes, my liege," and off he went.

"Come with me, Julia, let me show you how lovely my new rug, it brightens up our room. If the boys don't mind?"

"Not at all, my dear, take your wine with you."

When Aurelia and Julia had left the room, Marcus drank the whole contents of his glass, then gesturing to Romulus. "Another?"

"Don't mind if I do. It's a very palatable wine."

Marcus poured and refilled their glasses and said, "Yes, it's one of yours."

"I know," chuckled Romulus; ever since the successful mission against the deserters, they had become very good friends.

A knock on the door interrupted their conversation, "Come," shouted Marcus.

In walked Centurion Metelus saluting, "Yes, Sir. How can I be of assistance?"

"Apparently you like shopping," said Marcus.

"Me, Sir? Oh, no! Sir." Romulus couldn't help but grin.

"Well, you do now! I need you to escort Aurelia and Julia around the campus Martius for a couple of hours."

"When Sir?"

"As soon as they walk back through that door! Aurelia hasn't given me a moment's peace since she got back from Ostia!"

"Yes, Sir," groaned Metelus.

"I didn't know life in the army had become so easy," teased Romulus, which earned him a look of rebuke from Metelus.

Marcus laughed and said, "Never mind, Metelus. I know you are on duty but help yourself to a glass of that fine wine and sit down."

"Don't mind if I do," and licked his lips with a grin, he filled a glass and sat down.

"What did you make of those robbers attacking that merchant?" asked Marcus.

"Atticus didn't think they were robbers, and I'm inclined to agree with him," answered Romulus.

Marcus took a drink of his wine before carrying on the conservation, "And what does Atticus think?"

"He thinks they were killers sent to murder the merchant and his boy!"

"I wonder why," deliberated Marcus.

"Could have been having an affair with someone's wife?" said Metelus.

"Bit of an expensive way to kill a rival in the bedroom," said Romulus.

"Depends how good a shag she is?" Metelus laughed.

Marcus gave him a stern look and said, "You're not in the barracks with the other officers. Let's keep it a little cordial."

"Yes, Sir. Sorry Sir," replied Metelus.

"I suppose whatever it, was we may find out one day!"

The door swung open and in walked Aurelia and Julia; "I see our escort has arrived," said Aurelia with a smile.

Metelus stood up and bowed. "Good day, Aurelia, ready when you are." Then he smiled at Julia.

"We'll be on our way then darling," said Aurelia; she then gave Marcus a kiss on his cheek before leaving, and as they walked out Romulus shouted, "Enjoy your shopping, Metelus."

"I will make sure Julia spends plenty of your coin," Metelus retorted and slammed the door shut behind the three of them. Both Marcus and Romulus burst into a fit of laughter after the door closed.

Back up at the farm, Naomi who'd been showing Alesandro the animals, had now been joined by Lydia, and were walking down the fields to the vineyard. Alesandro had run ahead which gave Naomi time to tell Lydia of what she'd found covering Alesandro's tiny body. Lydia was quite appalled to find out and couldn't quite understand as to why anyone would do such a thing to someone so young.

"Look over there, Atticus and Zuma are back," shouted Alesandro with excitement, as he jumped up and down.

"Well, at least he's full of life," said Lydia.

"Good day," Zuma shouted as they rode towards them.

"And how are you, young Alesandro?" Atticus asked.

"Great, my new home is lovely, and I've had a big breakfast. Julia made me this tunic and I had a wash," replied Alesandro still full of excitement.

Zuma laughed and said, "He's full of beans, reminds me of when Atticus first arrived here."

"He does, but at least he didn't smell as bad as Atticus, if I remember it took me ages to scrub him clean and get rid of that smell," Naomi replied.

Alesandro ran to the back of the horses and asked, "What's that?" looking at several dead animals that were tied and were being dragged behind Fury and Lightning.

Atticus jumped down from Fury and asked, "Which one?"

"That one with those funny teeth."

"That is a wild boar, and those teeth are small tusks," replied Atticus.

"Who killed it?"

"Zuma killed that boar and three rabbits, and I killed the two deer and the other rabbit, so we'll have plenty of fresh meat to eat for the next few days."

"Would you like to come hunting with us one day?" asked Zuma.

"No, I couldn't kill anything," replied Alesandro shaking his head.

"He's not like you two big ruffians," said Naomi while ruffling Alesandro's hair.

"And he doesn't want to learn how to fight either," chastised Lydia.

Atticus lifted Alesandro up onto Fury's back, sitting him on the saddle; his legs only just reached the width of Fury's powerful body. Atticus led Fury up the fields back towards the stable. Lydia and Naomi walked at the side of Lighting and told Zuma about the wounds to Alesandro's body.

As Atticus walked Fury, he questioned Alesandro, "What do you want to be when you become a man?"

"Want to sail the sea and explore," he answered.

Atticus looked up at him riding and asked, "Where do you want to explore?"

"Across the sea to where all those boats bring the things to sell."

"So, you don't want to learn how to fight then?"

"Don't need to."

"Why not?"

"Because Naomi says if anybody hurts me, you'll chop their heads off."

"Is that so," replied Atticus looking behind him at Naomi who'd put her hands over her face trying to hide her blushes. Zuma and Lydia looked at Atticus with matching smiles.

"I can see why you two are a perfect match," grinned Atticus, then turned around to watch where he was going.

Zuma laughed and shouted, "A bit like you and Naomi, my little friend."

"Are you and Naomi getting married?" asked Alesandro gleefully.

"Yes, but only if she behaves herself," a small stone struck Atticus on the shoulder.

"Careful what you wish for my love," shouted Naomi throwing another stone at him which bounced off the back of his head.

"I'm hungry," said Alesandro.

"Don't worry, we'll soon have some of this meat cooked," said Lydia, "and there's fresh bread and cheese to be had as soon as we're back."

Down in the city, Romulus and Marcus were talking about the trip to Ostia, when the Legate Quintus walked into the room. Marcus quickly stood up and saluted while Romulus stood and said, "Good day Quintus," and bowed his head.

"Sit gentlemen, I've things to discuss with you both." Quintus walked around Marcus's desk and sat down.

"Right, first things first, pour me a glass of that wine you're both enjoying."

Marcus went to the table and poured the wine and set down a glass full in front of Quintus.

"I know you're retired from the legions Romulus, in case you're wondering why I'm including you in this discussion, but it will become apparent as we speak."

Romulus nodded his head in acknowledgement.

"We obviously have spies all over the empire, and we have been informed by a very reliable source, meaning the emperor and myself."

Marcus stiffened his back at the mere mention of the emperor, and Quintus paused to take a drink of his wine and let it sink in as to how high up discussions had taken place.

"How old is that son of yours, Romulus?"

"Atticus will be eighteen next week."

"Will he now?" Quintus then paused, stood up, and began to pace up and down the room deep in thought, "You have to be twenty to join the legions," Quintus continued.

"That is true," answered Marcus.

"How eager is Atticus to join and do Rome's bidding?" asked Quintus.

"I am quite sure that he can't wait to be old enough. It's all he has yearned for from a very young age," answered Romulus.

"An understatement if you ask me," said Marcus.

"Indeed, that's exactly what I thought, and he's to be married soon, isn't that so, Romulus?" Quintus had now sat down again behind the desk.

"Yes, he is," replied Romulus.

"And does the girl fully support Atticus in his thirst to fight for Rome?"

"She does," answered Romulus.

"Good," replied Quintus.

"As you both probably now know, I have the ear of the emperor and will endeavour to have Atticus enrolled in the legions sooner rather than later," said Quintus, "The spy has informed us King Ashur-uballit I, came to Rome with his son, disguised as a merchant. For what reason we are not quite sure, and an attempt was made to kill him," again Quintus paused for a drink of wine. "Now you can see why it's necessary for you both to be here at this meeting. It looks like Atticus intervened and saved his life."

Marcus and Romulus looked at each other in disbelief. "Looks like the Gods favour Atticus," said Quintus.

Then there was a knock at the door.

"Not now, do not enter," shouted Quintus.

"A couple of those Mesopotamian Kings' brothers, by all accounts given separate lands to rule, but are competing for overall control. So, it's quite obvious who orchestrated the attempt." Quintus paused again standing up and began to pace the room.

"And if they'd succeeded in killing him on Roman soil, that would have caused an uprising against us in the east," replied Marcus.

"Yes, indeed! War will come any way with those goat-fucking-inbreds. The Parthians seem to want the Mesopotamians to join forces with them and overturn our rule, but at the moment we need to build the legions back to full strength," replied Quintus, who then sat down again and swallowed the remainder of his glass of wine, before continuing. "General Maximus arrives at the fort in Ostia two days from now, his success at quelling that rebellion in Gaul. He is to be honoured by the emperor, but it has come at a great cost to his legions."

"How great was the cost?" asked Marcus.

"He's divided a whole legion between our forts up there to strengthen them and keep those buggers in line. His three remaining legions, returning with him, are only at half strength due to heavy casualties."

Quintus got up and refilled his wine glass before sitting back down, "We estimate it will take a full year to fully train and equip his legions ready to fight at full strength, hence the need for the calibre of Atticus even though he is only eighteen."

Quintus drank more of his wine and went on to say, "I have to go, but none of what we have spoken about goes beyond these walls understand?"

"Yes, Sir," replied Marcus.

"Agreed," said Romulus.

Then Quintus finished his wine, bid them farewell and left.

"Fuck me," said Romulus.

"What I don't understand, what was a potential enemy of Rome doing wandering around over here?" said Marcus.

While they were sitting discussing the reasons for the king to be over here, in walked Metelus with the ladies.

"Did you have fun, Aurelia?" asked Marcus.

"We did," she replied, "but I'm quite exhausted and need a lie down if you don't mind."

"We need to return home anyway," replied Romulus.

"Well, I'll retire then. I will call on you soon Julia," said Aurelia kissing her on her cheek.

"Goodbye, Aurelia," replied Julia smiling.

"I will let you know of any further developments regarding Atticus," said Marcus, as Julia and Romulus departed with Metelus.

"What developments?" asked Metelus.

"Sorry, my friend, but I'm not at liberty to say at this moment in time," replied Romulus with a deep sigh; he didn't like keeping secrets from friends.

"I see," answered Metelus.

Romulus and Julia collected their horses from the stable. On the way back home, Julia had questioned Romulus about the meeting in Marcus's quarters but had got the same answer as Metelus.

Chapter 23

It was now the day of Atticus's birthday. Naomi and Julia were busy organising the celebrations. Lydia was helping Aramea and Seema in the kitchen. Atticus had been hunting on his own at first light and had killed a deer which was to be roasted for the celebrations in the evening.

On his return, Atticus went to the training ground, practising with his swords and was watched by young Alesandro. Fury as usual was charging up and down the field chasing the other horses around.

The sun glared in the sky making it another extremely hot day. Sweat poured off Atticus, as he spun around slashing the swords in all directions, blocking, and lunging at imaginary attackers.

When he'd finished, Alesandro ran over to him with a jug of water for him to drink, but instead Atticus poured the water over his head to cool himself down. He then flicked his long dark hair towards Alesandro, wetting him which made the boy giggle hysterically. Alesandro then ran off and picked up a bucket and half filled it with water from the horse trough and ran back to throw it at Atticus.

Zuma walked up shouting encouragement at Alesandro, telling him to make sure he didn't miss. It wasn't long before Romulus arrived after hearing all the commotion; he quickly grabbed another bucket and filled it with water, joining Alesandro in throwing water over Atticus.

"Just you two wait until I get a bucket, and you'll know about it," Atticus shouted after getting soaked.

Zuma laughed, then picked up a spare bucket and joined in the fun; it wasn't long before all four of them were wet through after filling their buckets from the horse trough and soaking each other.

Naomi and Julia came out of the main house to see what was happening, and as they approached, Romulus and the rest of them looked at each other. Zuma smiled and nodded in the direction of the girls. The girls realised they were about to get wet and screamed, "NO! NO! Don't you dare!" and turned, running back towards the house, but they were not quick enough, and soon got a good soaking.

"Just you wait," shouted Lydia at Zuma.

Naomi shouted for Julia, "Come here and help us and bring a bowl of water."

Julia looked out of the doorway to see what was happening, laughed, and replied,

"I'm not getting involved no way," and she slammed the gated door shut. Naomi was well and truly soaked by now and said to Atticus. "As big as you are just you wait, I'll get my own back."

Atticus was laughing hysterically and slumped down on the floor, just as Naomi jumped on top of him and started tickling his bare ribs. Atticus, still laughing, pleaded with her to stop. Aramea walked out of the house tutting and muttering, "Grown-ups acting like children. We won't be ready for the celebration at this rate," and went back into the house.

Zuma picked up Alesandro and said, "Aramea has got a point. Come on, better help get things done."

Alesandro carried on laughing; he couldn't remember ever having so much fun.

Several wooden tables had been placed in the courtyard. Figo and Alepo were spit-roasting the deer over a fire, while the household slaves were busy running back and forth setting the tables with fresh bread, fruit, pastries, dates, and fresh fish.

The sound of horses filled the air as Tribune Marcus arrived with Aurelia, Metelus and Optio Clictus.

"Good day and welcome," greeted Romulus, as they dismounted and walked into the courtyard.

"It's been very hot today," Aurelia said to Julia as she greeted them on their arrival.

"It has," replied Julia.

"And where is the birthday boy?" enquired Aurelia.

"With Naomi helping her to get ready as far as know."

"Any further developments over the past few days?" asked Romulus.

A servant carrying a tray of wine and wine glasses entered the courtyard and placed it on the table offering it to their guests. After he'd gone Marcus replied,

"General Maximus has arrived in Ostia and has wasted no time in recruiting and training replacements. He also went to the fort outside Capranica on his way back and relieved them of four cohorts of Batavians, to the annoyance of the fort's commander. But needs must as they say."

"He strikes me as a man who doesn't muck around," replied Romulus.

"That's an understatement to say, he's been out hunting with his bodyguards every day! He's getting well and truly on with rebuilding his legions."

"Loves his hunting then?" asked Romulus.

"Can't get enough by all accounts," answered Marcus, before taking a large sip of his wine.

All the household and guests were now in the courtyard sitting around the tables deep in conversation. Figo and Alepo had carried out several large platters of hot venison and placed them on the main table. Romulus had gone into the main house and returned carrying a large box putting it down on one of the stone benches; Aurelia was very keen to find out what was in the large box and was whispering in Julia's ear as to its contents.

When they'd both finished with their hushed conversation, Aurelia smiled at Julia on hearing the answer to her question. Metelus and Clictus were too busy eating the venison and drinking the fine wine to even notice Romulus bringing out the heavy box. Zuma and Lydia were aware as to the contents and sat smiling. Alesandro had begun to pull at Romulus' tunic and pester him as to the contents.

"You'll find out in a moment," said Romulus, ruffling Alesandro's mop of hair.

Atticus and Naomi had arrived and were sitting talking to each other waiting patiently. Atticus knew it was something for him, but as to what, he didn't have a clue.

"Right then, everybody," Romulus began, "Eighteen, Atticus, eh! Boy has become a man." Then the crowd all started tapping on the tables. Atticus gave an appreciated nod.

"So, due to your preferred future occupation, I thought the contents of this box might come in handy," as he pulled items of a brand-new suit of armour out of the box.

Atticus's eyes lit up when Romulus lifted a bronze breastplate and held it up; even the Tribune Marcus marvelled at the workmanship.

In the centre were two black stallions facing each other, and underneath the words in Latin 'FYOORE' meaning *Fury*. Atticus quickly tried the armour on, and it was a perfect fit. "It's fantastic, father, I can't thank you enough," while running his fingers over the two stallions.

"Nothing more than you deserve, son," replied Romulus.

"You now not only fight like a soldier, but you'll also look like a soldier," said Zuma.

"He will do when he's had his hair cut," said Metelus, followed by laughter from everyone; even Aurelia couldn't help but giggle.

A few hours later Marcus, Aurelia and Metelus, mounted their horses to return to the city. Poor Clictus had to be helped onto his horse, feeling a little worse for wear after the numerous glasses of wine he'd drunk.

"Metelus will keep you updated, and I will no doubt see you shortly," said Marcus.

"You will," replied Romulus. Everyone bid their farewells and made their way to bed, as Marcus and his party returned to the city.

Chapter 24

Several weeks had passed, and summer gave way to Autumn. Work on the farm was in full swing as normal. The city's taverns and brothels were full of legionnaires spending their coin. Zuma and Romulus, along with the farm workers, were delivering the amphoras of wine twice a week. Atticus had been looking after the day to day running of the farm, while taking time out to go hunting early in the mornings. He spent the early evenings training without fail and donated as much time as he could to Naomi; the day for the wedding was not too far away.

Atticus had cleaned out the stables and put the horses out in the field just as the sun came up, but it was a very misty sunrise. The mountains higher up couldn't yet be seen due to the low cloud filling the sky around them.

Atticus then saddled Fury and strapped a quiver full of arrows ready for hunting to the saddle. He also strapped two javelins to Fury just below his saddle, after the attack from the bear he was always prepared for the worst.

Atticus had decided to wear his armour and try it out along with his swords; he wanted to make sure it did not hinder him in any way while riding Fury.

Naomi ambled into the stable yawning. "Well, don't you look the part," she said, smiling in admiration.

"No time like the present to try it out," Atticus replied.

"You're like a big child with his new favourite toy," Naomi teased and asked, "Do I get a kiss from my soldier boy before he goes hunting?"

"That depends," he replied walking over to where she stood.

Atticus towered over Naomi at six foot six, as Naomi was a petite five foot, and as he looked down into her face she asked, "Depends on what?"

"If you tell me you'll love me forever?"

"Do I really need to tell you?"

Atticus bent down, picked her up into his arms and kissed her like his whole life depended on it. When they'd finally finished kissing, Naomi opened her eyes and said, "Does that answer your question?"

Atticus smiled at her replying, "Yes."

"Good, now go get something nice for supper," she said and went back into the main house.

Atticus mounted Fury and rode off at a gallop towards the woods through the mist.

At the far side of the woods, there was a large clearing with a small cottage which belonged to a shepherd called Demitrious. It was only a small cottage as he lived alone. Demetrious kept about forty sheep in a field, which was surrounded by a stone wall. There was a barn and two small sheds at the rear of the cottage. Smoke came out of the roof from the oven, as the sound of the sheep bleating in the field broke the silence and was barely visible due to the mist.

Atticus did not normally come hunting this far down, but sometimes he would come and visit Demetrious. For some reason there wasn't any deer yet to be found, so he'd decided to go try his luck in the forest at the far side of the cottage.

As he rode past, he noticed the tracks of at least twenty horses, some of which were in the small yard at the rear of the cottage, which he thought to be strange as Demitrious didn't own any horses. As he looked down at the tracks, Fury had become alert and snorted, pricking his ears up then pounding his left hoof into the ground. Atticus knew all too well this to be a sign that something was wrong.

He immediately scanned the surrounding area, but the poor visibility caused by the mist and low hanging clouds didn't help much. Atticus had a keen eye and Fury to count on and all his senses said trouble.

Atticus slid down off Fury and drew one of his swords; he led Fury into the yard and began to search all around looking for clues. He began to knock on the door of the cottage, and as he did the door creaked slowly open, revealing the room inside which was quite dark as the shutters on the two windows were still closed. Atticus shouted, "Demetrius," and waited for a reply, but none came, so he shouted again, "Demetrius, are you there?"

Still there was no reply. Atticus then went inside and opened the shutters to let some daylight in, there wasn't any sign of Demetrius. There were several plates strewn about a table; some still had half eaten remains of bread on them, and all over the floor were bones that had been discarded after the meat on them had been eaten. Overturned cups and several wine jugs littered the floor, some of which had been smashed. The oven was still burning which meant whoever had been here with Demetrious hadn't long gone, but there was still no sign of Demetrius.

Atticus went back outside; Fury had made his way to the barn and as Atticus came out Fury lifted his front legs high into the air and stamped them down in front of the barn. Atticus strode over to Fury quickly still holding a sword out in front of him, and as he approached could see two legs sticking out from under some straw.

He spun around looking in all directions making sure it was safe to enter the barn; when he was sure nobody was in a position to attack him, he bent down and with his free hand dragged out the body.

Atticus then rolled the stiff body over onto its back revealing the identity of Demetrius who'd had his throat cut. His skin was very pale, with a blue tint to it, which made Atticus think he'd been dead for at least a few days as rigor mortis had set in.

Atticus had all sorts of thoughts flying through his mind now and said out loud to himself, '*Why would anyone want to kill you? but don't worry old friend I will find out and make them pay!*'

Atticus mounted Fury; anger on his face and revenge on his mind. He then picked up the trail of the horses heading towards the forest at the far side of the cottage and started to hunt for his human prey.

Back at the fort in Ostia, General Maximus had left to go on his daily hunt with his German bodyguards; this consisted of a dozen well-armed and formidable fighters. General Maximus was aged forty, and he himself was a battle-hardened fighter who didn't expect his men to do anything he hadn't done or wouldn't do himself. This and the fact he was fair but firm, made him very well respected by all under his command and beyond, and was also favoured by the emperor Augustus.

As Maximus rode with his bodyguard, he joked and laughed with them about the day's hunt in a very informal manner, because Maximus trusted his life to them on a daily basis. So, as soon as they were away from the formality of the daily command of his legions, protocol went out of the window.

"What do you hope to kill today General?" shouted Adelar, who was a strong, very muscular man in his late twenties, with long blonde hair and a thick beard; he was also a favourite of Maximus.

"Anything would be fine after the last two days, spending hours in those forests with nothing to show for it," groaned Maximus.

"We can't kill anything because the animals can smell Asken a mile away! He needs to bathe, he stinks of goat's piss," shouted Edelgard riding at the rear. Edelgard was an older German, coming up to the age of forty-five, but still as strong as an ox. Most Germans in the ranks of the auxiliaries didn't shave or cut their hair, but Eldegard had succumbed to the Roman way of personal grooming and kept his hair really short and trimmed his beard, he also took regular baths.

"Fuck off! you sheep shagger," retorted Asken, as everyone burst into fits of laughter as they approached the edge of the forest, even Maximus joined in laughing out loudly.

"Bit misty up here in the hills today," Dieter said with a bit of trepidation in his voice, he was a young warrior with no fear in battle but believed in omens and dark rituals from his ancestors back in Germanica.

"What's up Dieter, bit of mist and your balls have disappeared up your arse?" said Adelar jokingly.

"No, but mist on a morning is an omen for a warning," replied Dieter.

"Here we go more of that spooky shit." Asken laughed.

"Quieten down now lads, the animals won't just smell us a mile away, they'll hear us," said Maximus with a chuckle.

As they rode through the forest, silence now replacing the laughter, the mist swirled around them and there was not even the chirp of a bird, or the rustle of leaves could be heard. Dieter could feel his heart pounding like the beat of a drum deep within his chest.

"Are you sure, General, about this hunt? Something doesn't feel right," whispered Dieter.

"Why?" asked Maximus.

"Visibility is poor—" but before he could finish his sentence, a deer shot across their path.

Edelgard in a flash launched a spear, thudding into the deer's neck killing it instantly.

"Look, Dieter, surely that is a good omen?" asked Asken with a big smile.

"I'm still not convinced," answered Dieter while edging his horse forward peering into the mist.

"Keep your eyes open," said Maximus quietly.

Edelgard dismounted and pulled his spear out of the deer, then quickly trussed the animal up and laid it over the back of one of the mules they'd brought with them.

"First kill to me! That's a drink you all owe me back at the fort," said Edelgard with a grin, as he remounted his horse, and on they rode, deeper into the woods through the mist in silence.

On the other end of the forest, Atticus continued tracking his prey, determined to catch or kill Demetrius's killers, but still couldn't understand why he'd been killed. He pulled Fury up behind some bushes and listened, as he thought he could now hear the faint sounds of horses travelling slow and quiet.

So, without making a sound, Atticus nudged Fury on, silently stalking his prey. Both Atticus and Fury were ready for anything and moved forward as one.

An hour had now passed since he first heard the sounds of his prey; Atticus had now got his first sighting of them; they were just visible in the patchy mist.

His prey hadn't noticed they were being followed and carried on moving forward between the trees and bushes. Atticus could see his prey were all clothed in black and covered their heads with black headscarves; now things were becoming clearer to Atticus. He realised they were all dressed exactly the same as the merchant's attackers outside Ostia over a month ago.

Atticus began to flank his prey; as he got nearer to them, Fury stepped carefully, avoiding dead branches on the floor, and made as little noise as possible.

His prey came to a stand-still, so Atticus stopped again, just out of sight behind some bushes, but was now in earshot of them and could hear voices talking in a hushed tone.

They now began to split up and some had made their way across a trail leading through the forest which was barely visible in the mist floating through the trees.

It was now quite obvious to Atticus they were laying an ambush for someone 'but who?' thought Atticus. He'd counted twenty-three of them, all on horseback and they had spread out over a fairly wide area, as the trail entered a clearing further up. Atticus had seen it while following his prey, but from here couldn't be seen for the mist; all of them were carrying bows and curved swords. Atticus was sure they were assassins sent from the east.

All of them were dark skinned and wore charcoal painted around their eyes. He could see one or more had tattoos painted on their faces.

Atticus had come to the conclusion they were Parthian, but again he thought, '*Who were they going to try and kill?*' The enemy's ambush had now been laid. Atticus had decided the time to act was now. Demetrius's killers needed to die regardless of who they wanted to ambush, so, the thoughts to who they were going to kill were not an issue, he wanted revenge for the death of Demetrious.

Maximus and his bodyguards were now coming up the trail, oblivious to the ambush set for them, and rode on in close contact but spread out to each side of the trail still being quiet, looking for another deer or wild boar.

The sound of an owl broke the silence; Dieter reacted almost immediately and shouted a warning, "That's no fucking owl—" but before he could finish his warning, an arrow came out of the trees with a steel shaft and punched into his face knocking him off his horse.

Edelgard shouted, "Protect the GENERAL! Shields up!" and as they closed ranks to circle Maximus, a volley of arrows flew out of the trees on both sides of the trail, several hitting the shields protecting Maximus, but two of his bodyguards were struck by several arrows and were killed instantly.

"Quick! Dismount! We're too much of an easy target on horseback," demanded Maximus.

As they did, more arrows were fired at them, flying through the mist killing another bodyguard and several of the horses.

Maximus's bodyguards quickly formed a testudo to protect him. The few surviving horses darted off in all directions in fright, as did the mules. There were only eight of them left surrounding Maximus with their shields locked together tight.

Arrows flew in from all directions and clattered off the shields but were not able to penetrate their defences.

"Come on then you bastards and feel my steel in your gut!" shouted Adelar.

Another volley of arrows flew in and clattered their shields, still unable to penetrate them.

"COWARDS," raged Asken, shouting another challenge to their attackers.

Silence descended for a few moments, other than the heavy breathing of Maximus and his bodyguards, hiding behind their shields for protection.

They'd left a tiny slit to look out of, in case any of the attackers dared to approach. A loud scream suddenly pierced the silence, followed shortly by another.

"What the fuck was that?" asked Adelar, beads of sweat dripping off his forehead.

"Don't know," answered Edelgard breathing heavily.

All of a sudden, another deafening scream came from another direction.

"That's the sound of someone dying slowly in pain," said Maximus.

"So, it looks like we've got some help," Asken said with hope in his voice, "But who?"

"Get ready, boys," alerted Edelgard, looking out of the slit in the shields as one of their attackers charged at them out of the trees.

The mist swirling around the horse's legs as it charged at them, the rider dressed in black, screaming loudly, "DEATH TO THE ROMAN GENERAL!" while waving his sword in a circle above his head.

"Get your bodies behind the shields, men! If he opens us up, expect a volley of arrows" snarled Maximus.

"And that means we're fucked," growled Edelgard.

The rider charging was only ten yards from them; *wush!* came the sound above their heads, as a javelin flew only inches above their shields through the mist, punching into the rider's chest, knocking him backwards off his horse. The javelin had such force, it had ripped his chest wide open on impact; blood sprayed their shields, as the horse turned direction and disappeared into the trees. The body of the attacker laid spread eagle in front of Maximus' shield. He could smell the putrid stench of the man's entrails and bowel; steam from the warm organs rose, mixing with the cold misty air.

"Fuck me," shouted Asken.

Maximus quickly began to try and look out from behind the shields to see where the help was coming from.

"There must be more than one helping us," said Maximus, as another scream of death pierced the air from within the trees surrounding the clearing.

"There must be a patrol out here from Rome," shouted Adelar.

Two arrows then shot across the trail followed by thuds, and more cries of death. Edelgard and the other bodyguards started banging their shields with their swords loudly in rhythm which echoed through the mist.

The remaining assassins made one last charge from out of the trees, screaming their war cry; there was only a dozen left, but as they charged forward, arrow after arrow shot through the air in their direction, punching into their chests and throats. One arrow pierced an attacker while bearing down on Maximus in the eye. Screams of death and pain filled the air as they died, falling from their horses.

Maximus and his German bodyguards marched forward in-line, shields up, finishing off any survivors that were screaming in pain on the floor.

One last rider slowly came out of the trees; he shouted a challenge to Maximus and drew his sword.

"No! General it might be a trap, there might be more waiting!"

And quickly Maximus's bodyguards surrounded him, shields locking together, swords still drawn. As quick as a flash, an arrow clattered one of the shields covering Maximus; it was fired from the trees to his left.

"Coward," shouted Edelgard, as another scream erupted from the trees where the arrow had come from, which made the other assassin look to his left frantically.

"Wish I had a bow I'd kill that bastard," muttered Adelar.

A riderless horse ran across the trail, as Atticus rode out of the trees; blood dripping from his sword that was in one hand, the head of one of the assassins in his other.

Fury reared up and stamped his hoofs into the ground as he crashed his legs down, in a mark of defiance at the remaining assassin. Atticus then threw the head towards him which landed right at his horse's feet making it back up in fright.

"Who the fuck is that?" asked Asken, still protecting the General.

"I've never seen him before," answered Maximus.

"I don't bloody care, he's probably saved our lives," said Edelgard.

"He's not much more than a boy," said Adelar.

"That maybe, but we owe him our lives," answered Maximus.

Atticus rode Fury slowly towards the last assassin and said coldly, "Fight me and die or throw down your sword and surrender."

Maximus and his German bodyguards looked on, watching as Atticus closed in on his opponent.

"100 sesterces says the young lad wins," said Adelar.

Maximus smiled and replied, "As usual, you only back a certainty, I've never seen you lose a bet," which made the other Germans laugh.

The assassin charged his horse at Atticus screaming out profanities at him, sword out in front. But Atticus swiftly knocked the sword out of his hand and thrust his sword into the assassin's chest, smashing his ribs. The horse carried on past Atticus, as the assassin fell dead to the ground. Atticus then calmly turned Fury to face the General and his surviving bodyguards.

As soon as Atticus was a yard in front of Maximus, he dismounted Fury and bowed his head saying, "Good day, General," then looked at Maximus's bodyguards before nodding his head and continuing, "Greetings."

Atticus sheathed his sword as Maximus replied, "Well, young man, who do I have the honour of addressing?"

"My name is Atticus, Sir. It's a pleasure to be of service to you."

Maximus stepped forward and clasped his forearm; "The pleasure, Atticus, is all mine. You have saved the lives undoubtedly of myself and my remaining bodyguards, and for that we cannot thank you enough."

The bodyguards all muttered in agreement with their General.

The mist had now gone, and the full glare of the sun was in the sky.

"What brings you out here to the forest?" asked Maximus.

While Atticus explained to Maximus his events and reasons for being there, Adelar and the others went to recover their horses and mules; they also gathered up the bodies of their dead comrades. Maximus walked over to where the dead bodies of his bodyguards had been laid. He knelt down amongst them in deep reflection; these bodyguards had fought at his side for several years. Maximus placed his hand on the body of Dieter, who he had a great fondness for, somewhat like a father had for his son. Everyone stood in silence until Maximus stood up and said, "Strength and honour, see you one day in Elysium," Maximus then turned and faced the others.

Edelgard had recovered the mule carrying the deer, and said, "At least we will eat well at the fort tonight," to try and take everyone out of their dark mood.

"The same old Edelgard, thinking only of his belly." Asken laughed.

"It's a pity they're all dead. I'd have liked to have interrogated at least one of them," said Maximus with a long sigh.

Atticus replied, "Not to worry, Sir"

"What do you mean?" asked Maximus.

"If you would like to walk with me over into the forest there, I've got someone you might want to talk to!"

Maximus looked at Atticus, raising an eyebrow in bewilderment and walked with him into the trees. Followed closely by Adelar and Edelgard as the others stayed with the horses and the mules.

Asken had walked over to Fury to stroke him, but quickly backed off realising Fury wasn't happy for the attention which made the others laugh.

"See, even the horse doesn't like the smell of you!" Almut, another old German with dirty blonde hair who'd survived the ambush shouted, laughing as he did so.

"Piss off, you goat fucker," replied Asken with a grin.

As Atticus and Maximus, with the other two bodyguards walked into the trees, Maximus began the conversation between them.

"That's a fine suit of armour, where did you acquire it?" asked Maximus.

"My father Romulus gave me it for my birthday," replied Atticus.

Once they were in the trees, Maximus saw one of the assassins tied up to a tree, with part of his headscarf shoved in his mouth.

Maximus looked at him and smiled, as Edelgard said, "You were definitely busy in these woods young Atticus, and you seem to have thought of everything."

"My father and his friend Zuma taught me well over the years," replied Atticus.

"They certainly did that," Edelgard said with a grin.

Maximus walked towards the prisoner tied to the tree and stood looking into his eyes. The face of the prisoner was gripped in fear; Maximus turned to face Edelgard and said, "We'll take him back to the fort and question him later."

"Yes, General," he replied and cut him free, then dragged him back to the others.

"How far is it to your home, Atticus?" asked Maximus.

"Two-hour ride, that's all, but I need to go bury my friend, the shepherd Demetrius on the way back," replied Atticus.

"Good, we will come with you and help with the burial, and I want to meet the father of the boy who saved our lives," answered Maximus.

Asken and the others had buried their dead comrades and collected all the discarded weapons and tied them to another donkey they'd repatriated.

"Mount up lads and follow me and young Atticus, the prisoner can bloody walk," shouted Maximus.

They arrived at Romulus's home late in the afternoon, and on seeing them ride into the courtyard, the whole household had come out and were standing waiting.

Alepo had seen them coming up through the fields and ran to the main house to let Romulus know of their impending visitors arriving with Atticus.

Maximus and Atticus dismounted, as the others still sat on their horses. Romulus and Zuma were standing at the front of everyone.

"Father, may I introduce General Maximus."

At the very mention of his name, many of the faces in the crowd had expressions of amazement; Lydia looked at Zuma in shock.

Naomi was too busy to care; she just gazed at Atticus; glad he was home safe. Even though she did not know the events of the day yet, she had noticed the prisoner who was tied to a rope and had fallen to the floor with exhaustion.

"It's an honour to meet you, General," said Romulus.

Maximus immediately clasped Romulus's forearm and said, "Please call me Maximus, it's me who is honoured to be greeted by the father of the young man who has fought so bravely and saved the life of myself and my men."

"My son seems to have that ability lately," replied Romulus; Maximus looked at Atticus a little bewildered.

"He does that," bellowed Zuma.

"Aramea, bring wine and food out for Maximus' bodyguards."

"Yes, master," she replied and ran into the house closely followed by Seema.

"Father, I will go with Naomi and change out of this armour and clean the blood off it," said Atticus.

"Don't be long, we don't want to keep the General waiting," replied Romulus.

"Please, Maximus, if you would like to come with me and Zuma to my private quarters, I will have refreshments brought to us, and you can relax a while in comfort before your journey back to the fort in Ostia. Any matters you wish to discuss can be done in private," said Romulus.

"Excellent idea," answered Maximus; He then turned to his men who were still seated on their horses and said, "Asken after your horse is fed and rested, ride fast to Ostia and give a full report to the legate Octavian."

"Yes, General," he replied.

"They'll probably already be wondering where we have got to, and it wouldn't surprise me that they will have already sent out patrols to look for us," Maximus went on to say.

"Right, Romulus, lead the way, my friend," said Maximus; his bodyguard all dismounted and sat down on the stone benches in the courtyard, as Aramea and Seema brought out the wine and food, passing it amongst them all.

Alesandro had run and followed Atticus and Naomi to his room to wash and change, and while Atticus cleaned the blood off his armour and sword eagerly asked, "Did you chop some bad man's head off?" looking at all the blood stains.

Atticus looked down at him smiling and replied, "Yes but only because they were very bad men."

"I knew it," shouted Alesandro with glee and ran off back outside, skipping as he did so.

Atticus looked at Naomi with a grin. "See what you've started, telling him I chop bad people's heads off."

"Well, you do," answered Naomi before continuing. "Now let's get you clean we don't want to keep the General waiting."

Maximus, Romulus, and Zuma had sat and made themselves comfortable, as Figo arrived carrying a tray with wine and food for them; he placed it down and bowed before leaving.

"It's a very nice home you have here Romulus, and how old is Atticus?" asked Maximus.

"Just turned eighteen," replied Romulus.

"And what have you planned for his future if you don't mind me asking?"

Romulus gave a full account of how Atticus had come to Romulus's home as a young boy and how he had adopted him. And between himself and Zuma, they quickly gave a full account of his training and exploits already achieved, even at such a young age. Maximus couldn't help but sit listening with great admiration.

Just as they had finished talking, in walked Atticus wearing a clean tunic; his hair brushed and tied in a neat ponytail.

"Come sit by me," beckoned Maximus; Atticus sat on the couch to Maximus's left and picked up a glass of wine and took a sip.

"Your father and your great friend Zuma here have filled me in with your life story, short as it's been as your only eighteen, it is quite incredible," said Maximus.

Atticus replied a little embarrassed, "You know fathers and great friends will always exaggerate a bit. I've only ever done what has been needed at the time and I'm only able to do it because of their dedication to my training."

Zuma laughed and said, "I don't think you can play down your own ability with the General as he's witnessed it for himself."

Maximus looked at Atticus and asked, "How can I repay you for saving my life let alone for the lives of my men?"

"No need. It was an honour to be able to serve Rome, Sir," replied Atticus.

Maximus smiled and looked at Romulus and said, "Your son is truly a credit to you and is a very honourable young man."

Then he turned to look at Atticus and said, "If there was anything within my power to grant you what would it be?"

Atticus was about to answer when Maximus cut in saying. "Please I know what you just said so before you answer I really need you to think for a moment and ask me!" Atticus looked first at Romulus, then at Zuma who was sitting with a great big smile on his face looking at him.

Atticus paused, then looked at Maximus and said, "I want to join one of your legions as a centurion."

Maximus looked at him and replied, "You know you have to be twenty to join the legions, do you mean you want me to grant you your wish in two years' time?"

"No, I want to join now."

Maximus stood up and walked around the room in deep thought before replying, but Romulus spoke first.

"If it helps with your decision, the legate of the praetorian guards Quintus has wanted Atticus to join sooner rather than later, and to my knowledge has spoken with the emperor."

"Has he now," answered Maximus, then he paced the room again.

"Well, I have the emperor's ear and will go ask for an audience with him as soon as possible. I'll not have his talent wasted in the praetorian guards of all places," said Maximus grinning.

He then sat down on the couch next to Atticus again. "I think that it will be quite possible that in a couple of weeks young man I will be having the pleasure of your services as my first centurion in the ranks of my legion as soon as it can be formalised," said Maximus with a smile.

"But if you don't mind me asking why a centurion?"

"Two reasons: first, I get married quarters as I'm to be married in a few days, and secondly, I get to ride Fury into battle because where I go, he goes."

Maximus laughed and said, "I see you've got everything planned out then."

For the next hour, they all drank, talked, and laughed amongst themselves until the sound of many horses outside interrupted their conversations. The voice of Adelar could be heard at the gate. As it was opened, Maximus walked out of the main house followed by Atticus, Romulus, and Zuma.

They were met by Asken And the legate Octavian, along with several officers riding into the courtyard. and out on the road outside was a column of two-hundred Roman cavalry blocking the road.

Octavian dismounted and said, "Thank the Gods you're safe. I've had a report from Asken on the way here; we met while out looking for you, I've had patrols out searching everywhere."

"The thanks belongs to young Atticus here."

Octavian turned to address Atticus and said, "So you're the brave warrior Asken has described. If I didn't know Asken better, I would've thought his story to be a little over exaggerated, so Rome owes you it's thanks young man."

Maximus turned to Atticus and clasped his forearm. "I will come and inform you as to the emperor's response to our discussion when I have spoken with him."

"Thank you," replied Atticus.

"Adelar bring that prisoner!" Maximus shouted. He then shouted for Edelgard to bring his horse; after mounting, Maximus bid is farewell. Maximus smiled at Romulus and rode off with Octavian and the large escort of Roman cavalry, and his bodyguards, back to Ostia.

The gate was secured for the night, and peace and quiet, descended on the farm once again.

Chapter 25

The following week, Edelgard arrived at Romulus's home early in the morning, the day after the wedding of Atticus to Naomi. With him was an escort of thirty Roman cavalry. Figo had opened the gate on their arrival and sent Alepo into the house to fetch their master. Romulus walked out into the courtyard followed by Zuma.

"Greetings," said Romulus.

"Good day, Sir," replied Edelgard.

"How is that son of yours?" enquired Edelgard.

"Happy as a pig in shit, he got married yesterday."

The big German burst into a fit of laughter.

"He's still in bed," added Zuma with a grin.

"Nothing wrong with the warmth of a good woman, not that I get much chance these days," answered Edelgard, then he promptly asked, "I don't suppose you have some of your wine handy?" licking his lips in anticipation.

Romulus laughed and shouted, "Aramea, wine for our guest." Edelgard dismounted his horse as the wine was asked for.

"Come, sit here and tell me the reason for your visit."; Romulus pointed to the stone benches and sat down.

Zuma had gone to fetch Atticus as Aramea arrived with a jug of wine and several glasses. The roman escort dismounted on the road outside and waited by their horses.

Atticus and Zuma walked into the courtyard; Edelgard jumped up and bearhugged Atticus saying, "Greetings, my roman brother," then let go and stood back looking at Atticus and continued, "You look tired have you had a busy night?"

Romulus and Zuma began laughing, but Atticus just went red in the face. Edelgard grabbed his glass of wine, raised it, and shouted, "To Atticus and his new wife." Romulus and Zuma followed suit.

"By that is good wine," said Edelgard, drinking the whole glass in one go, some of which dribbled into his neatly cut beard.

He then asked for another glass with a grin, which Romulus filled saying, "You German's know how to drink!"

"Ah, yes, the reason for my visit, General Maximus requests you accompany me back to Ostia at once Atticus," he then drank the contents of the refilled glass. Atticus's eyes lit up.

"Go on, son, quick get ready, put on your finest tunic and say goodbye to your wife," Romulus exclaimed.

"I'll get Fury saddled," shouted Zuma and he went to the stable.

"Might as well have some more of that wine while I wait," said Edelgard and sat back on the bench grinning.

Atticus went to his and Naomi's room, Naomi was still lying-in bed naked, but sat up when Atticus entered in a hurry, revealing her ample breasts.

"What's happening?" enquired Naomi.

"I've been requested to go see General Maximus," he replied, and put on his best tunic and belt, then strapped his scabbards containing his swords. Atticus then tied his long black hair into a ponytail as Naomi watched him with adoration.

"Is it going to be like this when you are a Centurion of Rome?" asked Naomi smiling from her bed.

"Like what?"

"You rushing off and me lying in bed naked, wanting you lying next to me."

Atticus sat down on the bed next to her kissed her lovingly and then said, "Yes but I will always make up for it when I return," then he kissed her again.

"Well, hurry up back then."

"I will." He kissed her goodbye and rushed off back outside.

Fury was in the yard all excited, Edelgard gave him a wide berth. Atticus jumped straight up onto Fury. Edelgard mounted as Atticus shouted his farewells to Zuma and Romulus and rode off out of the gate at a gallop, quickly followed by Edelgard and the cavalry.

"I guess you have some idea as to why the general wishes to see you?" Edelgard suggested.

"I hope so," replied Atticus.

Edelgard grunted and said, "We didn't need to hurry, that wine was very good. I could have drunk another couple of glasses at least."

"Not to worry, here," Atticus threw him a full wine skin. Edelgard's eyes widened and replied,

"I must thank your father the next time I see him," then he pulled out the stopper and took a large mouthful followed by a large belch. He replaced the stopper and was about to return it to Atticus.

"Keep it," said Atticus grinning.

As they approached the gates to the fort, Atticus looked up at the great walls, full of sentries on the ramparts; the road was wide and as they rode in a column of twos. A large section of legionnaires were marching out on a drill. A big angry looking centurion was shouting orders, and threats if they didn't do as they were told immediately; they would feel his vine stick between their bollocks. The centurion nodded towards Edelgard and the column as they marched past. Atticus breathed in the smell of army life and couldn't be happier, having also just married his sweetheart, Naomi.

The guards at the gate saluted the party as they rode into the fort; soldiers were running around the training arena and others were practising with training swords attacking each other while being instructed by a tall, bare-chested instructor.

Edelgard pulled the column to a stop, as Adelar approached and said to Atticus,

"How do you fancy helping me win a wager with Matias over there?"

"Which one and how?" asked Atticus.

"The tall bare chested one," Adelar replied, "I'll challenge him to a duel with you with say odds of five to one!"

Fury barged his head into Edelgard's thigh, pushing him and his horse sideways.

"What's up with Fury?" asked Edelgard, a little startled.

Atticus looked at Edelgard with a grin and answered, "Fury wants to know what's in it for him." Then Fury snorted, flicking his head up and down.

"Your Fury is very intelligent," said Adelar with a smile. "How about a bucket of apples Fury."

Fury snorted again; "Looks like Fury agrees," replied Atticus.

"Just follow my lead and say nothing," said Adelar.

A few of the Roman escorts began to talk amongst themselves, "Quiet, boys, don't give the game away," said Edelgard.

"How do you know he'll take the bet?" asked Atticus.

"He's too proud not to in front of the men he's training," replied Adelar.

Then he nudged his horse to the edge of the training arena where Matias was instructing the sword practise.

"Good day to you, Matias," Adelar began.

"What do you want you hairy-arsed bugger?" replied Matias.

"That's no way to greet your old friend," replied Adelar.

"What do you want, I'm busy?" Matias asked, looking over at him.

"Fancy a little wager or are you still short of coins from our last bet?" teased Adelar.

Matias raised an eyebrow looking at him, sighed and asked, "What's the wager this time?"

Adelar paused before answering, "A duel between you and this farm boy for say, seven of your sesterces to one of mine and I will put up fifty sesterces what say you?"

Matias stroked his chin, looking at Adelar, then at Atticus, thinking, '*He's a big bugger for a farm boy but he can't be much older than twenty, probably even younger.*'

Matias was a good six-foot with a slender build, in his late thirties, skilled with the sword and a battle-hardened veteran of many victories alongside Maximus. But still for some reason, '*Adelar has a trick up his sleeve,*' Matias thought to himself, but looking around at his men, he needed to save face; surely, he couldn't lose to a young man not much older than a boy.

"I accept, bring the young man down here."

All the men who were practicing with swords now clattered their wooden swords against their shields and shouted support for Matias.

"Good day, young man," said Matias, then he offered him one of the wooden swords.

"Good day to you also," replied Atticus, as he took hold of the sword Matias had offered.

Matias began to twirl his sword skilfully in mid-air and then spin it around from one hand to the other with great speed. Atticus just watched, standing in front of Matias pretending not to be taking much notice, holding his sword in his right hand. Matias then lunged forward without warning, attacking Atticus first to his right, then his left, with great speed to the cheers of his men; but the cheers were short-lived.

Atticus quickly parried and blocked all of Matias's attacks with lightning speed and agility. He side-stepped Matias and rolled under the blade of his sword. He then pushed up with the balls of his feet and lunged at Matias with the point of his sword resting on Matias's Adam's apple, dead centre of his throat. Even Edelgard couldn't believe the speed of Atticus and was left sitting on his horse with his mouth wide open.

Matias smiled at his opponent and said, "Looks like that hairy arse bugger Adelar just got one over me again, may I know the name of the young man who's given me a short, sharp lesson with the sword?"

"My name is Atticus," he replied, lowering his sword then bowing his head.

All the soldiers who'd been cheering for Matias started talking amongst themselves, looking at Atticus; some whispered, "He's the one who saved the generals' life."

The roman escort cheered and shouted, "ATTICUS!" as soon as he'd defeated Matias. Adelar walked towards them as Matias began to dress; Atticus looked at Matias and recognising the uniform of a tribune.

"Sir, sorry. I didn't know your rank or I—" Matias cut him off.

"Nonsense, young man. I don't feel embarrassed, not in the slightest, and I can see why Maximus holds you in such high regard."

Then he turned to face Adelar. "You bugger," then slapped him on his back and went on to say, "One of these days I will get my own back."

Edelgard let out a loud laugh from where he sat on his horse; Adelar grinned feeling a little richer.

"Atticus, I will see you later up at the general's quarters, but I need to get these lazy excuses of soldiers back to their training."

Atticus and Adelar bid farewell and returned to their escort, where Edelgard still sat grinning. Atticus mounted Fury and said, "Don't do that again and Fury wants his bucket of apples."

"I will, as soon as we've seen Maximus."

They headed on up through the camp to the general's quarters; Adelar was smiling to himself over the coin he would be receiving later.

The general's building was in the middle of the fort, adjacent to the bath house. As they rode past one of the officer's barracks, several officers were resting sitting on stools outside. A centurion called Brutus walked out and looked at Edelgard and the others riding past. Brutus was a broad, muscular veteran in his early forties with short grey hair. He wasn't respected by the men under his command. Many of them despised him, some even feared him. They regarded him as a bully who didn't care how many of his men's lives were lost in battle, as long as he was getting put forward for promotion. Brutus wanted to be promoted to first centurion and didn't care what the cost to his men was, as long as he got it. He turned to a young optio called Linus, who was new to the fort and was still feeling his way around and trying to fit in with the other officers, and snarled, "Move, I want that stool," before pushing him off.

One of the other centurions called Cyrus said, "Leave the lad alone, Brutus."

"What's it to you?" growled Brutus.

"Nothing but he's new, no need to pick on him."

Brutus sat down on the stool and spat on the floor in front of Cyrus, he then returned his attention to Edelgard and the troop of cavalry passing by. He then noticed the young stranger riding the big black stallion.

"Who the fucks that young pup riding next to Edelgard."

"Not sure," said the young Optio Linus, who'd got up off the floor and dusted his tunic.

"I wasn't asking you turd," retorted Brutus, spitting on the floor again.

Brutus hadn't noticed Tribune Tiberius walking up behind him from the training arena, where he'd been assessing the new recruits going through their paces.

"That young pup as you call him," Tiberius announced; Brutus and the other officers jumped up and saluted shouting, "Sir!"

"As I was saying, Brutus, that young pup goes by the name of Atticus." Tribune Tiberius didn't much like Brutus, and that was clear upon Tiberius' face, as he looked at Brutus disgustedly.

"You know the one who saved the generals life along with some of his bodyguards or have you been asleep for a week?" Tiberius continued.

Brutus opened his mouth to reply but before he could Tiberius shouted, "Close it, Brutus. I don't need a reply!" Brutus shut his mouth straight away and kept looking straight ahead. He couldn't see young Linus trying not to laugh behind him.

Tribune Tiberius had noticed Linus smiling and chose to wink in his direction. He then carried on remonstrating with Brutus who was clearly not enjoying it in the slightest.

"Right, then carry on with your duties, as I am on my way to the general's meeting with Atticus and I never want to hear the words young pup referring to Atticus again, understand Brutus!"

"YES, SIR," he replied.

Tiberius smiled in the direction of Linus, then marched off towards General Maximus's quarters.

Cyrus laughed as soon as Tiberius was out of earshot.

"What are you laughing at?" demanded Brutus.

"Nothing," Cyrus replied, he then walked off shouting for Linus to follow him to check on the new recruits.

All Cyrus wanted was to get Linus away from Brutus before he could take his anger out on him. Brutus went inside and, in a rage, kicked over several stools, knocked over a table and pushed one of the barrack servants on to his backside.

Edelgard dismounted along with Atticus and the cavalry, Edelgard told one of them to take the horses to the coral.

"Come, Atticus, we still have time to use the bath house and freshen up before we meet the general, best we make a good impression. Don't you want to come Adelar?"

"No, thanks," Adelar replied.

Atticus laughed, "You mean you want to get rid of the smell of wine you've been drinking?"

"Yes, something like that," replied Edelgard grinning.

A praetorian cavalry escort arrived at the fort's main gate, led by Centurion Metelus who told the commander of the gate he had dispatches from Rome for General Maximus, and was allowed in without delay. He was taken immediately to Maximus's quarters, once there he was received by the general.

"What have you got for me?" enquired Maximus.

"Correspondence from the emperor Augustus, Sir!"

"Does the emperor require an answer?"

"No, Sir. I'm to report back straight away to let him know I have delivered it directly to your hand."

"Thank you, I won't keep you any longer, you're dismissed."

Metelus left and went straight back to Rome.

Maximus sat at his desk and read the dispatch and when he'd finished, he sat back in his chair and smiled.

Atticus and Edelgard left the bath house and walked over to the general's quarters; as they approached the entrance, they were met by Adelar and Asken.

Asken asked them, "Where have you two been, all the other officers have arrived?"

"I've told you they've been to bathe," answered Adelar.

"You should try it sometime and get rid of that smell of pig shit," replied Edelgard.

"Give it a rest you two, Maximus says we have to be on our best behaviour; no belching or farting while in the presence of all those fine officers in their best uniforms," said Adelar.

"Come on then, we better get our guest in there," said Edelgard with a smile. In they strode, acknowledging the guards outside on duty. Atticus entered first, followed by the others, and as he did, many of the officers took their first look at the general's saviour, and began to talk amongst themselves. Atticus noticed Matius standing to his left and nodded to him. Brutus was standing with Cyrus and Linus alongside Tribune Tiberius. There were at least ten other centurions, three other tribunes and various optio's in the room. Sitting behind a large desk was the General Maximus and the Legate Octavian, deep in conservation.

Atticus looked around at the splendour of the large hall; behind the desk were the four gold eagles of Maximus's legions, with a large bust of the emperor situated in the middle of them. All along the wall on the left were the legions standards, and like the other offices he'd been in, there were tapestries depicting roman victories.

Brutus was standing with a scowl on his face and wasn't happy to be there as he wasn't the centre of the proceedings. Maximus then looked towards everyone, and the talking ceased; silence now descended on the room.

"Please be seated gentlemen," Maximus announced.

Everyone sat, facing Maximus and Octavian; Atticus and Edelgard sat on a bench to the right of the room, while Adelar and Asken sat to the left.

Octavian was the first to address the officers.

"First things first, Tribune Tiberius what's your assessment regarding the complement of weapons for our legion's effectiveness for the up-and-coming campaigns?"

"Sir, our heavy weapons, arcuballista's have been replenished and are back up to full strength. Our scorpions though are only at half our requirements, but our engineers are working hard day and night to rectify that as we speak."

"And the catapults?" asked Octavian.

"The large stone throwers will be up to the legions full complement within a month, according to our chief engineer Publius."

Tiberius then took a few seconds to check his report that he was holding, then looked again towards Octavian and Maximus, carrying on his report.

"He also assures me our semi-automatic catapults will be at full complement within the same period and we have more than enough vespa's."

"Thank you, Tiberius, for your report."

"Tribune Matius, what is the strength of our legions and our battle capability?"

Matius took out his report from his satchel.

"Two legions are at full strength, but many of the auxiliaries' replacements are green, but are enthusiastic. Drill and weapons training is moving forward at pace." Matius paused to check his report before continuing,

"Our third legion, the Legio 11 Augusta is short of experienced officers due to our recent battles in Gaul, but with the four cohorts of Batavian auxiliaries you acquired—" this brought a loud chorus of laughter amongst the other officers and brought a smile to the face of Maximus. Matius continued,

"Is up to three-quarter strength, but replacements should be arriving from Germanica shortly, at the request of the emperor."

"And the fourth?" enquired Octavian.

Matius sucked in and filled his lungs before replying, "The fourth is less than half strength after suffering our worst casualties in Gaul. It is both well short of good officers and experienced soldiers," then Matius sat down after concluding his report,

"More work needs to be done with great haste. I received a report from the emperor not more than a couple of hours ago but will need more discussion between myself and Octavian before we reveal its full contents." Maximus paused and looked around the room before continuing,

"But believe me gentlemen we need to have our legions at full strength sooner rather than later."

Maximus and Octavian spoke quietly between themselves, and many of the other officers were now in quiet conversation amongst themselves too.

Edelgard nudged Atticus and whispered, "Won't be long now, and it will be your turn."; he looked at Atticus with a grin and continued, "Aren't you feeling nervous?"

"No," Atticus replied.

Maximus looked up from his conversation with Octavian, and looked around the room, which made all the officers stop talking and pay attention.

Maximus stood up and began to address the room, "Well, gentlemen, this brings me to the better part of our meeting." Maximus paused to make sure everyone was paying full attention.

"May I introduce my guest, Atticus. If you would kindly stand Atticus." Atticus, standing to his full height, which at six-foot-six, towered over most of the men in the room; only the German bodyguards were of similar stature.

"May I thank you for coming at such short notice," Maximus continued; Atticus bowed his head in acknowledgement.

"Many of you, if not all, will have now heard of my rescue from the hands of assassins sent to kill me." The officers in the room all stamped their feet on the floor in recognition.

Maximus then continued when the noise died down, "This young man not only risked his own life, but fought with such skill and courage, also saving the lives of some of my bodyguards shielding me." Maximus paused again as Edelgard, and the other German bodyguards stamped their feet loudly. When the noise died down again, Maximus carried on,

"When the final assassin was defeated at the hands of Atticus, the full extent of his heroics became apparent." This time Maximus paused to take a drink of water before carrying on,

"He had not only killed twenty-two of the assassins; their dead bodies strewn around the forest. He had the wisdom to capture one alive for us to interrogate." Again, the whole room, apart from Brutus who was skulking at the back of the room, stamped their feet in applause; some even cheered out loud and shouted Atticus over and over, led by Edelgard.

Maximus had to wait a while for the room to become silent so he could carry on addressing them.

"On this occasion, legion protocol has been set aside with the order directly coming from our great emperor Augustus! As Atticus is only eighteen, and as we all know enrolment into our great legions is twenty." Tribune Matius exchanged glances with Tribune Tiberius who was smiling to himself.

Maximus turned to the Legate Octavian and asked, "Would you like to read the emperor's orders?" and then sat down.

Octavian stood and picked up a scroll off the desk with the emperor's seal on it, clearly visible for all to see. Octavian then began to read it out loud,

"It is by the order of your emperor Augustus, that from two days hence, Atticus son of Romulus will be enrolled into the legions of Rome."

Edelgard could not control himself and jumped up punching his fist into the air and cheered. Maximus nodded to him with a smile and waved him to sit down, which he did straight away.

Octavian looked at Edelgard and asked with a grin, "If I may finish." Edelgard went a little red and answered,

"Yes, Sir! Err, sorry, Sir." Many of the officers had started laughing before silence was restored.

Then Octavian began to finish reading the order of the emperor,

"And by the power invested in me as your emperor, I enrol him with the rank of Pilus Prior 1st Centurion of the First Cohort of the Legio 11 Augusta." Maximus walked from behind his desk and approached Atticus, who was still trying to take it all in and clasped his forearm and said,

"Welcome to Rome's finest legions," the whole room was now shouting the name of Atticus while applauding.

Edelgard slapped Atticus on his back and said, "You've earned that my friend and I look forward to fighting at your side."

Tribune Tiberius then addressed Atticus, "It's an honour to finally meet you."

"Thank you," Atticus replied.

Adelar and Asken were next to show their appreciation, slapping Atticus' back; the rest of the officers were now in deep conservation, but Brutus had left, angry in the knowledge he'd been overlooked for Pilus Prior and was jealous of Atticus.

Back in Maximus's office, Octavian had gotten Atticus to sign the order, accepting his enrolment as Pilus Prior. Then one of Maximus's servants walked in and presented Atticus with his magnificent uniform. Most of the officers had now left, after meeting and congratulating Atticus, leaving Maximus and his bodyguards alone with Atticus.

"How about I pour that jug of wine into those glasses?" asked Edelgard.

"Good idea," replied Maximus; now that they were alone the conversation became less formal.

"Let's sit awhile, I bet you're glad that's out of the way," asked Maximus.

"Yes, I am a little, Sir," replied Atticus.

"When we're alone, meaning me and the boys here, call me Maximus," the general answered.

"No formality, Atticus, between us," said Edelgard, after swallowing the whole contents of his glass of wine.

"Your married quarters have been arranged and will be ready on your arrival to take up your post in two days' time." Maximus stated, he then continued, "It's Naomi, isn't it?"

"It is" Atticus replied.

"And what will she make of army life?" Maximus asked.

"She's always known from an early age that I was destined for the legions of Rome and where I go, she goes."

"Very good; behind every man is a good woman so I am told," replied Maximus.

"Are you not married?" asked Atticus.

"Yes, once, but she died of a fever many years ago while I was stationed in Germanica."

"Oh, I'm sorry to hear that," replied Atticus.

"Not to worry, it was a long time ago and I never bothered to take another wife."

After a while, Atticus said he needed to be home and get everything ready for his return in two days' time. Maximus said he would arrange for Edelgard and Asken to come and escort him and Naomi to the fort.

Chapter 26

The following day, the day before Atticus was to join the legions, Romulus was in a subdued mood even though Julia was doing her best to cheer him up by saying, "You knew the day would come when Atticus would start to fulfil his destiny."

"Yes, I know but…"

"No buts," Julia cut in which brought a small smile to Romulus' face.

Naomi was busy packing all their belongings ready for the move to the fort and was being helped by Lydia. Zuma and Atticus had gone hunting because it was probably the last chance for a while; preparations were on their way for a supper to be held in Atticus and Naomi's honour.

The evening celebrations had begun. Naomi and Julia along with Lydia were happily laughing, Romulus was doing his best to put on a brave face, while talking with Atticus and Zuma.

The smell of roasted venison filled the air, which had been killed on the morning's hunt; it was being slowly cooked on an open fire. Wine flowed freely and there was an atmosphere of expectation rather than sadness.

Romulus had given Atticus his final words of advice and seemed to cheer up a little. Atticus then went on to express his gratitude to Romulus,

"Father, everything you and Zuma have done for me over these past 12 years have made me into the man you see before you, I wouldn't be in the position I am, without your knowledge and guidance over these years," said Atticus, while holding his father's arm.

"That, as it maybe, Atticus, but the Gods put that heart inside you, and they have not finished with you yet."

Romulus took up his glass of wine, raised it to the sky and toasted the Gods Mars and Jupiter, then turned to Atticus once more and said, "I drink to you my son, because yours and Naomi's journey has just begun."

Romulus then shouted for Aramea, "Bring more wine. I'm in the mood to get drunk."

"I'm up for that," shouted Zuma. Lydia then said,

"If you're too drunk, you can sleep in the barn. You're not going to keep me awake snoring like a billy goat all night."

This made everyone laugh and the mood became more jovial, and as Zuma became more drunk, he started to sing out loud songs from his homeland.

Julia nudged Lydia and said, "Looks like he's sleeping in the barn then, and Romulus might as well join him, it won't be long before he falls off that bench at this rate."

"May the gods help us," answered Lydia smiling.

The celebration went on late into the evening before everyone retired to their beds, worse for wear.

The following morning, Atticus and Naomi went to the kitchen for breakfast, and as soon as Aramea set eyes on the both of them, a tear rolled down her cheek.

Naomi put an arm around her and said, "Come now, Aramea, it won't be long before we are able to visit, Ostia isn't that far."

"I know my pretty little Naomi, but what if Atticus is sent far away and you will follow. I know you will…"

"What will be will be, so no more tears," replied Naomi.

Atticus and Naomi sat down looking at each other, both a little sad that the time had come to leave. Aramea placed two bowls of nice hot porridge on the table, trying her best to smile.

"Thank you," said Atticus.

Then in walked Romulus and Zuma, both looking worse for wear. Atticus and Naomi both laughed while looking at them; Zuma had straw sticking out of his hair and Romulus was covered in straw that had stuck to his tunic.

"I take it you two shared the barn last night?" asked Atticus.

Romulus held a hand to the back of his head and replied, "I feel like I've been kicked in the head by Fury, Aramea pass me that jug of water please."

Zuma plonked himself down at the table, and due to his size and weight nearly tipped the table over. If it hadn't been for Atticus bearing his weight on the other side of the table, it would have.

"Is Lydia talking to you this morning?" enquired Naomi smiling.

"I hope so, I haven't seen her yet this morning," replied Zuma pulling out some of the straw from his hair.

"You two need to bathe," said Aramea while pushing two bowls of porridge towards them.

"That smells lovely," said Romulus.

"It smells a lot better than you two and It seems all that wine hasn't dampened your appetite then master," replied Aramea.

"Have you both finished packing your belongings?" asked Romulus.

"Only the things we need," replied Atticus.

Naomi and Atticus had finished their breakfast, Atticus stood up and said, "I better put my uniform on, Edelgard will be here soon."

"I can't wait to see you in all your glory," said Zuma, scratching his beard. Atticus and Naomi returned to their room, Naomi helped him put on his uniform, and when he was fully dressed, apart from his helmet, Naomi stood back with a glow on her face and said,

"You look wonderful. It fits perfect, now put on your helmet."

Atticus put it on and fastened the chin strap, he then eased his fingers along both sides of the helmet to make it more comfortable.

Figo and Alepo had taken their bags outside and strapped them to a pony in the courtyard. Julia and Lydia had gone for breakfast and fits of laughter could be heard coming from the kitchen.

The sun was now up in the sky, peering out from behind some clouds, and the warmth of the day could be felt. Fury had been saddled and was chomping at the bit, eager to get on with the journey.

Atticus's longbow and quiver of arrows hung from his saddle. Alepo had saddled a young grey mare called Thunder for Naomi to ride. Julia could never understand why Romulus had named the horse Thunder, with it having a very timid and pleasant personality.

Edelgard and Asken arrived at the gate with a troop of twenty cavalry riders, who'd been chosen from Atticus's legion, the Legio 11 Augusta, by Matius, the legions tribune.

On hearing them arrive outside the gate, Figo quickly opened it; Edelgard and Asken, gently nudged their horses into the courtyard, while the troop of cavalry dismounted and waited on the road outside.

Romulus and Zuma, along with the rest of the household, came out of the main house; several of the farm hands who'd been working in the fields and stable came running into the courtyard.

Edelgard addressed Romulus as soon as he saw him come out of the house saying,

"You look like you have been awake all night drinking that fine wine of yours."

Romulus gave a wry smile and replied, "You're not far wrong, my friend, but it was all Zuma's idea!"

"He did not need any encouragement," shouted Julia.

"I hope there is a jug left over for me," replied Edelgard with the look of hope in his eyes.

"Alepo run and fetch this bugger some wine, there's a good lad," answered Romulus, and off ran Alepo into the house.

"Where is that son of yours? Don't tell me he's still in bed!" asked Asken. Then out walked Atticus in his full uniform with Naomi holding his arm. Romulus walked up to him and pulled the breastplate of his armour checking to see if it was properly secured, knowing full well it was, but he was so proud of how Atticus looked in his uniform and didn't want anyone to see the tear in his eye.

Romulus then said, "Not bad, you'll do," and then he bent down and kissed Naomi on the cheek.

Alepo arrived with a jug of wine and gave it, along with a cup, to Edelgard, who filled the cup straight away and drank the contents in one. This made Zuma smile, as Lydia and Julia both went to fuss over Naomi, giving her all sorts of advice. Atticus then helped Naomi mount Thunder, and turned and embraced every one of the households, finishing with Zuma and his father.

Edelgard downed the remains of the jug of wine and mounted, bidding his farewell as they rode out with Atticus and Naomi riding in front.

Asken had taken the reins of the pony carrying their belongings and pulled it behind him. They were then followed into the road by Romulus and Zuma watching them leave.

As Atticus rode out into the road, the troop of cavalry quickly stood to attention and saluted, awaiting their order to mount.

Atticus, feeling a little strange, but ready for the task shouted to mount up; the sound of chinking armour and weapons filled the air.

Romulus looked on at Atticus, pride beaming from every part of his body. Then Atticus rode on with Naomi at his side, who was also beaming with pride for her man. Atticus thrust his hand in the air and shouted, "FORWARD" and the cavalry followed in a column of twos.

Romulus looked at Zuma and said, "I hope everything goes well for Atticus!"

"It will, it did for you," replied Zuma smiling with pride.

"Yes, but I had you fighting at my side. He doesn't."

"That's as it maybe, but there is a bond between Atticus and Edelgard just as it is with us."

When they were finally out of sight, Romulus and Zuma went back inside and closed the gate behind them. Romulus's eyes were filled with tears, but his heart was filled with pride. Atticus' journey had really just begun.